HEART
OF
DARKNESS

BY

STEPHANIE HUDSON

Heart of Darkness
The Transfusion Saga #10
Copyright © 2020 Stephanie Hudson
Published by Hudson Indie Ink
www.hudsonindieink.com

Heart of Darkness/Stephanie Hudson – 1st ed.
ISBN-13 - 978-1-913904-27-2

I would like to dedicate this book to all my wonderful fans,
those who are both new to the Afterlife and Transfusion world
and those who have support me for years.
I cannot thank you enough for keeping my dreams alive for so
long and I will be forever and always eternally grateful.
All my love,
Steph and family.

WARNING

This book contains explicit sexual content, some graphic language and a highly additive dominate Vampire King.

This book has been written by an UK Author with a mad sense of humour. Which means the following story contains a mixture of Northern English slang, dialect, regional colloquialisms and other quirky spellings that have been intentionally included to make the story and dialogue more realistic for modern day characters.

Thanks for reading x

CHAPTER ONE

TRUST

"Seriously?!" I said the moment I set a foot on the last step of the tavern, having hit my limit of waiting in the room for three Scottish shifters to come back and get me. Of course, when they told me they had something important to do before we left, I didn't think it was sitting around a table drinking and having a jolly old time in a pub!

"So, Hell's literally no different than being topside, other than the fact that there isn't a game on some flatscreen to swear at?!" I snapped the second I made my way over to their table, making all three guilty faces turn to me at the same time. This after their shoulders bunched, tensing at the sound of my voice. I swear I didn't think I would be starting this journey feeling like a nagging wife to three sexy Scots who I could barely understand at the best of times. Okay, so admittedly, only two looked guilty, the other one, however, raised a brow before frowning and switching the roles of annoyance by standing, taking me by the top of my arm and saying,

"I thought I told ye tae wait in th' room."

"Aye, that you did shifter boy, something I have been doing this last hour whilst pacing a patch in the floor and chewing my Gods be damned nails off, and why did I do this... all so you gits could have a beer!" I snapped, first taking the piss out of his accent, making him roll his eyes and say,

"We ur an' a' better acquainted wi' Hell than yer lass." I shook my head a few times as if this would help in understanding him, which of course it didn't. No, it just made me look as if I had some weird tick or hadn't yet mastered the girly art of flicking my hair out. Either way I followed it up with,

"Alright, now once again, only with a little less Scottish." He released a sigh and pulled me closer, now only putting a few intimidating inches between us.

"We. Know. Hell. Better. Than. You!" he said, over pronouncing each word like my brain was the size of a pea and I ate checkers in my spare time. So I pulled back a little and snapped,

"Oh right, so what is this, a chance to get a taste of some good ale before we move on... high up on the Hell's version of Tripadvisor is it?" Then I yanked my arm from his grasp so I could fold them across my chest, wishing I was wearing a slightly more kick ass 'take no messing' outfit and not looking like some bloody damsel from a regency romance novel. Gods, but what was next, kilts, bare chests and claymores?

"I dinne know whit that is!" Trice argued making me roll my eyes, something I knew I would never have gotten away with if it had been Lucius. Gods, but how I missed him. He must have been going crazy with worry!

"It doesn't matter what it is, all that matters is getting back to that sodding castle before Lucius kills who I am assuming is a brother he cares about, considering he made him ruler in his absence... you know, the one he is currently keeping in his dungeon and no doubt beating the shit out of right now!" I snapped making Trice release yet another sigh, something that I was beginning to think was a newly developed habit around me. Then he snapped back,

"Oh aye, th' one he cared sae much aboot that he kept it fae you… aye lot o' care there!" he said sarcastically.

"I am sure he had his reasons," I answered with a level of bravado in my tone that I definitely didn't feel. Because the truth was that I had been asking myself this question the whole time I had been left upstairs after the brothers had told me to wait for them. This was after first discovering the colossal mistake shortly after Gryph and Vern had turned up.

Because Trice was right…*Why hadn't Lucius told me about his brother?* Why keep something like that to himself? I couldn't understand it. But then again, he also hadn't told his brother about me either. Especially not in the beginning, that much was obvious or why else would he have had me thrown into a prison after first arriving.

Had he been ashamed of me?

Had the thought of admitting his Chosen One was human too hard to face down here? Would admitting it down in Hell end up as some kind of stain on his rule as King? The thoughts had me pausing my steps more than once when upstairs. Had that been the real reason for his brutal act in front of his kingdom, a large part of that I now knew included his brother?

It was a painful thought and one that had quickly overtaken the reasons he had given me, which had been and always seemed to be so that he could keep me safe. But surely as King he would have had the power to do that, just declaring me his… wouldn't that have been enough?

I honestly didn't know but since that Hex had been removed, I found my mind in a crumbling state of vulnerability. I just needed to get back to him and save him from doing anything to his brother. Like condemning him to death for a crime he didn't commit, after first questioning the Hell out of him. And when I say question, what I really meant was beating the crap out of him and kicking words from him like bouncing rings from Sonic the Hedgehog characters! Because this was Lucius we were talking about, what was he going to do, ask nicely and hope for the best? No, not my ruthless, brutal boyfriend.

Although, I did have hope that he would at the very least try and hold back, considering this was his brother we were talking about. In fact, I didn't know what I would do first when seeing him, scream a barrage of information at him or just fall into his arms and cry.

Seriously, my backbone was going to be a wobbling jelly mould by the time I finally got back to him. But with the reality of where I was now, I also knew I had to be stronger than that. And my biggest hope of all, was that it was only just for a little bit longer. Because I couldn't afford to fall to pieces now!

This had been the pep talk I had needed to give myself back in the room, after looking towards the floorboards where I had hidden the Eye. I had done this a little time after Trice had kicked open the door to his room and put me down. This, of course, was after first finding me downstairs in the tavern about to be lynched by an angry mob of Demons. Seriously, was a normal day ever going to be on the horizon for me ever again?

But one look at the Eye and I knew my mission was far from over. Hence why I hid it, at the same time telling Trice all that had happened to me and Nero. Although, I had to say, this wasn't the most ideal place to store what was essentially Hell's most powerful weapon. Then again, it wasn't exactly the type of room to come complete with minifridge and a safe in the wardrobe, so I did what I did best and improvised.

Talking about security…

"We are nae 'ere tae hae a drink," Trice said, making me look around him at the table behind and say,

"Could have fooled me… what you doing, playing invisible checkers?" He rolled his eyes again and said,

"If ye mist know, we are waiting fur th' portal keeper tae finish fucking th' barmaid before we kin be granted access." At this my eyes widened before I snapped,

"Are you serious!" He folded his arms across his leather strapped chest, one that tensed and looked even more muscley thanks to his new pissed off position.

"You're waiting while some guy gets his rocks off whilst Lucius' brother's life is on the line?!" I snapped making him once again lean closer to my face, bending slightly because of our height difference.

"Nay, I am waiting fur oor strength tae return by havin' a drink, sae that as soon as we mak' it through th' portal we kin shift 'n' git there a lot bloody quicker than walking. Noo, if some demon is getting his cock worked on 'n' havin' a jolly good polish whilst we wait, then good fur him… as fur us, we be getting a drink," Trice said, making my mouth open ready to argue again, only for it to then snap closed the moment his explanation was done. Meaning the next time it opened, it was proof that I had quickly lost my attitude,

"Can I have one?" I asked and at this, Trice smirked, making him look even more handsome than usual.

"I thought ye wid ne'er ask," he replied, making me smirk up at him.

"And I thought you would never buy," I quipped back before slapping him on the top of the arm and walking past him, smirking to myself when I heard him growl before grumbling about 'bloody woman', only doing so in his usually growly Scottish way.

"Well, it has tae be said, lassie, yer certainly resilient,"

Gryph said as I sat down at their round table. It was one that was in the corner in a back room, away from the ruckus of the bar area where they could no doubt get away with talking among themselves.

"That or mair luck than a moggie wi' nine lives," Trice grumbled as he sat down next to me.

"What the Hell is a moggie, because at this rate I think it must be one of the only things I haven't come across down here?" I said with a bite of sarcasm, one that left me feeling pretty foolish when Trice smirked. Then he draped an arm at the back of my chair and leant in close, before mouthing only one word at me that a toddler could have understood.

"Cat."

"Oh," I replied lamely making his brothers chuckle, something that ended quickly when I shot them my best death glare. They wisely picked up their ale and concentrated on drinking, though even that was done with a knowing grin on their faces.

After this I finally took the time to have a good look around the tavern, something admittedly I hadn't had much chance to do when first arriving. But then this was hardly surprising considering I pretty much managed to piss everybody off within the first two minutes of me being there. A new record even for me, but once again Trice had come to the rescue, saving me from what was quickly becoming an angry demonic mob.

But getting back to the tavern and how it looked now I had the time to take it in. The place was most definitely old fashioned, with a kind of medieval vibe to it that you saw all throughout England, with its wooden panelling surrounding the lower parts of the walls. It had been knocked, scratched and stained through countless years of abuse that no amount of varnish could remedy. As for the top half, this was a painted stone in a pale, yellow tone that at one time could have been white. But then, like the wood, it had no doubt been stained through years of tobacco smoke that had literally seeped into the walls.

It also looked like the plaster, that had once been used to skim the stone, had been mixed with bits of hay or animal hair, as there wasn't a flat or even surface to speak of. In between these sections were crossbeams of dark wood to match the panels. These beams also held another purpose other than being architectural, as they doubled as a place and means for demonic looking heads to be nailed to. Meaning it also looked like some sort of crude Hellish hunting lodge, and I almost questioned if its keeper was Hell's Huntsman?

I had heard tales of him through my family members growing up, and even read a few chapters about him in one of the books I had managed to get my hands on and sneak into my room. It was named the Hierarchy of Hell and admittedly, it was also one I had wished to have memorised, now knowing how handy it would have been for my future. Although, had I known, then I think my first choice would have been how to build an underground bunker and survive a lifetime of hiding.

Now, as for this famous Hell's Huntsman, not a lot of history is truly known about him, however in the Hierarchy of Hell, it speaks little of his life before being forced to sell his soul to the Devil. Though, in what little it did mention him, his name back then was Charietto. He was a German mercenary who was employed by the Roman Empire and would use barbarian bounty hunters to kill bandits, criminals and any dangerous rogue soldiers. He was famous during this time as he would stalk his victims at night and attack them at their most vulnerable, before cutting off their heads as proof of death necessary to receive the bounty.

Because of his expertise, he rose up through the ranks quickly within the Roman army but was finally killed in 365

AD by Alammanic forces, by what was known as the Raining of Spears. What isn't well known was that he was betrayed, set up by his enemies, who believed he was becoming too powerful too quickly. The story goes, that he then sold his soul in order to seek revenge, and as payment basically had to become the Devil's personal bounty hunter for a time. As in, a long time, because this was Hell after all. But after which he was free to do as he pleased in his Hellish afterlife and well, after looking at this place now, then I would say that freedom obviously equated into running your own pub.

What can I say, some people dream of fame and fortune, whilst others obviously dream of opening some crappy tavern in some shitty place named Turdville, where everyone wants to kill the new guy. Okay so admittedly that wasn't the most mature description of the place, but then considering my first impression of the joint, then I wasn't exactly going to call this place the Ritz.

Especially not with all the demonic heads mounted on the wall… because euww. And there were beasts of all shapes and sizes, that had been stuffed and preserved like some Hellish taxidermy.

Gods, but someone had even gone to the trouble of having the fangs and horns polished to a high shine. To the point that it made them look far too alive to be up there, as I wouldn't have been surprised in that moment if one of them had opened their mouths and breathed fire. Had it not been for the fact their bodies were missing, then I would have been reluctant to sit under one as I was doing now.

As for the rest of the place, crossbeams from the A shaped frame also held chained wheel chandeliers with every inch of them covered in wax and candles. Long icicles of that same wax hung down like frozen teardrops, and every so often a piece would go so far as to drip on the floor, hence why there wasn't any seating underneath. An even cobbled floor showed a carpet of wax at these points in the room, some with dirty footprints cast at their centres.

As for the furnishings, there was little to speak of, as there was nothing more than rustic wooden panel tables that were either round like ours or rectangles with bench seating for larger crowds. A mismatch of chipped stools and chairs were all the details I could make out considering nearly all of them were covered by a body, as it certainly seemed like a popular place.

"So, how long is this planning on taking? I mean I'm not one to rush you guys or anything, but we do kind of have an execution to stop," I reminded them, ignoring the urge to look down at a watch I knew wasn't there.

"Yeah, speaking aboot that, yer hundred percent sure oan this... right?" Vern asked after downing some of his ale and wiping his mouth on the back of his hand. Meanwhile, Trice had turned towards the bar area and raised four fingers before gesturing back to their table. Something which I gathered was indicating that he wanted another round, this time with my drink included.

"Well, I think you guys can gather that when it comes to Lucius and talking about his family, I am not exactly in the know!" I snapped before this became the beginning of my Lucius rant, something that couldn't be stopped now the 'Angry Girlfriend Beast' had been released.

"In fact, I feel like the last bloody person in Hell who does! So clearly this means we obviously haven't reached this level in our relationship, oh but being kidnapped together, being shot at by mercenaries, dates that include car chases and hijacked planes are the new relationship guidelines are they!" I snapped at the brothers who were starting to look at me as if I had officially lost the plot. Then Vern pointed a finger at me and said,

"Relationship goals right there." This was something I ignored because, well in truth I hadn't yet finished ranting.

"Oh, but he wonders why I might have trust issues when it comes to him, as let's face it, he hasn't exactly been Mr information…" I said, then turned to face Vern and finished off with,

"So, in answer to your question, I have no idea how many brothers Lucius has, because honestly, he hasn't told me about any of them, meaning that he could seven of the buggers, with each one being named the days of the fucking week! Gods alive, am I getting a drink or what!?" I was getting louder towards the end and looking around to see if anything alcoholic was coming my way as I think it was getting more obvious by the second that I needed it!

I felt my hand being taken in a large calloused one and looked back at Trice to see a soft comfort in his eyes.

"He should hae trusted ye, Lass." I gave him a warm expression in return knowing that I couldn't trust myself to say the right thing in that moment. So instead, I focused on what I could say, which was back to the point I was trying to make before my rant,

"All I know, is that the man that Lucius put in charge when he isn't ruling in Hell, is not who I saw as being the traitor." After I said this, all three brothers looked at each other, as if they were having their own secret conversation about it and it wasn't something they wanted me to know about. Great, just what I needed, more secrets. But then again, it wasn't as though it was with Lucius, because these guys didn't owe me anything.

"How come did ye nae tell us aboot him?" Trice asked making me frown,

"I've only just seen him myself and didn't have the chance to…" The shake of his head cut me off before his words told me why,

"I dinnae mean th' brother."

"You mean why didn't I tell you about Lucius?" I confirmed what I think he meant with that question, tensing my shoulders when realising that the time had come. Because, since that day down in the prison, this had been the real first opportunity that Trice and I had the time to talk about this. Of course, there had been when they had foolishly kidnapped me, believing they were saving me from a tyrant King. But even then, it wasn't as if that had been a good time to discuss my boyfriend, or more to the point that I had hid his identity.

"Yeah, because I hae tae point oot 'ere lass, that would hae bin a helpful piece of information whin we were walking yer ass across Hell tae tak' ye back tae him," Vern said nodding a head my way and pointing a finger at me from where he gripped his tankard of ale.

"That may be true, but in my defence, I didn't know the King was… well, *him*… meaning that I didn't know it was my boyfriend you were taking me back to," I said pointing out this fact and once again folding my arms.

"I tak' it wee things lik' that dinnae usually come up in conversation in yer relationship," Trice remarked before finishing off his own tankard of ale, and seeing as that comforting side to him was clearly gone, I gave him an evil glare. I was about to open my mouth to give him what for, when a barmaid swaggered over to the table with two tankards in each hand. She slammed them on the table, making whatever filled them splash over the sides and seep through the joints in the panels of wood that made up the tops of the tables.

"Cheers, darlin', be a sweet ass 'n' put it oan oor tab," Vern said, adding what was no doubt considered by most as a charming wink. However, right now this barmaid was having none of it.

"My boss says that if your tab gets any higher it will be

enough to buy this place," she said with a hand on her hip in a universally known stance as 'Pissed off'.'

"Here… gie him this," Trice said after producing another bag of coin and tossing it up in the air for her to catch. I was tempted to ask just how many purses of coin he had on his person but refrained, as let's just say that the barmaid wasn't the only one who looked pissed off.

However, this didn't stop me from saying anything, and I let my feelings be known the moment the barmaid left the table and was no longer in ear shot. Because even though I still felt slightly betrayed by Lucius keeping his brother from me, it didn't mean I was ready to hear other people making judgements on our relationship. So, call it bitchy or having double standards, I didn't care, I was still pissed.

"Not that it's any of your business, but since me and Lucius got together things have been a little busy dealing with kidnapping attempts, witch attacks, oh and rogue vampires exploding into dust… you know little things like that," I said sarcastically snapping before grabbing my ale and guzzling it down. Something that didn't look quite as effective when I started choking on what had to be the most disgusting drink I had ever had, Devil's rum included!

"Oh, Gods have mercy! What the hell is this, did she piss in a pot and stir it with some cider made from rotting apples?!" I wheezed out after coughing and trying not to be sick. Meanwhile, the other three started laughing whilst Trice patted my back to aid me. Something I brushed off with a wave of my hand because I was still pissed. Or should I say, I at least tried to before I found myself having to grip the edge of the table as if this would help.

"It's root water mead 'n' in truth, ye dinnae wanna ken whit it is, as I'm telling ye noo that her piss 'n' old cider wid taste better," Griff said, making me cough.

"You guys seriously need to get topside and find yourselves a good old English pub to drink in, I am thinking Guinness would be right up your street," I said, before pushing away my tankard and scrunching my nose up when Vern and Griff both tried to reach out for it quickly, only Vern got there first making his brother hammer a meaty fist on the table in his annoyance.

"Or clearly you could just stick to that shit, which by the way, tastes like a topside club being squeegeed down at the end of a Saturday night." At this, Trice finally chuckled next to me.

"Getting back tae yer list 'n' how much shit has happened, I wid lik' tae say a'm surprised by it all... bit in fact, a'm only surprised that it isn't longer," Vern commented, making me sneer at him before telling him,

"Well, I did miss out the part where I had to kill a load of mercs, then jump out of a helicopter, or the part where I had to fly a plane after first shooting the pilot with an ice bucket on his head." At this both Vern and Gryph choked on their mead and I grinned over the rim of the tankard but before I could drink, Trice put his hand over the top and applied enough pressure until the cup was back on the table.

"That's mine 'n' if ye don't mind, I wid prefer it wi'oot yer spit," he said making me remember how much I hated it.

"Of coorse, ye'r exaggerating… she's exaggerating… isn't she?" Vern said with a nervous chuckle. But then before I could respond I found my chin in the grasp of a strong hand as my face was turned up to face Trice. I swallowed hard as the breath suddenly left me and as he studied my eyes for a few seconds, he then let go and turned back his attention to his brother, answering him,

"Nay, she's nae exaggerating," then he promptly went back to his ale leaving me confused at the exchange. Thankfully, after this, talk turned to their plans of getting through the portal and from there the plan was shifting into their combined dragon like form. They then informed me that it should only take them an hour to reach the castle.

I had been about to argue at this, when I was told that Lucius' brother had until morning before his execution. This meant we had most of the night left on our side and I had to admit, it was welcome good news for once. Because I knew that I would never forgive myself if Lucius not only lost his brother because of me, but even worse, Lucius ended up being the hand behind that execution, as I knew he would.

Lucius was that type of ruler. Whether it was being the very first person at the front when leading his armies into battle, or whether it was being the one to make the difficult choices and being the hand that carried them out. But I also knew that because of this, he would never be able to give forgive himself when he did. Which would make two of us, for he wouldn't be the only guilty soul that committed the crime against his innocent brother.

Hence, why I was angry that Lucius had kept this from me, because if he'd have told me about Dariush being his brother then none of this would have happened! My comments to Nero would have been about a brother that he didn't know he had, not the one that's by his side and ruled in his absence. It was a cruel twist of fate indeed and one that no matter how much I tried not to think about it, I found I could fixate on little else.

Thankfully, after this there was no more talk about my relationship with Lucius and I was more than glad of it. Although, I could tell that all three of them still had questions. But at the very least, I think they could now understand the start of our troubles hadn't been when I had first stepped foot into Hell but in fact long before that. Oh no, because Hell had just ended up being the icing on the poisonous cake!

Besides, I had a feeling that after these three noble shifters had kidnapped me and I had been returned, Lucius had obviously thought it best to put together some sort of team. This much was clear seeing as Trice had been charged with finding a way to remove the hex. Something he had explained to me after finding me putting myself up for sale in way of a bounty.

Of course, my disappearance, or should I say more to the point, after the harpy Queen had kidnapped me and Nero, then removing the hex had come secondary to finding me. This side of the story had come from Trice, as he told me it was the reason that Vern and Griff had been called back to the castle.

Now, as for those two, it was soon their turn to explain what happened after they returned back to Lucius' kingdom, as shortly after arriving was when it had all begun. Starting with Lucius supposedly being overpowered by some kind of vision of me at the harpy Queen's lair. Because after this, Lucius had quickly left the castle telling no one of his plans other than letting Vern know that Nero was still alive. After that, it was easy to assume that Lucius hadn't been long behind us as he had found Nero and been able to save her life before she really did die.

I had to be honest but hearing this the moment Vern had appeared would have been some of the happiest news in my entire life! That was, had it not then been tainted by the fact that Lucius was about to kill his own brother, as something like that certainly had the power to put a downer on any happy occasion!

But getting back to trying to prevent that from happening, not long after this conversation, the brothers finished up their drinks and I watched as Gryph nodded to someone by the bar that I had my back to. I turned and looked over my shoulder to see a male demon that had light, aquamarine coloured skin. It also glowed in a yellowish tone around the symbols that seemed to have been cut into his flesh. Around his neck was also some kind of webbed skin that joined up to his ears and fluttered whenever he spoke.

He also had what looked like gills on each side of his head, that could be seen thanks to a thin strip of hair he had running down the centre of his mainly bald head. One eye was covered up by a patch sown directly into his skin, and the other was a dirty yellow colour framed by the harsh slant of a dark jagged brow. He looked mean and menacing, despite the fact that he winked his one eye at the barmaid he had obviously just had his manhood serviced by... or what had Trice called it, having his 'cock polished'.

As for the barmaid, she was a red skinned demon with pointed ears and black lines around her features in the places an old woman would have wrinkles. She also had two sets of eyebrows and a pair of glowing horns that started from her forehead and framed the crown of her skull. Long, dark ebony hair flowed down her back, and was interlaced with plaited dreads and beads reaching the beginning of a tail. One that was allowed to snap out freely due to the hole in her gypsy style skirt. She also had a piercing in her nose that was like a bull's ring passing through the nasal septum, and a chain attached to either side that was joined to the piercings on her double row of eyebrows.

She winked back at the 'creature from the blue lagoon guy', a person who I had gathered was the portal keeper we had been waiting for. Her eyes flashed, glowing in excitement, and this wasn't all she flashed as she also yanked aside her low-cut top giving him what I assumed was a memory for the road in that of a bare breast. The demon smirked and purposely licked his lips, paying attention to the tip of the largest fang as if reminding her where it had recently been.

"Come oan, lass, let's go git yer package," Trice said standing and wrapping his thick long fingers around the top of my arm, and doing a little more than just encouraging me to stand. He then looked to his brothers as he pretty much lifted me from my seat and nodded a little towards the bar, delivering a silent message for them to do something.

"We wull catch up wi` ye outside," he stated firmly, before walking me across the room and to the staircase at the back that I knew would lead to the room we had been staying in.

"You know I'm perfectly capable of walking unaided," I grumbled, making him scoff,

"Aye, that may be true, bit a'm still playing th' part o' th' hunter 'n' yer still mah bounty."

"And now?" I asked, referring to the empty landing we were stood on after I had been practically dragged up the stairs. Hell, but at this rate I was surprised that he hadn't just thrown me over his shoulder like last time and carried me up there, caveman style.

"As fur now…" he responded, letting his answer linger at the same time backing me up towards the door. The same one I now felt come into contact with my back as I was pressed firmly against it… no, not pressed, but more like caged.

After that he said three whispered words that soon filled me with dread…

"Alone at last."

CHAPTER TWO

UNLUCKY STRIKES AGAIN

O kay, so being backed into a doorway by Trice's big muscular body was so not what I wanted to happen right now!

"Err, Trice?" I questioned, now not sounding as cocky as I had done only moments ago. He let go of the top of my arm and instead placed it above me with his palm flat against the wooden frame. He took the last step needed to eliminate the space between us and I had nowhere to go but to hold my breath, creating not even a centimetre of extra space between us by doing so. He was so tall that I had to arch my neck all the way back just to keep sight of him. But then the second I did, I instantly regretted it. this was because of the intense look he was now giving me, with his eyes turning glacier as honestly... *it was like looking directly into ice.*

"Trice," I whispered, this time doing so on a breath that nearly caught in my throat and became captured there just like I was.

"I wull nae git another chance tae tell ye this, bit I need ye tae know…"

"Trice, please don't." He ignored this plea and instead grinned through it, doing so in a cocky, self-assured way, before he then told me,

"I dinnae care if ye'r with th' King, fur I wid fight them all, every last one under his rule 'n' above fur if ye only asked it o' me…"

"Trice, please…" I begged again, but he only got closer and continued as if my words had meant nothing but a desire for him to continue,

"…For if ye only spoke o' a word o' chance or hope that ye may one day be mine, I wull forever fight for ye 'n' if ye speak it noo, then I wull send my brothers thro' th' portal tae save th' King's brother, fur no man deserves an unjust death." I swallowed down the hard lump his words of devotion had stirred up, forcing me to speak again,

"And me… what would you do with me?" I asked in a shaky voice, making him duck his head low enough so that he could whisper the words directly in my ear.

"I wid tak' ye tae my own Kingdom 'n' fight fur th' right tae claim my throne, just so I had th' power tae keep ye 'n' make ye my Queen." The moment he finished with the word queen I gasped, making him grin against the shell of my ear when feeling me shudder for himself.

"Oh, Trice, I can't…" he pulled back a little at the sound of my nervousness and took hold of my chin once more, doing so now to prevent me from turning my head away like I tried to do. Then he told me,

"One word is all is needed… just one word, Amelia, 'n' I wull mak' ye mine, always remember that." After this and what I knew was his solemn vow, I nodded my head in what little space he gave me to do so. This was before he finally took a much needed step back, now that he had told me what he desired of me.

I had so many questions and none of them were about being his Queen, but only about him being King and claiming the throne he spoke of. However, because of what had happened between us I didn't have the right and more importantly, I didn't want him getting the wrong impression by my asking.

As it was now clear to me that just because Trice had seen me with Lucius, it didn't mean that he was ready to give up on trying to claim me for his own. And to be honest, with a man like Trice, I would have been tempted had I not already been utterly in love with Lucius. Tempted had my soul not already been claimed, locked and merged with his own, for I honestly could never imagine myself with anyone else other than Lucius. There was no-one but him. Lucius was my everything, and right now all I needed to do was to get back to him. In fact, that felt like my life's motto at the moment, as all I ever had to do was get back to him!

But I didn't say any of this to Trice because I didn't want to hurt him. Whether that decision was right or wrong, I didn't know, but in my heart all I could think was that there was no point inflicting pain where it was not needed. Meaning it was like Trice had said, he needed only one word from me to be enough to give him the go ahead and claim me. Just one word that I honestly could promise to both myself and any God that could hear me, that it was one that I would never say…

Yours.

After this, I felt him reach behind me close to my waist and the moment I felt space created behind my back, I knew he was opening the door. It meant this was also my cue to get my ass inside to put even more space between us. I liked Trice, I really did, but I was in love with Lucius, which meant that times like this spent alone with him caused me nothing but guilt. Because despite how innocent it was from my side, I knew that Lucius at this moment in time was no doubt in his castle waiting for my return and worrying about me every second we were apart. And my being here alone with Trice didn't feel fair… *at all.*

It was of little wonder then, that the second I stepped inside I released a breath of relief and quickly hurried over to where I had hidden the Eye of Janus. I used the loose nail that was raised up from the plank, as it had been how I'd found the hiding spot in the first place. After pulling up the floorboard, I continued to pull up the next and then the next until the gap was big enough for me to free the Eye from its hiding space. It was still covered in the torn piece of the harpy Queen's skirt, wrapped up like a present I couldn't wait to hand over to Lucius.

Trice took one look at it and grabbed what looked like a discarded sack that had been used for carrying kindling to the room for the fireplace. He gave it a shake and then held it open so that I could put the Eye inside, purposely looking away from it as I did so. I didn't need to ask why as the myth of this thing was obviously enough to have people wary of it, even powerful beings like Trice.

I pulled on the rope and knotted it so it wouldn't come open, and then used the leftover rope as a strap across my chest.

"I wid offer tae carry it, bit something tells me th' Eye has found its new owner 'n' wid only try tae tempt me tae use it," Trice said making my eyes widen in shock.

"It would really do that?" I asked.

"It already is, lass." I gasped in surprise and before I could ask him anymore about it, he looked down at the floor and off to one side as if he could hear something. I, too, took pause to see if he could hear someone coming up the stairs or something, but then after a few seconds of nothing he looked up and said,

"Time tae go."

This made me wonder whether the three brothers could communicate with each other using telepathy, because this hadn't been the first time I had witnessed something passing between them in this way. And it would make sense considering when they all combined and became the same creature, then surely they would need some way of communicating with each other.

Either way, I think it was safe to say that this was something I wouldn't be long in finding out considering Trice had mentioned that flying was going to become our preferred way of travel. Well, just as long as it got me to Lucius' castle quicker and with more than enough time to save his brother.

We soon found ourselves downstairs and making our way across the tavern towards the exit but as soon as we were close, I felt something. It was like a creeping sensation along my skin, as if some dark entity had been walking its fingertips up my spine leaving behind an icy cold trail. I even found myself shuddering then trying to pinpoint where that feeling had just come from.

It was as if there was an ache on my back from where the hex had once been, and the crawling feeling that I got was also a reminder of the evil who had put it there.

I turned and looked back at the bar, scanning it quickly to see if there was any reason for the feeling, but all I came across were the same patrons and bar staff that had been there before. Nothing looked out of the ordinary, although I was in a tavern in Hell, so what was now becoming ordinary to me was actually a bit worrying to my state of mind. Was I really going to get back to the mortal realm and find myself questioning the state of things when going into a normal pub? Would I find the lack of horns, scaled skin and more claws, fangs and teeth than beer caps, as being unusual?

I decided to put the uneasy feeling down to the tendrils of

power that still lingered on my body from the hex, so I ignored the strange looks I was getting, which included a questioning look from the red skinned barmaid who had obviously been the service of choice for the portal keeper we had been waiting for.

"Come oan, lass, mah brothers be waiting," Trice said, jarring me from my questioning thoughts. Then we left the tavern and thanks to the cloak Trice had given me, it meant I had some protection against the cold as I pulled it closer over my shoulders. I could feel the Eye of Janus as a comforting weight at my back, telling me it was secure and above all, hidden.

Although, considering what it actually did to people whenever it was touched by an unworthy soul, then I very much doubted it would get pickpocketed and not be noticed. As even in Hell I was sure people all of a sudden bursting into a cloud of black sand wasn't the type of thing that people ignored. But what did I really know what people considered as normal here, as it certainly wasn't red skinned demons flashing their tits or little green goblins creating handsome projections of men so that they could get their little goblin rocks off?

Outside, Griff and Vern were waiting for us along with the aqua blue skinned demon who was looking impatient, as if he had better things to do. Well, of course he did, I thought with a giggle, wondering if he actually had a boss of any kind and what they would say if they knew he was taking breaks in a tavern to get his own rocks 'polished'.

"I do have shit to do, you know," the demon grumbled, making me utter under my breath,

"Oh yeah, we know." Trice smirked down at me knowing what I was referring to, before we all set off down the street. I had to say it looked slightly different now that I wasn't running for my life wringing wet and covered in mud. Of course, it also helped that it was no longer raining but this didn't help the cobbled street from being covered it puddles, one of which was considered more a pool of water and after a quick glance around, I didn't see any other way to negotiate it other than getting wet. But then, before I had chance to dip my foot in, I swiftly found myself being swept up into a pair of strong arms as I was shrieking out from the loss of stance.

"What are you doing?"

"I wid say tis obvious, unless ye fancied spending th' rest o' th' journey soaking wet fae th' knees down," Trice said sloshing through the water, that thankfully only came up to just above his ankles. As for me, I was kept from being soaked thanks to his thick leather boots and his strong hold on me. But after this I didn't know what to say, so decided to keep my mouth shut and ignore that cocky handsome smirk of his. One, I had to say, was not even affected by the scar on his handsome face, as it most certainly didn't detract but only enhanced his rugged beauty. I would have been tempted to ask what happened and how he'd received that scar, but I refrained, as I didn't want to give him the wrong impression by asking personal questions.

Although, on a purely irrational front, I had to confess being this close to him made me want to reach out and touch it, tracing the line with part of my fingertip. Trice, along with his brothers, most certainly had that lovable rogue thing going on. Something all three of them definitely worked to their advantage.

This theory was confirmed when Vern looked back over his shoulder and winked at me. I would have rolled my eyes if it hadn't been for the fact that these three were yet again here not only to save my life, but to deliver me safely back to Lucius.

Something that was beginning to look like a full-time job of theirs, making me wonder if they were looking forward to getting back to their usual jobs of hunting people for a bounty, instead of human Fae-sitting. But it also had me wondering if they would claim their souls back from Lucius like they had bargained for, and if they did, then what? I knew it was strange seeing as they hadn't been in my life for very long, but I had to admit that once this was all over, I would most certainly miss the McBain brothers.

Even Trice.

Speaking of the broody Scottish Hero, the second my legs were released from Trice's hold was when I was jarred out of my thoughts of the future. Because we were now on the outskirts of the town and seeing as there wasn't a River in sight, I knew it must have been on the other side from where I had pretty much broken in and legged it through the muddy streets.

The whole town was surrounded by a wall, so it wasn't surprising to see a guarded entrance as we approached. Which, thankfully, was one that didn't have the same enraged gatekeeper that had chased me only hours ago with the intent of killing me.

No, instead the guards positioned either side of the colossal double doors simply nodded to both the portal keeper and the three shifter Warriors. Three guys that admittedly looked far more imposing than I did when first turning up at the gates looking like a drowned rat. It just goes to show what a lot of muscle and weaponry can do when you need intimidation to get you into places.

When we walked through the gates, I found a rudimentary path that led into a forest area, one that was covered either side by only one type of tree. It was what I was soon informed to be named the crooked forest, and for good reason. Because this didn't really surprise me, considering all the tree trunks sprouted from the ground and curled in S shapes before leaning to the right. The strange forest floor was also covered in dead pale leaves, telling me that the unusual shaped tree trunks and their eerie thin branches once held a bouquet of foliage. One that would have created a canopy above had those leaves still been there. However, now it just gave the forest a creepy, abandoned look and one seemingly void of all life.

Pretty soon the pathway became lost to a bed of dry, dead leaves that crunched under our feet as though we were stepping on a packet of potato chips. I had to question how this had happened considering it had rained not long ago and should have been a soggy mess of sludge. Yet here we were, crunching our way through the forest with the silence only welcoming us again whenever we stopped. I didn't know how long it was that we walked, but I couldn't imagine much time had passed seeing as when I looked back over my shoulder, I could still make out the glow of the town we had left behind.

"Not far now," Trice said as if he was reading my mind. and he was right, it wasn't more than a couple of minutes before we stopped in front of what looked like a manmade cave. The rounded entrance had been decorated with carved stone blocks that went from the ground level all the way round to the other side. The only break in the circular decoration was a V shape keystone mounted at the centre at the very top. It was carved with some sort of demonic symbol I couldn't read, if I were to hazard a guess, I would have said it held information about the destination the portal led to.

But other than the stonework, there wasn't really anything else that would have led you to believe this was a place of significance. Nothing screamed 'here lies a portal to a different realm' or that there was anything special about this place, as it could have been the entrance to some hibernating demon's home.

However, that was about to change, as the portal keeper pulled a glass vial from inside his jacket, one that looked like it belonged as some fancy handle on a dagger as it was that type of shape. From this distance I could see it was decorated in swirls of hammered gold, and it was only when he twisted them that it made the same symbol that was carved on the keystone.

After he did this, the glass filled with some sort of blue cloud before it was released, seeping out of the end in a glow of tiny blue sparks. There were thousands of them that looked like little fireflies that all started to group together to form what looked like a giant key. The portal keeper then extended his arm out with the key in hand, and the closer to the centre of the opening he reached was when something happened. A curtain of power appeared in a shimmering wave of fabric as if caught in the breeze. It reminded me of the near invisible force that kept Lucius and me apart back at the Tree of Souls temple.

But then the gleaming wall began to turn into something more, and as the key was pushed forward it became that of a solid keyhole. The moment the key was inserted, the shimmering wall intensified and became a swirling colour of purples, blues and greens, with an ominous black framing the edges. This was obviously now signifying that the portal had been opened.

It was nothing like the portal I'd first stepped into when coming to Hell, after stepping through the centre of the tree. For all I knew, every portal in Hell was something different to the next, most likely depending on where the destination led you to. But all I cared about was that this particular destination was going to be closer to Lucius' castle because I feared that time was quickly running out.

I went to take a step forward, and stopped the moment I felt it. That creeping feeling that I felt dancing up my spine when in the tavern just came back to me and I couldn't help but look over my shoulder, feeling as though we were being watched. In fact, it became something so tangible that I could almost reach out and touch it. I could taste the metallic bitterness in the air as if something wasn't quite right.

"Trice, do you feel that?" I asked, making him look down at me first before he looked to where my eyes were rooted in the forest behind us.

"Aye, we ur bein' watched," he said with a frown, making me thankful that I wasn't being judged for being nervous or paranoid. Although, to be fair, I think being paranoid down in Hell was probably a regular occurrence, and one that kept you alive.

Added to these suspicions was thanks to the portal keeper as he turned the key, pulled out the handle and took a step back giving the four of us a wide berth.

"What's gaun oan here?" Trice asked just as Gryph said,

"Aye, how come dae ah feel…?" That sentence died in his throat the second the portal keeper suddenly threw his head back and let out a blood curdling scream. After that I didn't have long to question anything as his skin started to ripple as if his flesh was being cooked from beneath. I felt myself start to gag at the sight of his skin bubbling before it popped and blood burst from the opening. Trice was stood in front of me in a second, protecting me from both potential harm and the view of the portal keeper being boiled alive!

I just caught sight of him falling to his knees before his agonising cries reached a crescendo. The stench of cooked flesh was ripe and clung to the air, which meant that I had to continue to breathe through my mouth just so I wouldn't vomit. I also knew that for as long as I lived, I would never get that smell out of my head, for it was burned to the horrific memory section in my mind for all eternity.

I was just about to speak, ready to ask one of them to do something, when the sound of an arrow whistling through the air ended both his suffering and my question. I knew that Vern had been the one to put him out of his misery, and also ours by being forced to witness such horror.

"Look, see anythin' we recognise?" Vern said, and I looked around Trice's big body to see him placing a foot on his chest as he yanked his arrow from the portal keeper's head with a sickening sound. Then he used the same arrowhead that was all bloody to peel back the shirt and reveal the mark of a hex. It was clear then that he had obviously been coerced into fulfilling his task and now it was done, a gruesome death was his only reward. Unfortunately, as all four of us were too busy staring at the body on the floor, we hadn't noticed the cause of the hex creeping up behind us.

All four of us turned the second we heard the cackling laugh of a wolf in sheep's clothing.

"You?" I questioned the moment I saw the red skinned barmaid, quickly piecing together how lover boy had received his hex. She shrugged her shoulders and smirked before telling me,

"You have something my master wants."

"Oh, and let me guess, you're just the chick to get it back for him?" I said with a fold of my arms, and Trice tensed next to me. This was before I felt his hand at my side as if put there by instinct.

"Oh, it isn't just the Eye my master wants," she replied with a cunning sneer, making Trice tense to the point that his knuckles cracked. It was in that moment that I knew something was going to happen, as I could almost taste it in the air.

"So, you're taking over other bodies now... *witch,*" I sneered back at her, hissing the last word like an insult, making her lip curl in anger at the sound. At this, Trice growled and I felt his two brothers step in closer as they too waited for trouble. You could have cut through the dangerous tension with Trice's icy blade as we all waited for what the witch was planning next.

"Whatever gets the job done, now the way I see it, you have

two choices, Princess…" This time I was the one growling at what was most definitely an insult back.

"…you can either come with me and I will allow the shifters to leave and walk through the portal, one that will lead them to Lucius' castle so they may save his brother, or I will send you all into an even deeper realm for you to try and crawl out of," she said, making me clench my fists at my side, allowing the anger to start to fuel the rage I knew was strong enough to beat her.

"I think we'll pick option C," I said as I started to lift my hand, feeling the power rising within me. But unbeknownst to me she had the upper hand, for her own power was far quicker than mine.

"Very well, say hi to the King, after all… he is an old friend and he's just *dying* to kill himself another dragon!" she said emphasising the word dying, and before I could think too much about it, suddenly a Demonic tentacle lashed out at us, coming from nowhere!

It headed straight for me, and at the same time she raised her own hand making a gust of power fly straight from her scarred hands. I knew then what she had intended to do, which was grab me, whilst pushing the others back and forcing them into the portal. However, what she hadn't accounted for was Trice's quick actions. He had partially shifted enough to bring forth his wing, shielding me and at the same time knocking back the tentacle with enough force it severed a meter length from the end, making the squirming piece fall at our feet.

But this all happened in seconds, and as the witch screamed in anger, it was the last thing we all heard before we were pushed back by an invisible force. We headed straight for the shimmering portal, and I watched as first Vern then Gryph disappeared through it. Then it was their brother's turn to follow as my last glimpse of Trice was him desperately shouting my name a single second before he vanished. As for me, I could feel myself falling right behind them and I braced myself for whatever it would feel like to fall through… however, *it never came.*

My body came to a painful halt as it was tugged back just before my body was able to make it through. I first looked down across my chest to see where the pain was coming from, as the rope from the sack cut into my skin. I then looked over my shoulder to find the cause, as there was another tentacle that had grabbed hold of the sack and was using it to keep me in this realm.

"LET ME GO!" I screamed, and this had been all Trice had needed. Because suddenly a clawed hand came back through the portal and snagged the rope just enough to cut through it, releasing me from the witch's hold. I screamed as the pain sliced through me, where Trice had accidently caught my skin whilst trying to save me, before everything else was lost to sensation. This was the nauseating feeling of being sucked through some kind of vacuum as all four of us found ourselves flying beyond the portal like the witch had intended. I cried out, but my voice became lost in a dazzling echo that surrounded me as if there were hundreds of me all screaming at the same time. I then felt Trice's hold on me disappear as he too was ripped away, with his clawed fingers losing their grip on my clothes.

My body felt as if it was being torn apart in a painless attempt at trying to create more of me. It was the strangest sensation I had ever felt, and thankfully it wasn't one that lasted long. I landed in an ungracious heap with only the smell of freshly cut grass to tickle my nose. Then the pain hit, and it felt like every part of my body ached after spending twelve hours at the gym!

"Owwww," I moaned, before putting my hand beneath me

and pushing up so I could take a look and see what new shitstorm had landed our way or should I say…

Where we had landed.

When I took one look at my surroundings, the first thing that came to mind, also came whispered from my lips…

"Oh shit, well, we are not in Kansas Hell anymore."

CHAPTER THREE

DASH IT ALL

I shifted painfully, pushing my body even further up from the ground, taking in my new surroundings again. Unsurprisingly, it was something that looked vastly different than the realm I had once been in moments ago. The grass beneath my fingertips was unlike anything I'd ever felt before, as it was so soft, I almost questioned whether I was in fact sat on some giant creature's back and was now stroking its fur. It wasn't even a familiar green colour, but instead was a strange beige that faded to a soft peach tone at the tips.

I shook my head and tried to rid myself of the dizzy, unsettling feeling that had rattled my brain as I'd been forced to travel through the portal. I didn't know how I knew, but the gateway we had just travelled through, was something much more powerful than we expected to find. Because one thing was abundantly clear…

We were no longer in Hell.

Which begged the question… *where the Hell were we!?*

I expected to hear the groans, grunts and curses of three Scotsman, however all I heard was the wind rustling the strange looking trees up ahead. I looked to be in some kind of meadow as there was a strange arch of wilderness in the distance cutting off the view from up ahead. The trees were a strange amber tone that started off the same colour as the grass and then turned white as if the tree bark had been bleached. Then came a canopy of orange leaves that created a warm glow as though the sun was setting lower than the horizon. As for the sky above, it was the only usual sight I could take from my surroundings, being that it was a bright blue and cloudless day. I knew then I most definitely wasn't in Hell anymore for I hadn't seen a sky like that since entering the realm.

I turned around and looked in the opposite direction from the forest to find an endless sight of mountains in the distance. They were beautiful, even if they were nothing like the rolling green hills of my own mortal countryside, but instead were blanketed in different shades of oranges, yellows, and reds. In fact, it looked like a sunset had fallen from the sky and landed on the Earth like some Persian comforter. But then, there in the very distance, I could just see what looked like turrets rising out on the top of a hill, but it was too far away to make out many more details other than that.

"Where am I?" I questioned aloud, knowing that it was unlikely that I would get an answer. Gryph, Vern and Trice were nowhere to be found, and I couldn't help that sinking feeling in my chest from rising. It was the same feeling I had on realising my mistake when first stepping into Hell back when Lucius had tried to stop me. At the very least, I liked to think that I hadn't made too many bad decisions since then. Although, despite that, it obviously hadn't exactly got me far. No, in fact, all it had gotten me was kidnapped and finding myself face to face with the harpy Queen… oh and not forgetting a brother Lucius didn't know he had. And speaking of brothers,

"Gods alive! What's going to happen to me now?" I muttered looking around at the ethereal looking landscape, one that the witch had only ever intended to send the three brothers to. Because it was obvious she had other plans for me, thankfully Trice had intervened. But this was when it really hit me…

"Fuck no! Shit, shit, shit!" I shouted at myself after spinning on a foot and finding it was true…

The witch had the Eye, meaning that I had failed.

I had failed Lucius.

And now I was here, and my failings were mounting by the minute because unless some miracle happened, then the chance of getting back before Lucius executed his brother was looking less and less likely. Which also meant that the sight of me sat on some therapist's sofa telling them how I couldn't ever forgive myself and writing my feelings down in a book just wasn't cutting it, is one that was becoming clearer by the second.

So, here I was, the witch had managed to get the Eye and I couldn't help but feel like the biggest failure ever! I don't know why it had chosen me to be its keeper or Guardian or whatever the hell it wanted to call me. But for some reason it had and now that it was no longer in my grasp, I felt its connexion with me stronger than ever before. I had to question whether this was so that I could find it again, and I could sense when it was near. Either way it was in the hands of the witch and her Master, whoever he may actually turn out to be.

My only consolation with this shitty turn of events was the knowledge that the witch's master didn't have the power to touch it like he obviously thought he had. But then, did he actually think that the Eye of Janus should have chosen him?

If that was the case, then why did he have harpy after harpy sacrifice their lives touching it? Was it to test its strength, to test its ability at killing and taking life? Once again, I was struck down with too many questions and not enough answers, and just then I had to question where my head was at considering I had my own problems to face, ones surprisingly more important than the Eye right now… like finding three Scottish shifters.

"Well, I'm not going to get anywhere by standing around here all day feeling sorry for myself," I said before I started walking in the only direction that looked like it led anywhere. The strange grass brushed up against my ankles and tickled my skin, and I was about to reach down and touch it when suddenly I heard shouting. I started running towards the sound, making my way across the flat part of the meadow before it started to incline into a hill. There was no way of knowing what was on the other side, but all I could hope for was that I wasn't as alone as I thought I was, and I would be trying to decipher some heavy Scottish accents again in no time.

This was thankfully confirmed the second I heard a very distinct swearing that was more of a feck than a fuck.

"We need tae find th' girl, nothing is mair important!" I heard Trice saying in an angry, almost panicked tone.

"We wull split up if we need tae, bit dinna worry, lad, wull find her," Gryph assured him.

"As fur ye, wull ye hurry up 'n' shift yer Wyvern arse!" Trice snapped, and this was the last thing I heard said before I made my way over the hill and could see them. However, I sucked in a quick breath of surprise and squealed in fright the second I saw the dragon in front of me… no not dragon…

A Wyvern.

I didn't really know what the difference was between a dragon and a Wyvern, other than Vern in his shifted form had two legs not what I gathered was the usual four you would see on a dragon. But either way this didn't detract from his magnificence, and seeing as this was the first time I had seen a creature of his kind, well, it was easy to see why I was stunned to silence.

He was incredible!

Most of him was black with hints of red, the majority of which was on the flaming colour of his scaled underbelly. But I could now see elements I recognised from when they were all shifted and merged as one. Like his black tail that had red spikes running down the length and ended into a narrow arrowhead. The large feet with the curled black talons was a sight I knew intimately, as I had once travelled clutched in its tight grasp curled up like a baby.

Then there were his wings, black like the night, where different size scales ranged from the smaller ones at the centre to larger ones towards the tips. Prominent finger bones were brushed with hints of red along the ridges and each finger was tipped with a large deadly talon, matching those on his feet.

But, most magnificent of all, was his head. A dragon's head that had strange, webbed fins running down the side of its cheeks and down its neck. Row after row of sharp teeth could be seen sat in between two sets of fangs, one slightly smaller than the other. A single, giant horn surrounded by spikes lay at the centre of his head and glowing red eyes were slanted, and also spiked by hardened skin giving the appearance of an eyebrow. His eyes were burning like red hot coals that had been carved from cooled magma, as if chipping away to get to the lava underneath. They reminded me of the shape of a cat's eye, with the horizontal slitted black pupils that looked as if they were sneaking through the cracks of a door.

"Amelia! thank th' gods!" Trice said as soon as he saw me

coming over the hill. He then looked directly to where my gaze was rooted to and teased,

"Vern git yer arse back tae human before she thinks ye'r going tae gobble her up." The dragon, or should I say, Wyvern, as I clearly needed to get into the habit of doing despite how he looked, bristled at this, shaking his head a little. Then something started to happen, and I gasped, unable to help the shudder that wracked my body. I hadn't even realised that Trice had reached me, and my reaction made him take another step closer to me.

"Tis all right, lass," he assured the moment the air around his brother started to turn into a vapour. It was as if an immense heat had warped the elements around him and the very fabric of time was shaking and vibrating. In fact, any minute I expected him to be sucked into some kind of alternate universe. Then again, I had seen way too many sci fi movies and was admittedly a massive geek.

But whatever was happening to him started gaining momentum, as pretty soon it started to warp the image enough that all I could make out was colour. The black and hints of red started to merge, until eventually more colours were added and the jumble of a distorted image started to create a shape once more. This meant that soon, Vern was stepping through the chaos, leaving it behind him the moment he did. His cocky grin said it all, and the dimples shown at his cheeks said even more.

"I don't know which one I preferred, but I have a feeling that if I said this one, then that will probably go straight to his head," I commented, making his brothers laugh. But with that cheeky grin still playing at his lips, he strode over to me with a cocky stride and then said to me when he was no more than a foot away,

"My lady, I cannot express what it means to see you

unharmed and looking ravishing as… oh darn…" The moment it was out of his mouth he stopped whatever else he was about to say, and his eyes widened in shock just as ours did the same.

Then in an overly posh English way, he said…

"Dash it all… I am a gentleman again!"

CHAPTER FOUR

A FLY BY SHOOTING

The moment this came out of Vern's mouth, his two brothers burst out laughing as if their hilarity could not be contained.

"I fail to see how this is amusing," Vern said as well as crossing his arms and tapping his foot. Which I had to say, in that moment, all he was missing was a tweed suit, a large glass of brandy and a springer spaniel stood next to him with a dead pheasant hanging from its mouth.

"I think ye'll fin', brother, tis very funny," Trice said in between laughter. As for poor Vern, well, none of us seemed to know why it happened, only that the moment we had made it through the portal, Vern had been affected in a way his brothers hadn't been.

To begin with, he had been the only one to fully shift into his other form. Which made me question if because of it, it had some kind of reverse effect of the spell Nero had put on him? A spell that back in Hell had naturally worn off after a time, making me now wonder what it was about this realm that had brought it back?

"Well, at least one good thing comes out of this," I said rolling my lips inwards to try and prevent myself from laughing along with his brothers.

"And pray do tell me what that is, my lady," Vern said in a voice that didn't match his pissed off demeanour. I smirked and told him,

"At least I'll be able to understand one of you." Then I gave him a wink that made him roll his eyes at me. I patted his chest once and teased,

"Now that wasn't very gentlemanly of you." At this, Griff burst out laughing yet again, making his whole muscle clad belly shake, and Vern just granted him an unamused look in return. As for Trice, he was now the one with his arms folded across his chest, scowling as if the idea of me being unable to understand him was one that vexed him greatly. But as for me, well I just kept the big smirk on my face as I walked over to him, smacked him on the side of the bicep, and said,

"Come on, broody, let's get this journey over with."

"And whit journey may that be, lass?" Gryph asked as I started to make my way down the hill. I looked over my shoulder at all three of my Scottish saviours, and instead of crumbling to the floor in a girly mass of hysteric tears crying over the fact that the situation now looked helpless, I pulled up my big girl pants and said,

"Well, knowing my luck, for all I know we could be off to find the fucking Wizard of Oz!" Trice shook his head a little with a grin playing at his lips as he made his way over to me.

"Then I guess that mak's ye Dorothy," Trice said after patting me on the top of the head and proceeding to take the lead. To which I grumbled to myself in a childish voice,

"I guess that makes you Dorothy... whatever, tin man." At

which point Gryph and Vern looked at each other and said at the same time,

"A'm th' lion!"

"I will claim the lion." I scoffed a laugh before informing them,

"Okay, but why you're fighting over being the cowardly lion, I don't know… plus the scarecrow is the real hero," I reminded them, making them both shout again at the same time that they wanted to claim the scarecrow. But I knew that this was just camaraderie to mask what was actually going on, which in truth was nothing more than a dire situation. Though none of us wanted to say that, because admitting it out loud would also mean admitting something far worse than just being lost…

It would mean a death was on our hands… or should I say,

A death on mine.

I don't know how long it was that we walked before it finally twigged on me to ask,

"So, how come you're not shifting, because no offence, wouldn't that get us there a lot quicker… *wherever here is?"* I muttered this last part to myself as it was hard to know where we were going, seeing as we didn't know where we were to begin with!

"It wid, bit considering we dinnae ken where it is we are, I think tis best we save oor energy fur whin something bad happens 'n' nae offence, Dorothy, bit around ye something always bad happens," Trice said, making me want to growl in return and ignore the extended way he said the name Dorothy due to his accent.

"Gee, thanks, and *of course why would I take offence to that?"* I muttered sarcastically making him grin down at me.

"So, any idea where we are?" I asked thinking this would be an important fact to know right now.

"No, as it isnae a place we've ever bin tae before, althoogh if I wis taw hazard a guess I wid say 'twas in one o' th' elemental realms," Trice said, just before Gryph walked up beside us and added,

"You've git that right, as nowhere in Hell looks as nice as this place!"

"It's a jolly lot cleaner than some of the… oh darn it, please do continue, for I fear my explanation on the matter will come out as sounding rather droll and like my fellow brothers, I surely do not wish to offend you, my lady." At this, Trice and Gryph burst out laughing when Vern smacked himself on the forehead in shame. Gryph then waited for him to catch up before slapping him on the back and telling him,

"Stop yer lollygaggin', yer posh twat 'n' git a shifty oan before yer britches git any tighter 'n' squeeze aff yer bollocks completely, yer big pansy!"

"That's hardly helpful now, is it?" Vern said in return after putting a hand on his hip before he could stop himself posing in the girly stance.

"Well, as lang as yer posh ass hasn't forgotten how tae shoot a feckin arrow, yer still useful," Gryph teased, making Vern cross his arms and quip,

"Charming, brother." Gryph held out both sides of his tunic and pretended to curtsy, but with such a big bulking body of muscle it was more awkward than anything. Hence why I couldn't help but giggle at the sight, granting me a wink from the big guy in return.

After this we continued to walk along the unique countryside and I had to confess, that after about an hour of navigating up and down hills my thighs were screaming at me and begging me to stop. Also I could have drunk a well dry and wished that I had asked for a water back at the tavern. Now, as for the three brothers, well they barely looked as if they had taken a leisurely stroll around someone's garden, despite the fact that together they were carrying an arsenal of weaponry strapped to their bodies and weren't exactly dressed light for the journey.

However, it was when we were coming to the top of the next hill that we finally saw life of a different kind. It was in that moment when I heard Trice swear next to me that I knew it wasn't going to be good. This was confirmed when about forty men all started to pull weapons from their behind backs and take aim at the four of us who stood at the top of the hill looking down at them now running towards us. In fact, I think I would have preferred the sight from Jurassic Park to see a speeding stampede of dinosaurs running towards us, 'cause my only response was,

"Ah crap, what now?!" I took pause and Trice gave me a single look as if to say I told you so, making me hold up a hand and warn him,

"Don't say it, don't you dare say it!"

"Ye git it, Dorothy?" Trice replied with a condescending pat on my head, making me groan,

"And cut the Dorothy shit, would you?" My reply to this was his smirk that said it all.

"So, what do we do now, because no offence, but I'm getting the impression that these locals aren't all that friendly?" I asked, thankful at least that the McBain brothers didn't look all that worried.

"Whit gave it awa' lass?" Gryph asked with a one sided grin.

"Oh, I don't know, must be the Attila the Hun thing they've got going on, plus those weapons don't exactly look like anything they bought in a toy shop!" I snapped out the obvious, making Vern pull his bow free along with an arrow from his quiver.

"I say we give them a bloody good thrashing!" he said, and I couldn't help but raise a brow in question before I mocked,

"Wow, brutal much, you were almost terrifying." Again, just like his brothers, his look said it all. But then Trice gave Vern a slight nod of his head, making him lower his arrow and relax ready for battle stance.

As for the small army that was now racing towards us, one that looked nothing short of barbaric, they were getting closer by the second. Each and every one of them was clad in black leather and thick furs around their shoulders, giving them the appearance of an army of two legged beasts charging our way. Their weapons and basic armour were all a mismatch of designs with only the colour of darkness in common. Whoever they were, they were organised enough to fight as one, just like any trained army would.

But they also looked like a band of brutal killers that had only one common goal, and in that very moment it was to reach us. Yet despite this, it was still clear that they were most likely mercenaries or a group of travelling raiders as it didn't seem as though they were part of anyone's army but their own.

"So, again, what is our plan here?" I asked as my voice got more panicked knowing that I didn't have a weapon of my own and we were most definitely outnumbered.

I felt Trice's heavy hand rest at my shoulder before telling me,

"Now we shift, lass." He finished this with a wink down at me before warning,

"I wid stand back if I wis you." Oh, I didn't need asking twice as I started walking backwards, giving them a large enough space to do whatever was needed to create the beast that could easily take down this army of... *whatever they were.*

As soon as I was far enough away, all the brothers stepped up to one another and clasped each other on the shoulder creating a triangle of muscle. Then, each of them took in a deep breath and the moment they did, the air around them started to change. It was as if a pulsating power was vibrating out of them, turning the air around them into something tangible, as though they had started commanding the weather, sucking it to them to focus it into what they needed. As if they had sucked in any supernatural particles that may have been around them, forging them into their own power and creating something magical at its centre.

In truth, I didn't know whether I was glad or not that the sight of them shifting was kept mainly behind a veil of magic, like they were caught in the middle of a vortex and all I was left looking at was a blurred version of the world around them. It was one that grew bigger and bigger and with each time, I wisely took another step backwards, fearing that I hadn't given them enough space.

Then, just before the vortex could drop, a great and mighty beast flew up from its centre, roaring in a boom of sound as it did. I gasped the second it was out of the top before the magic that had been around them could vanish, dropping down to the ground like a dissolving wave hitting the shore. Their combined dragon rose in an impressive display of raw power, and the deafening roar of its fury echoed along the landscape. This was amplified by the mountain range that surrounded us and made the treeline shake.

A sound escaped my lips that wasn't just shock, because I had seen this before, but more in utter awe of seeing it once again. They were incredible and not a sight that anyone would ever get used to seeing, for it would literally take anyone's breath away!

It was also a sight that was strong enough to stop the small army in their tracks as they too obviously never seen anything like it before. The dragon swooped low after circling the men, roaring with all three heads before rising back up the hill to fly straight at me. I sucked in the shuddered breath through my teeth as I forced my feet to stay where they were and hold my ground as I knew the beast wouldn't hurt me.

I felt the ground shake beneath me as the beast landed, and I was left looking up at the underbelly that was a combination of fur, feathers and scales. It opened up one of its large, clawed feet that I knew belonged to Vern, telling me silently to get in and hold on for the next part of the journey, because Trice had been right, they had waited until absolutely necessary for them to shift so we may have some hope of escaping any trouble that may arise. One look at the barbaric soldiers that were shouting out in some anger fuelled war cry and banging their weapons on their shields, and I knew there was no better time than now.

So, I ran the short distance to the clawed foot and gently lowered myself into its clutches, trying to get as comfortable as possible. This was somewhat of a challenge, but I managed it and clung on to the thicker part of his talon that curled around me as gently as it was capable of doing. Then I let out a small yelp as three sets of mighty wings above me started to manipulate the air around them. Now using it as a force to lift their large body from the ground and take flight once more.

We circled around, and I swallowed hard trying to ignore the pit in my stomach that threatened to bring up what little food I had eaten, especially seeing as the small mouthful of root water mead I had drunk was now churning in my stomach as if it had been a drop of acid I had taken.

"Just hold on, Fae, nothing to do but just hold on," I told myself, hoping this little mantra of mine would work in calming my bodily functions. The last thing the shifter brothers needed right now was me losing my big girl bladder or being sick on them.

I looked below, thankful at least that I wasn't afraid of

heights unlike my mother, and saw the barbaric bandits congregating together and hiding something in between the centre of them, as they seem to be working frantically on something. That's when I started to have a really bad feeling about what was to happen next.

"Now, what the hell is that?" I questioned, squinting, and trying to see if it would help in discovering what was going to be thrown our way next. Of course, by the time I could actually make out what it was, I was too late, as it was just that… something being thrown our way as…

The trap was being sprung.

CHAPTER FIVE

WHEN THE MIGHTY FALL

After this, everything happened so quickly that I barely had time to scream in warning. Thankfully, I wasn't the only one who noticed when the glowing net was fired from what looked like a handheld mediaeval cannon. The McBain brothers had seen it for themselves, which wasn't totally surprising considering they had three heads, so you would expect at least one of them to have seen it.

But this meant that I had to hang on for dear life the second the brothers had to freefall to move quickly enough to avoid it. They did this by tucking in their wings and by a fraction of space, they were able to dodge it just enough from it catching them. It was in this moment I almost seemed cocooned, as their legs tucked under their belly at the same time a pair of their wings wrapped around itself... me included.

This meant for a short period of time I couldn't see what was happening, until the wings opened at the very last moment before we collided with the ground. I screamed when I saw how close we were and kept my eyes closed as if waiting for the impact that never came. No, instead the beast rose up back up the hill to where we had begun this flight, and as soon as it came closer to the ground, it opened up its claws without warning. Then, with a little flick of its foot, it dropped me so that I was rolling onto the grass with a bone jarring thump.

I then looked up in time to see the cockatrice lower its head enough to convey with me its plan, silently telling me to wait here while it went to deal with the threat. Something I was assuming it couldn't do whilst it had me in its grasp, and after free falling in a spin and plummeting to the ground, I had to say that I readily agreed. I was just thankful that I wasn't going to be on that particular ride again as I definitely didn't think my stomach would be able to take round two.

After this, I watched as the combined beast of three flew closer to the men before releasing a long stream a fire, one that came from Vern's Wyvern. This had the small army covering themselves in an interlocking shell that created a dome of protection above their heads, doing so with their shields. It was also when I realised that whatever those shields were made of, they were obviously fireproof.

"Oh shit, that's not good," I muttered to myself, and the dragon roared in anger as it too realised that fire was not penetrating the shields like it hoped it would. No, instead it merely left scorch marks in a sunburst shape around where the army stood compacted together.

The beast snarled down at them as it circled the army yet again, and this time came at them with a different approach. Again, it was Trice's cockatrice's head that lowered and instead of fire, breathed out a long stream of ice that covered the small army like an oversized igloo. It froze the tops of the shields making them now a large mound of ice, and only left me wondering if the bodies beneath it were frozen too?

Boy, I hoped so.

I didn't have long to wait until I found out. The brothers' dragon was getting ready to circle back around to take another hit at them. At the same time there was an echoing sound of cracking ice as the army all raised up their shields as one. This caused them to burst from the icy cage together.

But it was in this moment that the dragon had its back to the army, and all they had to do was take only seconds to aim before they were again firing their weapon. It looked like a glowing golden net that flew through the air like a torpedo before opening up big enough to catch its prey. Because the dragon's back was to them, it left me screaming in a desperate attempt to let them know of the danger flying towards them from behind…

But I was too late.

Because now the beast was falling.

"NO!" I screamed again, as the sight of a tangle of wings, legs, heads and tails all plummeted through the air in a twist of golden rope. And what was worse, was that this time there was no hope of them saving themselves before they hit the ground. I cried out again in horror as the beast hit the ground, tearing up the landscape as if a meteorite had cut through a slice of this realm. The McBain brothers had fallen, and I was just left questioning what would happen to them when the army reached them, as they were now closing in on them.

I knew then that there was only one thing left to do, and I just hoped that I had enough power to be able to do it, because over forty men were a lot more than the four I had knocked down the last time. But then I remembered the harpies that my power had managed to eradicate in one blow, and all I could hope for was that I could achieve the same thing again, only this time without the power of the Eye. There were just too many ways that this could go wrong, but it was only that one reason to try that was all I needed. All I needed to have me racing down the hill ready to take on an entire army of barbarians!

The dragon in the net rolled as streams of fire, ice and air were bursting from its mouths in a desperate attempt to escape. But this didn't last long as I could see the problem for myself when its large body was being constricted, preventing their breathing. Because the net that was tightening around them, was doing so the more they moved and struggled, coiling around them as if the very net was alive.

"Oh, Hell no!" I snapped as I could feel the anger burning inside of me, and I let it grow with every second that I was forced to watch as the brothers struggled against their restraints. I let it fuel my instincts in getting there sooner, ignoring the pain in my muscles that were already aching from all of the walking we had just done. All that mattered was getting to them in time, as I saw the barbarians all point their weapons at the dragon who was at their mercy.

The closer I got, the more I could hear a strange language being spoken by them but then a buzzing vibration went through my head, penetrating my skull and bringing me to my knees with the power of it! Something about the sound of their voices had me cradling my head and trying to push past the pain that shot through my brain. Thankfully, it didn't last long, or I knew I wouldn't have ended up being able to get back on my feet. Something I needed to do to make it the rest of the way to save them. I would have questioned what it had been, if hearing their voices being spoken now hadn't started to morph into one I could understand, as if it was naturally being translated through my mind...

"I've never seen three heads on one dragon before," one said, whilst another replied,

"You know what this means!"

"Three times the pay!" another shouted, and his answer to this was,

"The King's bounty will be plentiful indeed!"

This was the tail end of a conversation that I could overhear as I got closer to them, until suddenly my approach was known.

"Look what we've got here then, lads."

"Looks like our bonus came early with this little piece of fluff." They sneered with yellow teeth grinning at me, and one even licked his lips as if he could already taste the spoils of their kill. But yet again, this was something that added to the anger inside me as I took a widened stance ready for the blast of power I could feel illuminating my veins.

"Oh, it's bonus time alright... it's just not one you're expecting!" I said in a cocky way that spoke of the damage I was about to inflict. Then I thought of what made it happen the last time, as I held out my arms with my hands turned up with palms pointed to them ready for the blast of power to erupt like the Gods' fury and then…

Nothing.

Nothing fucking happened!

Then I tried again, first lowering my arms and bringing them up quicker this time, as if I were trying to push my way against an invisible wall. But in the end, after five attempts, I just looked like an idiot, because nothing was happening other than the men now being half convinced I was crazy and the other half finding my actions an amusing sight.

"Gods be damn it! Work will you!" I said, shaking my hands as if this would kick start them into action. I didn't know what was happening or more to the fact, why it *wasn't* happening, and had to question was it because I was no longer in Hell?

I was no longer in a realm I… *I belonged in?*

I don't know where that thought had come from, but it was

one that seemed to be born from some hidden absolute certainty. A certainty that Hell was... *was my home?*

But how could that be, how was that even possible? I was human... *wasn't I?*

"Okay, now is so not the time to start going crazy, Fae," I muttered to myself, as now the leader of the barbarians nodded my way. This silent command meant that half the men were now surrounding me instead of the three headed dragon. I couldn't make out most of their features as the lower half of their faces were covered by swathes of black material, reminding me of ninjas. Darkened eyes were surrounded by painted skin, making me wonder if they did most of their killing at night, for they would surely blend in.

Thick, padded material made up for strange boots and the rest of an outfit that looked as if they had been crudely sewn together from the carcasses of the creatures they killed. A strange patchwork of different textures made up a tunic style top underneath long jackets cut into sections for easy movement. Strange helmets were made from blackened skulls of even more poor creatures they had slain over the years of barbarity.

But wherever they were from, it was safe to say it was probably far from here, as this serene ethereal world around them made them stick out like black bruised thumbs. Like marks and stains upon the beauty of this new world. I just hoped that my remains weren't the next in line for some depressing barbaric fashion statement.

I held up my arms in a universal sign of surrender, hoping that in this realm it didn't just mean fuck off and kill me. Who knows, maybe it was a universal sign for take me to your leader? Either way it was doing at least one thing right, as it was focusing most of the attention on me and not on the brothers who had finally given up struggling.

"Look, I know you may think you've hit the motherload here with a three headed dragon, as clearly killing is your occupation. But I can assure you we are much more valuable alive than dead, skinned or made into a tailcoat," I said which in turn made the leader, who was the biggest of the lot, push some of his comrades out of the way so that he could take over what I supposed was the beginning of negotiations.

"Yeah, and who might you be then?" the big guy said, and I had to force down the urge to laugh as the sound of his voice was remarkably high pitched considering the size of him. Meaning the sight of him was a lot more intimidating than the tone of his threat, that was for damn sure! I coughed down my laugh and pretended that I was clearing my throat before I answered.

"My name is Amelia Draven and I belong to a King in Hell, Ruler of the Kingdom of Death, someone who will pay a handsome reward for our return." The leader looked me up and down and then burst out laughing before looking back over shoulder, telling his men,

"It's our lucky day, fellas, for we will feast tonight, for behold, we not only have the three headed beast to present to our King of Sin, but a lost Queen as well, our dark lord will be most pleased!"

"Err, what now?" I said, but he ignored me as it was drowned out by the sound of all his men raising their weapons in the air cheering as one. Meanwhile, I was still stuck on things like, 'dark lord', 'King of Sin' and 'Lost Queen' playing over in my head like a bad jingle or even worse, 90's rap!

However, this was cut short, both their celebrating and my freaking out, as a whizzing sound cut through the air. The zip of sound was the only prewarning I had as to what came next as an arrow came from nowhere and embedded itself in the leader of the group. This made the last sound heard from his lips an undignified high pitched squeal that reminded me of a piglet being stepped on. Then he fell on the ground backwards and ignited into blue flames as if the arrow itself had some kind of spell on it.

The rest of the barbarians froze for a heartbeat before they frantically started to look around, now raising their weapons in self-defence instead of victory.

"Dragon fire!" I heard this being hissed from one of the men, before another arrow came from nowhere and hit him square in the eyes making his head explode into blue flames. I screamed and automatically ducked down and at the same time, covered my head, as I didn't particularly care to be next.

After this I heard the same whizzing sound time and time again, all coming from different directions, which was followed by the sound of bodies thudding as they dropped on the floor. In the end it was like waiting for popcorn to be done in a microwave, you waited until the popping sounds slowed to a near stop before you checked it. And sure enough, I was right, as soon as the sounds ended, I looked up to find everyone dead but myself and the growling dragon still in the net.

I didn't really know what to do because I couldn't see where the arrows had come from, so in the end I did the lamest thing yet, and that was throw my hands up in the air and shout,

"I'm not with them! See, no fur in sight and my teeth are still white!" Then I grinned a cheesy grin, that even in the back of my mind had me asking myself what the hell I was doing but mainly, what the hell must I have looked like?!

Well, whatever the case, something I did must have worked as for one, I didn't end up with an arrow in my body before becoming Miss Crispy of the Realm! Oh, and secondly, the air around us started to shimmer just like it did when opening up a portal. Only instead of it being confined to the space of a doorway, it was all around us. However, when it started to open up, it did so in slices, as it looked like people sized tears being made in the world around us, where another world could be seen beyond.

I rose to my feet, feeling compelled to get closer to it, but by the time I took my first step, a man emerged from beyond the opening. This happened over and over again, as pretty soon a whole regiment of soldiers appeared, now being the ones to surround us in place of the barbarians.

I wisely staggered back until my back was against the McBain's dragon form, feeling some comfort in this as I felt it breathing heavily with the rise and fall of its stomach that was obviously now at my back.

Once the new army had us completely surrounded, they all stood to attention the second their own leader obviously stepped through, and he couldn't have been further from Mr Piglet Squealer, who had just died by a flambéing.

I turned my head slightly, patted the dragon's belly in comfort and told them all the only thing my irrational brain could come up with in that moment…

"Well, Toto, it looks like we just found the Wizard."

CHAPTER SIX

LAND OF DRAGONS

The dragon at my back whined slightly, and I wondered if this was due to my bad joke in sight of the army now surrounding us, because if it hadn't been impossible odds before, then now there was no masking the chance of escape from being near impossible. This was because calling them an army was exactly the right word for they were the polar opposite of the bandits that had been slain in seconds. The same bandits that now lay in patches, bleeding on the grass like this area of the land had just been infected.

Each of the men now surrounding us were all wearing matching armour of the highest quality, and trust me, I had seen enough in my time to know the difference. It was simply exquisite and exactly what I would have expected to see from a Kingdom of Fae beings. This being the more fanciful term for elves. However, what they themselves preferred to be called was still yet to be discovered.

But the sight of them was what confirmed we were indeed now in the Elemental Realm, as this show of strength was also one of beauty. As line after line of tall, slim men dressed in black and gold armour that gleamed under the sun was proof of that. Gods, but there wasn't even a speck of dirt in sight, making me randomly wonder if polishing the uniforms every night was part of the job description?

Matte black steel was contoured to every muscle in sleek flowing lines that were adorned by the high sheen of gold inlays, pieces of which created a design that reminded me of an art nouveau period. The flowing lines on the chest plate created a V shape and housed a symbol like a shield of nobility that I guessed represented a certain Royal house in these parts. The design was two twisted trees that framed the edges of the symbol in the middle, one that looked as if it could be some sort of ancient Elvish language.

It curled inwards and then out again with the branches reaching up to form deadly points. This centrepiece was also surrounded by the unmistakable form of a Dragon's head, one created in simple thick lines and not lending itself to too much detail. It was just enough to give you the appearance of exactly what it was... guardian of the symbol of the King in the centre.

A belt of gold broke up all the black and tapered down into a V shape before the rest of the armour split off into two sections, which covered the tops of the soldiers' legs. Two shoulder pieces framed the top of the overall design, adding strength and movability to the arms, along with protection from any oncoming blows from above. These were black plates that interlocked in teardrop shapes that ran down the biceps, whereas directly over the shoulder was a large gold leaf. Attached to these shoulder pieces were long, flowing black cloaks that barely even moved, becoming a testament to how still each warrior was at holding his nerve.

To complete the soldiers' look, narrow pointed boots rose up past the knee, with the same gold edging that matched the helmets they wore. Helmets that covered most of their faces and were topped with an arched horn like a blade down the centre of their head, one that would point towards the enemy. One that glinted in the sun with its razor edge that too was plated in gold, becoming a beautiful weapon in its own right, as I wouldn't have fancied getting headbutted with one of those things!

Now, as for the leader, he was the only one who was dressed slightly different, for his armour was the opposite image. It was all gold, with black accents showing behind the chest plate in the chain mail tunic he wore underneath. He also wore gloves and the crest on his chest was bigger than the others. His helmet matched his amour in colour, as it was all gold with raised swells twisting around the sides. These curled back on themselves and down the centre of the nosepiece. Each helmet was the same in style, only showing a slither of skin in a Y shape, this was because each helmet only let you see the eyes, the tip of a nose and a thin section of the mouth, so the army was protected from head to toe.

"Who are you… are you a King?" I asked, thinking that it was better to get introductions on the way. I couldn't see much of his expression, but I was almost certain that I saw a slight twitch of his lips. Something that at least told me he was most likely smirking at my question.

"I am captain of the Dragons Guard and have been sent to protect the creature at your back and deliver him to my King," he said, and at least I had my answer as clearly the idea of being a king, amused him.

"Where are we?" I asked, making him cock his head slightly to one side as if he was trying to determine whether or not I'd lost my mind.

"You have entered the dragon lands, but then this should have been obvious considering you have one at your back," he commented dryly, and I refrained from the urge to roll my eyes.

"Oh, you mean these guys. Well, see that's the funny thing as they're not from around here either," I told him, making him narrow the part of his eyes I could see.

"Excuse me?"

"I brought them with me," I informed him before taking the time to think if this had been a good thing to say or not.

"And where exactly is it you think you are from?" he asked in a disbelieving tone, and I suppose I couldn't really blame him. Not considering most likely we looked like we just dropped out of the sky, which wasn't exactly that far from the truth.

"Well, that's where things get tricky. Where do I start?" I said making him suggest,

"The beginning is usually a good place," he replied, and I knew with his tone that it was an underline warning to start explaining myself. I laughed nervously and before I could stop myself, my inner filter had no chance at stopping me.

"Well, I could start by telling you that I'm a human who accidentally on purpose stepped into Hell believing that she could save, not only her boyfriend and her mother, but her boyfriend's entire kingdom..." I paused to hold up a finger and continued,

"...which I may add, ended up not being the case, as in at all! But pretty much resulted in me getting attacked by giant spiders and crazy weird tree pod people, which I managed to survive thanks to these guys," I said cocking a thumb over my shoulder at them and definitely this time making the captain frown. And this really should have been my cue to shut the hell up, but it was as if verbal vomit was just spewing out of me.

"So that was before the dragon behind me saved my ass, which don't let this big three headed beast fool you, because they are actually three shifters by the name of the McBain brothers… well, anyway, they saved me and took me back as their bounty to the King…"

"You're bounty?" he questioned, making me laugh nervously again before waving a hand in front of myself and saying,

"Oh, it turned out fine in the end you see, as the King turned out to be my boyfriend… Ha, I know what you're thinking, crazy right…? Like, who knew, not me, clearly?!" I said now laughing like he would find this funny, but instead he just folded his arms across his chest and said,

"Indeed."

"Err, well anyway, I found this out before I got thrown in prison by his brother who thought I was a witch… which I am not by the way!" I pointed out quickly, making him nod and say,

"Continue."

"Oh, okay, well the King came back, was not happy to find his girlfriend in prison as you can imagine," I said as though he could, making him once again comment dryly,

"Indeed… and you ended up here how?" he asked, making me say,

"Oh, right, that… well, I got kidnapped by harpies but don't worry, I killed them all," I told him, making him finally react as if this was the most shocking part of all, one I didn't focus on but instead continued to tell him my tale of insanity.

"But then I got chased by Hellhounds, jumped on a boat of death and then thankfully the McBain brothers found me in a shitty tavern before a mob could attack me." Hell, but even saying all of this out loud was making me disbelieve myself, so Gods only knew how much of it this guy was believing!

"That's quite a tale, and one I hope ends soon with how you came to be here… which you have still yet to tell," he said, obviously now prompting me to do so and telling me in a really nice way that he was getting impatient.

"Ah, yes, well we were on our way back to the Realm of the Dead, which I should point out is where my boyfriend rules as King, but we got double crossed by the portal master who had been hexed by this witch, who kind of wants me dead sometimes and kidnapped the other… okay, well I'm not actually sure what she wants with me but anyway, we got pushed into this realm." At this he released a sigh, and with a glance spared at the dead bandits scattered around the place he said,

"Hence the raiders."

"And hence not really knowing where we are, oh, and why we are here, that would include the dragon at my back not really being from this realm… although coincidence, much." By the time I had finished this very quick recap on I don't actually know how many days, because really, they all started to merge into one a while ago. So, by the time I had stopped speaking, I think he was ready to throw me in whatever version of the Dragon Lands loony bin there was. I knew this when he tore his helmet off his head and demanded in disbelief,

"Do you want to explain the dragon part of that to me again?"

"Oh Gods, not really, I mean it was hard enough saying it the first time," I admitted on a sigh, that in truth was one that related to the handsome face I now found staring at me.

But this was unsurprising, being the type of being he was as Fae were known for their beauty, as in… every way. And this guy was no exception to that gene pool, apart from he had a slightly more rugged beauty than I had expected. But then again, he was a captain and obviously spent his days killing raiders.

He had long, dark blonde hair that was plaited at the sides in neat rows and looked to have been brushed to a high shine, despite all the killing I mentioned. Which made it clear that this was no doubt a natural form of his beauty, along with his bright green eyes that stared back at me with a regal look to them, that matched his high cheekbones, thin nose and pointed chin. Chiselled lines that mirrored the shape of his hairline, one that came down slightly into a V shape on his forehead.

He was definitely someone of power and great importance, that much was clear even without him declaring it himself by being named the captain of the guards. Yet I was still to learn his name, making me wonder if he had kept it from me on purpose. Maybe I just wasn't important enough to him to be granted it, as his next question to me certainly suggested so.

"What is the name of your master?"

"Err, now just wait a minute, I said boyfriend, not master… let's get it straight right now, for I belong to no one!" I said, clearly being affronted by the terminology he used as I was starting to think the equal rights obviously didn't exist in this realm. Just then, before I could open my mouth to say more, I watched as the captain nodded to one of his men to go ahead and cut the dragon free of the golden net.

However, the second they were free the brothers didn't just fly straight up in the air as I had expected. Instead I felt the vibrations at my back before the air whipped around my hair, knowing now that the brothers were changing back. This was when I wisely took a few steps further back, that put me closer to the man in charge… *whoever he may be*.

Although to give the guy credit, he was still gentlemanly enough to put an arm out in front of me as if to protect me from what was happening. Because one thing became clear to everyone witnessing this incredible sight, for this may have been the Land of Dragons… but it wasn't the land of shifters that turned into them.

This meant that when the whirlwind of power disappeared, the captain sucked in a startled breath when it left three men stood at the centre that none of the army were expecting to see. I knew this the second the army's weapons were quickly pointed in the direction of the McBain brothers.

"No! Don't they're with me, they're harmless!"

"Speak fur yersel', lass!" Trice said with a fold of his arms and standing dead centre with his brothers either side him, oh, and looking as menacing as ever.

"This is impossible!" the captain shouted, obviously witnessing the first of their kind in these lands.

"I told you they are shifters, and they came with me... they are, well, like my bodyguards," I said, trying once again to get him to understand that they weren't a threat, although considering they had just shifted from the sight of a three headed dragon, then I guess this still needed to be proven as my words were a little above being useless right now.

"What th' girl says is true, we wur sent tae escort her back tae oor King whin a witch sent us 'ere instead," Trice stated firmly, and I sighed in relief when the captain made a hand gesture to get his men to lower their weapons. This was before shocking us all and telling us,

"Yes, I am aware of your troubles, for was all known before your Princess here told me her long tale of woe."

"Seriously, you let me just keep..." I was cut off when he winked at me and Trice snarled,

"How the fu..."

"I believe what my brother is trying to say, or ask, for a lack of better phrase, is if you would be so kind as to explain how it is you knew we were coming?" Vern said in his posh and diplomatic way, something that ended up being pointless when his brother added,

"Yeah, so lik' I said, how th' fuck!?" Trice asked again, ignoring his brother's exasperated sigh.

"Because those raiders weren't the only ones looking for you," the captain informed us, making me frown as I had a bad feeling about this.

"But how?" I asked in a wary tone that spoke of my distrust, and for good reason when he said…

"The King knows of your witch."

CHAPTER SEVEN

A KING OF DRAGON FIRE

As soon as we were told of the King's knowledge of the witch, Trice, Gryph and Vern all took action by arming themselves. This naturally caused an adverse effect by the army once more raising their weapons and pointing them our way.

"Come 'ere, lass," Trice ordered in a stern voice that said he meant business.

"But I…" I started to try and ensure peace when Trice practically growled at me, cutting me off,

"I think ye hae said more than enough, don't ye lass?" Trice said, giving me a pointed look and referring of course to my overload of information I had offered up on a platter of words with no real prompting. Meaning that, yep, the look he gave me that said, 'you're a pain in my ass, woman' was totally warranted this time.

However, the moment I was about to walk towards him, giving Trice what he wanted, was when the captain intervened, stopping me with his words.

"That won't be necessary," he stated, before he raised an arm again and ordered his men,

"Lower your weapons." I let out a sigh of relief as I knew with one look around us that we didn't have a chance of escaping this type of soldier. But I also knew that the McBain brothers would never give up without a fight and they were proving that point by not yet lowering their own weapons. So I made the decision to prevent a chance of anyone getting hurt and instead of walking to Trice, I turned to the captain, ignoring the growly shifter's demand.

"Explain how your King knows of the witch?" I asked.

"I'm afraid you will have to ask that of him yourself, for he wishes to meet with you, young Princess," the captain replied with a bow of his head to show his respect, doing so for what I guessed he thought was addressing royalty.

"So you do know who I am?" I tested.

"As I said, you will have to take it up with my King," he replied, not giving me an answer.

"What mak's ye think we're gonnae follow ye, especially noo ye hae admitted tae knowing oor enemy?" Trice said, making the captain smirk before informing him cryptically,

"Every kingdom has its spies, shifter, you should know this." I frowned in question, but it was one I didn't get chance to ask before the captain was voicing his orders once more.

"Now ready the gateway!" he shouted, and at the very back of his men, four cloaked Fae beings emerged. However, none of them showed much of themselves, not from beneath the heavy veil of thick material of their cloaked robes. Robes that covered every inch of their bodies, including the large hoods that swooped down low over their faces. Each of which was edged with a thick border of elvish symbols that looked magical in origin.

They each took their positions, spreading out along the rows of soldiers, before raising up their hands and chanting in an ancient language I had no hope of deciphering. I only knew that it was the source of power needed to reopen the gateway that they had first stepped through. This was after they moved their hands at the same time, as if they were each spelling out something secret, because a light started to emerge following the path of their fingers as if igniting some forbidden message on an invisible page.

Seconds later, the same glowing symbol emerged before each of them. It was one that looked like a number 2 was connected to a vertical key at its side. A key that had two fang shaped lines where the head of the key would fit inside the mechanism. It finished with a sideways V shape underlining these 'fangs'.

But then the moment the symbol was finished, the air surrounding us started to distort as if heat was rising from the ground, creating a shimmering wave of colours. It then started to split as if a rainbow wall had been slashed in two, reminding me of when petrol lay on the top water before someone ran their fingers through the effect.

Then suddenly each of these portal masters made a slashing gesture with their hands cutting across in front of them before pulling back as if they were taking the part of the portal with them. This in turn made the opening bigger, as they took back the symbol they had drawn, now creating that same tear in the space ahead like before. One that obviously lead back to the Kingdom from where they had first appeared.

Once this was open, the captain stood side on and held out an arm in a gesture that told us to proceed him, no doubt making sure we weren't going to try and make a run for it. It was the reason I looked back at the three shifters I had come to call my friends and saw now the uneasy looks they gave me in return. This was when Trice shook his head and told me not to do it, when I just shrugged my shoulders and told them,

"I don't see any other options here, lads." Then before any of them could stop me I ran at the portal, holding my breath as I did and hearing Trice's roar of anger in response. But what was done was done and I was only thankful that this time, it was as easy as stepping through an open door. In other words, entering this new world was far easier than ever before and admittedly, I had been through quite a few portals. Not enough to write a book on the subject or anything, but I wouldn't have called myself a novice either. Although, at this rate, then a book titled, 'How to survive Hell and beyond' was starting to look like a very possible business venture in my future, especially seeing as I wasn't even sure I had a job to go back to when this was all over.

I looked behind me when I heard Trice's frustrated groan from the other side, before he said to his brothers,

"Let's git this shit done." This was because what I had said had been the truth, we didn't have any other options, as we simply didn't know where we were, or how to get back to Lucius' realm. Besides, we were outnumbered by a lot more than just a band of raiders who had simply been out for a payday. No, these were skilled fighters, who were well armed and even better equipped to withstand three shifters that had clearly run out of juice. That had exhausted their power to shift, which left three hard as nails fighters and a human girl who could mainly kick human ass. Now, as for the ass of the Fae, then as far as I had read, they may have been pretty, but they were also known as hard motherfuckers. Although, to give the brothers their due, they had been no match when facing giant spiders and weird tree pod people, so what the Hell did I know.

Besides, I was curious to know what this King knew, as from the sounds of what the captain had said, it may be possible that we had a common enemy. And that age old saying 'my enemy's enemy is my friend' had never been truer than at this point in time.

"Ye ur one big pain in mah ass, lass," Trice said the moment he'd stepped through and stopped next to me. I looked up at him and gave him a wink, telling him,

"I love you too… erm, you know, as a friend and all," I added quickly when I realised my mistake, but the huge grin on his face told me that the last part definitely didn't mean as much to him as the first.

"Gosh, upon my word, would you look at that," Vern said as soon as he made it through, and when it was quickly followed by another gasp of shock, it was enough to gain our attention towards the direction both brothers were now looking.

"Gods' blood, it isnae possible!" Gryph had added the second he too made it through.

"Holy mother of…"

"Dragons, yes," the captain said behind us, before motioning with a nod of his head and saying casually,

"This way."

"Okay, so I'm confused, did we just step into Game of Thrones or Lord of the Rings?" I said, at the sight of all the Dragons that dominated the surrounding landscape. They were every shape and size and colour of scale, and they were either flying in the clear blue sky or sleeping at leisure in mounds of hay that had obviously been laid out for them. They were dotted along the vast rolling hills, creating spots of colour against the palest green grass.

But that wasn't the only sight that dominated the land, as in the middle of this incredible sight of these magnificent creatures was the heart of all beauty. A city unlike any other, and one surrounded by a gleaming white wall that was so polished, it almost looked like a milk white mirror. It was one that reflected the moat of sapphire blue water surrounding it. But then, after a more intense look, I realised that it wasn't just water at all, but in fact, liquid blue flames. An eternal fire that was constantly licking and hissing its dangerous forked ends at the wall, as if guarding the city.

But the real beauty was found in what it protected beyond the wall, as at its core was a castle of the likes I had never seen before! It rose up as though it was one giant sculpted gemstone, making it look as if it had been made from a pale blue glass. It was curved and rose up in a twisted design as if mimicking the flames that surrounded it. Then, with a series of gleaming white staircases wrapped around sections, it ended up making it look like white vines had grown around the structure. Turrets, like twisted branches reached higher at different points of the castle and the two tallest were what framed the incredible entrance.

A giant arch, what must have been at least a hundred feet high, joined in an elaborate carved design of what must have been a Royal Crest, for it was the same one that adorned each of the soldiers' chest plates.

"Welcome to Calidad," the captain said before proceeding us, and leaving me to question,

"Calidad… What does that mean?"

"Nay, it cannae be true," Gryph said nearly stuttering on the words.

"By the Gods, but I fear my sanity lost," Vern said in his overly posh accent, until finally it came to Trice, who looked utterly rooted to the spot, muttering,

"Bit tis but a legend… tis… tis…"

"Alright, please can someone fill me in here?"

"Had I not, in this moment, been a gentleman then I fear there was chance at an inappropriate jest made at the lady's expense," Vern said rolling his own eyes at himself and making me frown at him, before snapping,

"Not that type of filling in, genius!" Gryph laughed and commented,

"Nice try oan getting yer humour back, brother."

"It wis aye a myth, a land o' Dragons... twas ne'er real," Trice told me, until the captain corrected,

"Calidad means Land of the Dragon Flame... now follow me, for the King is waiting," he said making me be the first to follow, and when I realised the three McBain brothers were still rooted to the spot and frozen by the sight, I shouted back,

"Well, if it's as amazing from up here, then it will be even better the closer we get... right!" When they still didn't move, I released a sigh and said,

"Yeah, that was your cue to move your asses, boys!" Thankfully, this finally worked, with Trice shaking his head grinning to himself.

The portal had opened up on the top of the hillside looking down at almost the exact same landscape we had just left, for there were mountains in the distance and the forest on our left-hand side. In fact, the main difference was the colour of the grass, as it was most definitely more familiar to my home world. Oh, that and of course the ethereal looking castle that faced us now and one surrounded by fantastical creatures, that would have anyone believing they had just stepped into a fairytale land.

But then every myth, story and fantasy all had to be born from some element of truth... didn't it? To be born from some small seed planted in someone's mind that eventually let it bloom into what it was today and told for a thousand years to come. After all, that was even how most Gods gained their power, doing so through the belief of their followers. And looking towards the incredible sight before me, well quoting the awesome Willy Wonka, it was as if I was stepping into a world of a pure imagination. As though I had unknowingly had the ability to step through my TV screen into any one of the amazing fantasy movies made, my mind was going crazy at the endless possibilities.

Because it was exactly what your mind was capable of conjuring up when thinking of an elvish city... that and much more. It was stunning in every way, despite its guardians being what was most likely considered as the most dangerous creatures alive, and this place had a city of them!

However, this had me thinking back on what the captain had said when he had first announced himself. How he was the Captain of the Guardians, meaning they hadn't originally been there for me but to guard the beast at my back. To retrieve the creature and ensure its safe return back to these lands.

The army hadn't just been the protectors of their King, but they were also the guardians of the very beasts that gave their land the name, Land of the Dragon Fire, and I could see why, even if the dragons had been absent from the picture ahead. The city was clearly dedicated to them, with the castle being at the centre of that shrine. The colossal wall itself that surrounded the city was thick enough to be a palace in its own right and one that could clearly have housed hundreds, if not thousands of Fae beings.

Of course, the view from up here offered you the ability to grasp the sheer scale of the place, as the wall surrounded a place that could have easily been as big as Manhattan!

In fact, we were so far away from the main castle that I almost questioned why they hadn't opened up a portal closer to the entrance. This meant that it wasn't really shocking that we had a good few hours left of walking and in all honesty, I wanted to cry. Or at least my legs did!

I was just thankful when the captain had obviously taken pity on me and handed me a silver flask of some sort of juice. It was delicious and I couldn't help but comment with a moan of appreciation, making him again smirk down at me as if this was a common trait of his. I had to say, it was one of those smiles that was infectious and not solely because it came with a pretty face.

He was at least gracious enough to grant me his name when I asked for it, but then in true Amelia fashion, my way of doing this was,

"So, does everyone call you captain, because, no offence, that kind of reminds me of a pirate." At this he laughed, and it was a warm, comforting sound that strangely reminded me of someone drizzling honey.

"My name is Balin."

"That's a nice name. Actually, if history serves me right, it means knight." He grinned again at this and gave me a soft look that Trice obviously didn't like because he was giving the captain daggers with his eyes.

"That may be so in your human realm, but here it means trust and not something I imagine your shifter friend is all too eager to grant me yet," he replied with a knowing grin.

"Ah, yes, well, he doesn't trust easily," I said defending Trice, even though he was making it increasingly hard to do so, especially when he started flicking a small blade in and out of his fingers.

"Um, I wonder?"

"Wonder what?" I asked making him look down at me with a mischievous glint in his eye before telling me,

"If it is because I am a Fae being or the lack of trust is because I am speaking to a girl he is *obviously in love with?"* he tested, whispering the last of this sentence closer to my ear and making me swallow hard. Then I naturally start stuttering out my excuses,

"Oh no… no, we are just… well, you know… we are friends and he's just protective of me… of our friendship, I mean… Gods, I am so bad at this aren't I?" He laughed and said,

"Yes, but then again, you are human," he said with a wink, obviously teasing me and it made me laugh back, which in turn made Trice growl. Something I chose to ignore on account of I wasn't doing anything wrong and he just kept adding fuel to the fire… pun intended because, hello, we were in a city named after Dragon Fire, so totally needed to be done!

But as for Trice, well it wasn't as if I was flirting with the guy, flicking my hair seductively out of my face and laughing in some sing song way at something he just said that wasn't even funny. I was just talking to the man!

So, I purposely looked over my shoulder and snapped,

"Calm down, Growly, I am just pumping him for information to take back to our leader so we may take over their world one day! Jeez, testy much!" I joked, making Balin throw his head back and laugh a full belly laugh, which impressively didn't make his armour move even an inch. As for Trice, he just rolled his eyes at my antics, despite his brothers joining in and laughing too. Gryph even nudged him and said,

"Lighten up, brother, afore yer ass starts squeaking, yer that uptight." Trice growled again and the second Vern opened his mouth to add to the jest, he raised a finger at his brother and warned,

"Not a single posh word oot o' yer mouth, or yer wull be making yer way doon this hill quicker than a'body else… and oan yer ass!" Then he stormed past them before catching up to me, grabbing me by the top of my arm and snapping,

"A word, princess."

"Oh, goodie." I muttered sarcastically as he started to pull me off to one side, so we put some distance between us and the captain who was now looking considerably less amused.

"Seriously, what is your problem?" I snapped even though I was pretty sure I knew.

"Oh, I hae plenty, bit then, sin meetin ye thay just keep mounting up noo, don't they?" I staggered back a step as soon as he said this, and he instantly knew he had hurt me.

"Wow Trice, you know if you wanted a less hurtful blow you could have just hit me!" I snapped, making him rake a frustrated hand through his hair causing the scar on his face to stand out even more.

"I dinnae mean that th' wey it sounded," he said, looking guilty.

"No? Because it sounded exactly how you meant it, Trice!" I snapped back not letting him off the hook just yet.

"Look, I just meant that we hae enough shite going oan richt noo, wi'oot ye trusting th' wrong people."

"Oh, I am sorry, can you tell me again what I would gain by being an awkward, rude bitch to these people who, by the way, haven't done anything bad to us so far and newsflash, they could have shot us all to death with a wave of magically flambéing arrows that made our heads explode!" I pointed out, making him scoff as if this could never have happened. I swear it was at this point that I rolled my eyes before reminding him,

"Look, I didn't ask for any of this to happen or to get you guys involved. Because let me remind you, it was a job you took because Lucius is your King, and he trusted the three of you enough to get the job done!"

"Alright, noo just a…" Trice started to say but I interrupted him as I was way too gone in the midst of my rant.

"Oh, and you can trust me, Trice McBain, Mr growl at the human at lot! That if you don't think I feel guilty enough as it is that I got you dragged into all this shit, then you're wrong!"

"Alright lass, I think yer have made yer…" Again he tried once more but yet again, I ignored him or when he raised his hands in a 'please for the love of the Gods stop, woman' gesture.

"But am I going to lie down and quit just because I am overwhelmed by guilt? No, I am not, because that isn't me. I am a fighter because I was born a Draven! And Dravens always get up. They always fight. They keep going even if it means against impossible odds!"

"Aye, a'm getting that, lass," he muttered with a knowing look, and it was one that ended up landing on something behind me. But again, I was too far gone to notice and as I continued, I also didn't take notice of the heavy beating of wings, or the way the ground shook as enormous feet landed, or even the way Trice moved so he was now protecting me.

I only heard the sound of my own anger being expressed like water gushing from a dam he'd just destroyed.

"It's in my blood, Trice, so call me Princess all you want but I am sick of that shit being said as though it's some kind of insult! I am not weak because of it… I am strong because of who it makes me, I am a Gods be damned Princess and proud of it!" I shouted at him, something that ended with the sound of clapping and I turned, ready to storm off in some dramatic fashion when a sight stopped me dead.

This was because I was now facing…

The Dragon King.

CHAPTER EIGHT

A KING'S FLIGHT

The moment I turned around, I couldn't help but do so slowly, with my widened gaze taking in the mythical image of an incredible, enormous white dragon now stood before us! Naturally, I sucked in a shuddered breath whilst taking a couple of steps backwards because well, despite what Trice thought, I did have some self-preservation!

But it was strange when being faced with this mythological beast, because it wasn't as if I hadn't seen an impressive dragon before. In fact, not to brag, but I had seen what was most likely considered as one the most unique dragons of all, as the shifter of three brothers when combined was an incredible sight to behold.

Three creatures all merged as one that created the appearance of a three headed dragon with three sets of wings, three tails and three pairs of feet, was a sight that was bound to stop anyone in their tracks. Even someone who lived here where dragons seemed to roam free like wild horses. Hell, for all I knew this was a dragon wildlife reserve and the man who sat upon the white dragon, now riding upon its back like his Noble steed, was the park's manager.

However, despite these facts and what was my close relationship with the most impressive beast of all belonging to the McBain brothers, one fundamental truth was what changed my reaction. I knew that whenever faced with the combined shift of the brothers, that they would never hurt me. They would only protect me, because at the centre of all that thick scaled skin fur and feathers lay three Scottish hearts belonging to the three bounty hunters that knew and cared for me.

But as for this majestic pale beast in front of me now, well that was no shifter. He was just a dragon and what looked like a mighty one at that. This of course meant that the threat was very real and one I was taking seriously despite it being tame enough to be ridden on. Even if all evidence did point towards the fact that it had been tamed by a master…

It's rider, the King.

It was easy to deduct as much considering the crown he wore on his head, and I was at least thankful that the handsome man was smiling despite the imposing figure he presented. Of course, if I'd have ridden in here on top of that mighty beast, dressed as one of the Teletubbies, then even I would have been considered imposing.

Parts of the beast looked as if it had been carved from white stone, as its body was overly muscular and covered in what looked like a sheen of velvety skin. Now, as for its feet, tail and underbelly that reached all the way up its neck, this was covered in large, thick scales. Lines of black could be seen in between the cracks, giving it the appearance of darker skin beneath. As for its face, this was domed with a fin at the very top of its head. It looked to be made of hardened scales, making it look as though it had a horn connecting to the bridge of its nose and finally ending at its beak-like mouth. Rows of teeth could be seen running along the sides of its face as they were not hidden when the beast had its mouth closed but instead, they overhung the bottom part of its jaw. A series of slits either side of its snout that were obviously nostrils, blew out steam when it grew restless.

Its incredible eyes were set back with darkened skin framing the spiked arches of its brows, the scaled head bristled like feathers when it snorted as if in an impatient manner. This made the King coo down at it, asking for it to calm. It obviously didn't appreciate being stood there idly as its master was yet to make a command of it. But on hearing his voice, its eyes glowed like blue crystals with a permanent flame behind them.

As for its wings, these were connected to two giant arms that branched off with large finger bones that were knuckled and interlaced with paper white webbed skin. A pair that was currently tucked close to the side of its body, and once more it snapped out its tail as if it just wanted to be in the air catching the wind.

Now, as for its rider, the King was most definitely no less of an impressive a sight as he too was enough to take your breath away. I couldn't tell how tall he was, not while sat on top of his pale beast, but from what I could tell, he was certainly a striking figure to behold, with his square shoulders and hint of impressive biceps that were slightly strained against the material covering his arms. Long, straight chestnut brown hair, wasn't even windblown, and for a girl, trust me, I was questioning this for good reason.

A mischievous grin played at kissable lips on his handsome face, yet I could see that just as easily those easy features could turn into the hard eyes of someone serious, thanks to the deep slant to his eyebrows. This combined with the strong line of his nose, the high slope of the cheekbones and fuller bottom lip, screamed nobility and power, as he held himself well. But these were just some of the minor details I could make out from down here, like what he wore, was also easy to see.

It was a grey blue tunic that clung to his muscular torso and down his strong thighs, thanks to a split up the centre that allowed for ease of movement. He also wore a plated silver chest plate, where it was plain to see that its design had been made with his dragon in mind as it resembled the scales of his pet. This matched the ice blue material beneath his silver shoulder pieces that were attached to long, mediaeval style sleeves that brushed the top of his knuckles. The hint of dark grey leather trousers could be seen tucked into high boots, that also appeared to be made of silver metal plating.

But his breastplate was what interested me as it was inlaid with the glowing blue Insignia of his Royal house, the same that was shown on his army's armour. To complete this impressive look of a King, was the white sword he wore attached to the thick belt that hung low on his hips. It was one that looked as if it had been made from quartz, resembling a shard of ice topped with a handle that looked to have been carved from a white horn. In fact, I had only ever seen one like it before and that belonged to Trice.

As for his crown, this too was a combination of interlocking plates to resemble scales, and at the front it held a single tear shaped blue crystal that had the same glow as the Royal Crest on his chest and that of the eyes of his dragon.

"I must say, I enjoyed the show immensely," the King said with a distinct royal lilt to his tone. I made a strange, nervous laughing sound when I looked around and realised that we were the only ones still standing. This was because the rest of his army, along with his captain, had lowered to one knee to show him their respect. However, this didn't seem to faze him as he seemed more amused by the sight of us, than anything else. Or should I say… *the sight of me.* This was because he hadn't once taken his eyes off me, much to Trice's growing annoyance.

"I take it these are the ones my brother also seeks?" This question was aimed at his captain, who also took this as his cue to stand.

"Yes, my King, we found them near the borderlands. It must have been the closest portal to the Kingdom of Souls, for we found the raiders surrounding them." The King nodded, now looking lost in thought before asking,

"My brother's raiders, I presume?"

"They were men from the Astyllen mountains, yes, my King." I easily followed this conversation between them and had to force myself not to ask the long list of questions that were mounting up by the second.

"Then lucky for you that you now find yourselves here and not there, for your welcome would have been quite different," the King informed us, and I had to hold back from asking whether his brother also had a dragon or not, as it wasn't exactly the cute doggie welcome you usually received from a pet.

Speaking of which, the dragon was really getting restless now as he padded his claws on the ground scratching up great chunks from grass.

"Ease yourself, Othello," the King said, making me want to ask if he was a fan of Shakespeare, but I wisely refrained.

"You are destined to belong to one of the Kings in the Hell's Realm… yes?" he asked as if confirming a rumour of some kind. I nodded, thinking this was the smartest reply I could give, although he quickly wanted it confirmed when he said,

"The one name Lucius Septimus, Ruler of the Kingdom of Death and son to Lucifer himself?" Again, I nodded which was when I realised this obviously wasn't enough for him as he raised a brow expectantly. So, I swallowed the hard lump named 'intimidated by yet another King' and answered him,

"Yes, that's my boyfriend… erm, I mean, the King I am destined for," I said after my childish sounding blunder, because Lucius was right and especially in a setting like this, it did sound juvenile. And the moment he smirked in response I knew that he felt the same way. But then he nodded to his captain, giving him some silent order, and one I only understood when he stepped closer to me. This caused a chain reaction when all three of the McBain brothers went on high alert and were about to intervene before I held up a hand stopping them.

"Please don't," I said looking back at them before focusing on Trice who looked as if he wanted to argue. So, I looked back to the King and said,

"Can you please give me a minute?" I saw his gaze scan to where my problem lay as the three brothers all had their hands itching to go to their weaponry. But this was one fight I wanted to prevent, because hello… Dragon Fire didn't sound fun.

The King bowed his head slowly, granting me my wish, so I turned on a heel and slapped a hand to his captain telling him,

"Take five, Balin." He chuckled before stepping out of my way. After this I walked up to Trice, but when his dark gaze wouldn't leave that of the King's, I grabbed one of the straps across his chest and used it to pull him my way so we would have the appearance of privacy. Even though one look round at these guys and I knew it was an impossible task for they would no doubt be able to hear us… especially with those pointed of ears of theirs. Either way, it didn't matter as there was only one person who I needed to listen to what I had to say.

"Look, I'm sick of fighting, not to mention I'm thirsty, I'm hungry and I feel as though I could sleep for a week. Look around you, Trice, we are outnumbered, and I doubt you guys will be able to shift again for a while… right?"

"We are nae wi'oot oor powers, lass, 'n' ah think ye remember that we are mair than capable in a fight," he said referring to the first time they had saved me against the two battling sides.

"That may be so, but they haven't hurt us, and by all accounts they saved us from the raiders." Trice didn't look convinced as he cast his stunning dark brown eyes that were edged with a dark green ring over towards what he most likely considered the enemy and narrowed them even more.

"Come on, Trice… look, it sounds as though it was his brother who was the one that had the raiders out looking for us. I think that was the King that the witch was in league with. Just please don't do anything rash and let me go with them," I said with that pleading tone.

"And if tis nae as it appears, whit then?"

"You heard it yourself, he knows who Lucius is, so perhaps he can help us in getting back to him, because unless you have forgotten, we are kind of under a very tight time constraint here." At this Trice softened his gaze and lifted a hand so he could soothe the apple of my cheek with the pad of his thumb. Then he told me the hard reality that I already knew I couldn't disregard as being a possibility.

"And if we're already tae late?" I closed my eyes against the thought of it, and released a sigh before I told him,

"Then that is a new nightmare I will face when I finally get back to him, but until then I have to hope and do all that I can to turn that hope into a possibility that he might still be alive, and if that means going with these guys and being compliant, then that's something I need to do too."

"I think ye'r making a mistake," he told me, and I softened my gaze and said,

"You might be right, but if there's even a chance that you're wrong and we save his brother, then I have to hope for that outcome too, which is why I'm going to ask you please, Trice, please trust me by trusting them." For a moment when his features turned hard I thought he was going to refuse me, and I would have no chance at stopping the three brothers from trying to take on the King's army. But then he took one look at the odds stacked against them and knew that if they fought then there was another strong possibility, one he didn't need to say for his expression said it for him… he thought I might get hurt.

This was confirmed when he assumed,

"Ye hae no powers in this realm, dae you?"

"It doesn't look like it, no. I tried with the raiders when they had you guys in that net thing, but I just ended up looking as though I was trying to drip dry my hands." At this he finally smirked, giving me a hint of that handsome smile of his. He released a sigh before this was obviously what he needed to hear before he made his decision and thankfully for me, it was the right one.

"Fine, Princess, fur noo we dae it yer way bit despite how much ye trust these guys I wull be oan mah guard." I nodded in agreement before I tapped the back of my hand to his hard stomach and said,

"I wouldn't expect it any other way, shifter." Then I winked up at him before turning around and walking back over towards the captain and the King, someone who looked as though he had been waiting for this outcome.

"Captain, escort these men to the throne room as I will personally take care of the Princess myself." It was at this point I was starting to regret my decision as I held up a hand when I was being led over to the dragon and said,

"Erm, actually, on second thoughts, maybe I should just go with…" I didn't finish my sentence as the King laughed heartedly before giving his pet a command in another language. One, that if I was to hazard a guess, was most likely elvish. This was when the dragon got low to the ground and stretched out a wing on his left side making me wonder if this was some fantasy world version of one of those inflatable slides that pop out when a plane lands in water. Although, you didn't see very many of those passengers trying to walk back up it, so what they expected me to do now I didn't know. Either way I was going to end up on my face sliding down on my belly every time I tried and looking like a grade A idiot doing it. Oh, and Gods only knew what the dragon would make out of this, I thought with a mindful eye roll at myself.

Meanwhile, the King chuckled as if he could hear my inner rambling and grabbed hold of what I could now see was an elaborately carved saddle. He did this so he could lean over and hold out a hand to me. I opened my mouth about to tell him that I still wouldn't reach, when suddenly I was heaved off the floor by the captain and handed up to the King. I yelped at both the shock and impressive show of the King's strength. It was incredible as all he needed to do was to grab hold of my wrist, shackling it with his large hand, before lifting me straight up in the air. Then he brought me closer to the front of him and said with a hum of words,

"This would go far easier, beautiful, if you spread your legs."

"Excuse me!" I said in a high-pitched tone that had him laughing harder before whispering in my ear,

"Straddle the saddle, my lady." Gods, but it was like he was the voice of sin.

"Oh right, of course… silly me," I said feeling my cheeks now melting through the embarrassment. But I did as I was asked as he made room for me by shifting back on his large saddle so I could be tucked in front of him. Then he placed a hand on my stomach, and I sucked in a startled breath, making him tense behind me before he was once again whispering comfort in my ear,

"Relax, this will go far easier if you lean back against me,

for I will not let you fall." I swallowed hard before trying to do as he asked, although the moment he gave the dragon a command, he had me tensing again knowing what was coming. I instantly looked to Trice in my moment of weakness as if he was my saviour and his face said it all… disappointment.

He hadn't wanted me to make this decision and watching me flying off with someone he didn't trust looked as if I had left after first stabbing him in the heart. I wanted to mouth that I was sorry. That I was okay. For him not to worry. But the only thing that came next was my scream of fright the second the dragon launched itself up into the air, as it was one thing taking flight tucked safely under a dragon and caged in its grasp, but it was quite another riding freely on its back, flying on top of the beast and feeling as though there was nothing around you to stop you from falling. But then that wasn't quite true, as the second my fright was heard the King's arms circled me in a cage of muscle as he grabbed hold of the saddle in front of me. It was a horn shaped carved piece of wood that acted as a way to steer the beast. I knew this because I could see the leather straps that connected to different parts of its head. They were clasped under the hidden parts of its ears and horn like scales that were longer than any other part. I wondered if these we're the most sensitive parts on a dragon's body, for it seemed it took the barest of touches of the horn before the dragon knew where its master wanted to go.

"By the Gods!" I uttered in awe, for seeing the world around me now at this height was a beauty of the likes I had never seen before. It was like a Kingdom that had been gently brushed with every colour as far as the eye could see. Because surrounding the city were the rolling hills of faint greens that created an ombre effect from where they would turn darker towards the forests and mountains. Beyond that was even more colour, for the mountains themselves reminded me of a night sky with swirls of blues and purples. But instead of the moonlight reflecting off the stars and moon, it was the sun that was reflecting off mountain rock as if glass shards were rising up from the rough terrain.

"Like what you see?" The question came from my back and startled me as again it was whispered close to my ear. This was no doubt so I could still hear him over both the roaring sound of the dragon's breath below us and the wind that cut across our skin when travelling at speed.

"It's stunning."

"I am biased, but it is indeed the most beautiful out of all the four of the kingdoms, and I am happy now to have such magnificence grace it with her presence, for your beauty will be its gift for the time you will be here." I had to say, if a compliment like this had come from anyone on Earth, it would have sounded cheesy or even laughable, but coming from the King at my back who didn't have a cheesy bone in his body, it was quite a compliment, and one I took seriously thanks to the intimidating presence it came from.

"Thank you, but I…" his laughter cut me off from being about to dispute this fact as he told me,

"Pride is not a sin I think I will find in you, isn't this so?" It was a strange response to my reaction to his compliment, but he wasn't wrong. I didn't look in the mirror and consider myself something special or to hold a beauty beyond compare. But that didn't mean I was necessarily unhappy with how I looked. I mean, I had my father's dark hair and his sun kissed complexion, along with my mother's nice eyes. Although how long those eyes I would actually continue to see out of I didn't know. As I was still on Nero's borrowed time for however long her 'seeing eye powder' would last.

Which meant that I really hoped that I got back to Lucius before blindness struck this already clumsy human, as I couldn't imagine the King at my back classing me as magnificent then, not when I was falling at his feet. And yeah, it was true that the guy was handsome, but he was nowhere near as handsome as Lucius… not in my mind anyway, there was only one man who had that power to have me falling at his feet.

But this thought just had me wondering what Lucius would think on hearing about my current escapades. I remembered back in his Lamborghini when telling him how I had jumped out of a helicopter and I had to wonder which one would win on the fury scale… me riding on the back of a dragon with the King at my back who had his arms around me, holding me flush to his chest like he would never let me go, or shooting another pilot?

I had a feeling that because this time included another male, this one would win hands down. Because if Lucius had been tempted to lock me up before or have me shackled to him, then after this particular moment in time, I just knew that temptation would soon become an absolute certainty in his future and mine!

In fact, as I tried to imagine what Lucius was going through in this moment, I'll be honest, the thought had tears in my eyes. Ever since I had stepped through that damn portal in the Tree of Souls I had caused him nothing but heartache and worry.

Every single decision I had made just felt like the wrong one, one that I continued to make over and over again. And yet, all I could hope for as the sight of the King's castle came into view, was that getting on the back of this dragon with another King wasn't yet another…

Terrible mistake.

CHAPTER NINE

DEALS WITH HANDSOME DEVILS

I couldn't help but shriek out in fright the moment we started to descend to the ground in a great arched sweeping motion that tilted us both to one side. The King had been ready for this and braced himself, for he had been the one commanding the dragon's descent. I, however, had not, which meant the moment I started to shift in the saddle was when his arm strengthened around me, tugging me back once more into his close embrace.

"Easy now, Princess, for I will not have you falling and breaking this pretty little neck on my watch... not when I have plans for you," he said, making me want to question what he meant by that and what those plans of his were exactly. However, this was hardly the time as I feared for my life and had no choice but to cling on to the strong arm that was banded across my stomach, anchoring me to him.

Thankfully, it was shortly after this that we lowered enough to land, doing so in what looked like a private, rooftop garden that was situated near the very top of the castle. I was surprised that the sight of the mighty beast landing didn't have the people scurrying away like frightened bystanders, but then again, what was I saying, as one look at the land and all the dragons that resided here, I could imagine that seeing any dragon was as common as seeing a cat in someone's garden back in the human realm.

And back to the dragon in question, as soon as it was down it lowered itself as far to the ground as possible, meaning this must have been a natural reaction for when his master needed to get off its back. After this the King loosened his hold on me and I could finally breathe freely, taking in a shuddered breath as quite honestly, it didn't feel right for me to be in another man's arms.

The King, unbeknownst to my inner turmoil, then swung his leg over the dragon's back and let his body slide a little way down the dragon's wing before jumping off and landing nimbly on his feet. Then with a flick of his hand casting his flowing robes out of the way, he turned back towards me and said,

"Your turn." When I didn't respond quickly enough for him, he tried to hide a knowing grin, obviously amused at the sight of me rooted to the saddle and not in any hurry to leave it. Not considering my only option was to do the same as he had done and knowing that it was most definitely going to go terribly wrong. My silly notion when first getting on the dragon that he was a living version of an aeroplane was now coming to fruition, just minus the water landing.

"Come on, Princess, considering which realm you have just come from I'm sure you have no doubt done far worse, than to give reason to play coy with me now," the King said in a teasing way I failed to see until it was too late, as I was already taking the bait.

"I'm not playing coy with you!" I stated in a tone that was verging on huffy making him chuckle. Then he crossed his arms over his chest, making the material at his arms tighten even further.

"No? Then prove it," he challenged.

"Prove it by getting off the dragon?" I confirmed before looking around me and trying to find a way off this thing that didn't include a slip and slide.

"Prove it by trusting me to catch you when you get off the dragon," he confirmed, and when I didn't do it quickly enough for him he gave the dragon another command, which made his pet tip even further towards where the King was stood. This made me shriek in fright and soon I couldn't get my leg its back over fast enough. However, in my haste to get down the dragon, I caught my foot and fell face first as my fear of making a fool out of myself was quickly becoming a reality.

Thankfully, however, the King must have for foreseen this calamity about to happen and managed to catch me before I fell face first on the ground before him.

"Whoa, and there she goes," he commented in an amused tone before lifting me up and setting me down on my feet.

"Note to self, clumsy people should not ride dragons," I mumbled, making him throw his head back and laugh.

"I shall have to remember that," he said looking down at me, for now I could see that he was extremely tall, even taller than Lucius. In fact, other than Ragnar and what little time I had spent around Caspian, it was the shortest I had ever felt. Which was why I blurted out without thinking,

"How tall are you?" He grinned down at me, before lowering half his body bending at the waist and whispering a single word,

"Tall."

After this he motioned me to follow him by sweeping out an arm, causing his wide sleeves to sweep barely an inch from the floor. Honestly, I kept on expecting some director to shout cut, and the King here to then shake himself out of playing his character and introduce himself as Dave. Because it was like being in some damn movie! It had me wondering if Tolkien himself had accidently fallen into this realm and that was where he had got most of his ideas from… apart from the dragons of course. I swear but I came a foolish heartbeat away from asking him if he knew of any hobbits, and even found myself checking his hands for a gold ring… *one to rule them all*… I thought on a silent snigger.

Of course, this also had me itching to ask if Rivendell was his neighbouring kingdom or if he knew anyone called Elrond or Aragorn. Thankfully, I refrained from the urge as I didn't think it would go down too well. Besides, right at that moment there were much more important things that I wanted to know, and I was already an expert at Lord of the Rings Trivial Pursuit. I wasn't, however, an expert on the Elemental Realm.

This was why I let him lead me into his stunning crystal castle that I could see now was carved and decorated in a series of art nouveau designs, that I would have expected from Fae life. I knew the elemental beings existed as I had read enough books to suggest that they were real. And even if I hadn't, I was still in the know thanks to my aunty Pip, as she was born in this realm. Which naturally meant that given my curious nature (thanks, Mum) I would often ask her to tell me stories about what it was like.

However, considering this was a place she had also been kicked out of and banished from, this then meant that none of the stories she told really reflected well on its people. As it soon became clear to see that she was a tad bit bitter on the subject, and rightly so as these types of stories would often end with,

"...if the pompous ass willies could only see me now!" I didn't really know what an 'ass willie' was, but coming from Pip in this tone, then I was sure it was a great insult. Though I could see now where she had got her assessment from, as one look at the sheer wealth and prosperity of the place and it was no wonder that its people came across as arrogant. It wasn't exactly a place that screamed Pip anyway, as it was all clean, curved lines, expertly carved to a high standard of beauty, where every inch of the palace was designed with thought and executed with the greatest craftmanship.

For example, the floor was polished to such a high sheen it looked as if when stepping on it you would go straight through it, as it could have fooled you into believing it was water! The white trees I had seen in the forest that had a strange ombre effect, also reflected in the designs used, just like the grass, as it was what added colour to what could have been a very stark palace. Muted pastel colours ranged from peaches, oranges, pinks and even reds the further and deeper into the castle we travelled. It was like a sunset getting closer and closer to the horizon burning the sky with its descent.

The furniture was all intricately carved pale wood and it had been done as if sympathetic to the shapes of the trees, never losing the memory of where they had come from. The designs often mirrored branches reaching up, into some archway. They curled and entwined in some creative way to produce the back of a chair or the legs of a table. It was craftsmanship at its highest standard, and it left me wide-eyed and mouth agape as I took in as much as I could when walking through a large open hallway, one adorned with handmade treasures.

However, it was only when we came to a set of double doors the size of a four-storey building that I realised we had reached our destination. The colossal doors had pure white panels that were decorated in silver metalwork representing the castle, as when the doors were opened by the guards on each side, it split the image down the centre of the castle's main entrance.

As for the guards, they were dressed the same as the ones that had been under the command of Captain Balin and unsurprising, when the doors opened, there were more of them inside. However, what was inside made me gasp at the sight of the sheer magnificence and beauty of the Great Hall in front of me.

"Welcome to my home," the King said, obviously pleased with my reaction as he was smiling down at me, before making a gesture for me to continue to follow him. I did this but with wide eyes and my mouth near fully agape, as it reminded me of some mighty cathedral. This was down to its long line of giant pillars that each seemed to hold up a network of decorative arches covered in vines, leaves and flowers all made out of carved stone. These interlocking beams also created a large open space above but had clearly been made from different trees this time, as they were much bigger and most definitely straighter. The same went for the pillars that ran the full length of the hall, as the beginning of each pillar looked like the original tree, making it seem as if they had just grown up out of the ground and were only decorated the further up they rose once stripped of their branches.

In between these pillars, joining them, was a lattice of vined arches that held great chandeliers hanging down from silver chains. These were made from antlers of some kind of beast that unsurprisingly, I hadn't seen before. Each end of the antlers held a disc of blue flames. These were reminiscent of the same flames that protected the walls of the castle by the dragon fire that shimmered on top of the moat.

At the very end of this colossal space was exactly what I expected to find, for it was definitely a common theme within these mighty castles. For what was a Kingdom without its grand statement, one for its King to sit upon. Lucius' was the same as I remember seeing it for the first time with him there to occupy it. I remembered being intimidated by not only the site of his actual throne, one made from the horns of his killed enemies, but by Lucius himself when sat there in all his demon glory, like the Hellish master he was.

But this was as far from a Kingdom in Hell that you could get, for everywhere you looked was a beauty that only the wildest of imaginations could have conjured up without first seeing the magnificence of this place. As for the throne, it was nothing short of a piece of artwork. One that began as a group of trees that I had seen in the forest. Four of them to be exact, that were all grouped together and exactly as you would have expected to see them before being plucked from the ground.

They rose from the ground to the height of my shoulders before that natural bend of theirs started to take shape. This then made it a perfect and organic shape for a King to sit on before the tree straightened and started to branch out, separating from one another, each becoming its own tree the closer to the ceiling it reached.

It was as if this throne had been planted with four seeds in a row at least 200 years before being ready for its first King to sit on it, making me wonder if some kind of magical spell had been used to make them grow as a solid entity rather than letting time do all the work.

I could just about see that there was a hidden staircase that wrapped around the back so it could be accessed with ease. This in itself stood at the centre of a raised dais made up of layers of half-moon shapes that got smaller and created steps leading up. Each tree that started to branch out held an insignia carved into the wood, making me wonder if this represented the joining together of four kingdoms? Had there at one time been one King to rule them all? If that was true then how did they get split up in the first place? Again, my curious nature was rearing its head and had me eager to find out if I was right?

As for its current King, he now ascended the steps, making his way to his throne and upon reaching it, he then motioned for me to come closer. It was like our first meeting all over again, when he was sat upon the dragon looking down at me as he did now. In fact, I was actually surprised to find that his throne wasn't made out of some giant dragon's head. But then, thinking back on it, other than the few elements outside, there hadn't been one thing inside that referred to dragons. This then made me wonder if the Kingdom came first and the dragons second?

"Now, as to why you are here," he said, surprising me out of my inner questions and coming right to answering them.

"Wow, I have to say that's refreshing," I commented making him look intrigued.

"And what would that be, my dear?"

"Well, I'm never quite used to anyone just coming right out and answering questions that I haven't even had a chance to ask yet," I told him, saying without so many words that I was curious.

"Ah, I see, so people underestimate your ability to handle things?" he guessed and again I was surprised.

"Wow, you're perceptive too, the Queen must be one lucky girl," I stated as a way to see if he was married and hoping that he was... *happily.*

"I am afraid that for one of the four Kings of the Elemental Realm, finding a Queen isn't as easy as you would think," he admitted with a bitter edge to his tone that was understandable if what he said was true. But then again, I don't suppose there was a dating app for looking for Fae princesses to marry.

"Why, do you have to marry royalty?" I questioned, making

him smirk once more and lean forward after bracing his forearm on his knee.

"Why, are you offering, *Princess?*" he said emphasising my title, and at this I choked back a cough and said,

"No, trust me, I have my hands full with my own King… and I would be too much of a handful in a place like this."

"And what is it exactly about being here that is so unfathomable to you?" he asked seeming now as if he was insulted, so I quickly back-tracked.

"Are you kidding me, I would be a nightmare for you."

"How so?" he asked again and with more patience this time, especially after going with the whole, 'it's not you, it's me' thing.

"Well, you saw me getting off your dragon, think of that as small taste of the clumsiness my boyfriend faces on a day to day basis and you will understand why my being here for too long is not a good idea," I admitted making his lips twitch.

"Because you're clumsy?" he enquired with mirth.

"Yes, and you have a lot of nice things, half of which I am sure are breakable and not Fae proof."

"I am afraid you lost me, little Princess, for we are all Fae here." On hearing this, I felt like smacking my forehead and cursing my shortened use of my middle name, Faith.

"Ah, yeah, that… I think now is the time to let you know we have something in common, as my name is Fae, well, it's Amelia Faith, but people call me Fae… for short and yes, before you say it, the irony isn't lost on me either." At this he burst out laughing and told me,

"Well, I will admit, little Amelia Faith, or Fae as you so sweetly named yourself, that you amuse me greatly and I do confess to looking forward to our time together whilst you are here," he said kindly, making me have no choice but to move on with my next point.

"Ah, right, well about that, you see I am hoping that my not so subtle charms and all, will persuade you to help me."

"Is that so… hmm, now I am intrigued as to know in what way do you think I could, help you that is?" he said still clearly amused with me.

"Well, as you know we got sent here by a witch and we are just trying to get back to my boyfriend's realm."

"And I wonder, if this boyfriend of yours is currently doing all he can to get you back?" the King asked and before I could focus too much on the strange question, I answered him without restraint,

"Oh, I know he is, as he would do anything."

"Really, now that is interesting," he said more to himself than to me. But again, it didn't yet penetrate my mind deep enough to really ask why, not at first.

"Yeah, Lucius would stop at nothing to get me back and you see I have to get back before… wait, now why is that interesting?" I asked, finally having a bad feeling about this, and what was soon to realise was my runaway mouth!

"Because I need to know what your King would be willing to do to get you back."

"Why do you need to know that… I thought… I thought you were going to help us?" I said stumbling on my words as that dread started to sink deeper and deeper into my chest.

"Oh, I am and soon, if what you say is true, we will all have what we want."

"What do you mean?" He leant forward again, and this time his tone was less playful and more serious as he started to confirm my worst fears.

"What I mean, little human, is, if what you say is true, then your King will give me whatever I want to get back his intended Queen… or should I say, *who I want.*"

"Who?" I questioned on a barely there whisper.

"Yes, who, for you should have realised by now that it wasn't my brother who made a deal with your witch after all…"

This was when that dread doubled and was confirmed to be warranted when he finished that sentence and said…

"It was me."

CHAPTER TEN

NOW CHILDREN, BEHAVE

The second I heard him admit this, a few things happened simultaneously, the first being me turning on my heel and making the first step forward in running from him. At the same time, the huge, colossal doors at the very end of the throne room echoed as they were forced open and three shifter brothers walked with purpose towards the throne. That was when I realised that shifting into their mythological beast wasn't their only gift, as enhanced eyesight must have been another. I knew this when even from their distance away they could see the moment I was grabbed from behind and dragged up to the lap of the Dragon King.

Once there, I quickly found a hand collaring my throat and this was all that was needed in controlling me, because the moment I tried to squirm out of his hold and was about to elbow him in the gut was when his strength became my greatest enemy. I knew this the moment I started choking with what seemed like very little effort made on his part. He eased his biting fingers from my tender flesh a second later, and whispered down in my ear,

"That time was a mere warning, the next will be painful for far longer, so please don't make me hurt you."

Trice was the first one to see this, and the next of their abilities was proven when all three of them crossed the large space a few mere seconds later at blurring speeds. Speeds that would be equalled to that of a vampire.

"LET HER GO!" Trice roared at the same time the army split into two lines and marched their way with purpose down the length of the hall. They ended up running parallel with the shifter brothers at the centre, along with the captain who was now striding with purpose behind them.

"Ah, such care they show for their bounty," the King said, releasing a sigh before speaking to them in a strong, commanding tone that was now without a shred of ease and amusement I had been getting used to,

"Despite how this looks, I do not wish to hurt the girl. However, I can assure you that should my terms not be met then I could snap her neck with a mere flick of my wrist, and I think we can all agree, that would be such a waste."

"You want tae bargain, then fine, let th' girl go 'n' we wull talk," Trice demanded, making Gryph pull his war hammer from his back and twist its gilded handle in his hand with skill before he agreed with a short,

"Aye... *talk.*" Then he smirked as if this was the very last thing he was going to do. And that massive demonic foot dipped in black steel that was his hammer was warning enough.

"After all, communication is key," Vern added calmly, whilst pulling his own weapon free and arming his bow with a flaming arrow quicker than any of the King's men could react to.

"You are in no position to make demands of me!" It was in this moment, after the King had said this, that something in Trice completely snapped. It was something I had never seen before and from the looks of things, it was something his brothers hadn't seen in a long time either.

The air around him started to ripple just as if he was about to shift but instead of bringing forth the cockatrice creature in him, what actually happened was he started to manipulate the power of the shift. This meant that instead of losing sight of the man in the shift, he forced the reverse effect by forging his creature to his human host and now creating a demonic version of himself.

Then he rose up higher and continued to grow until he was a mountain of a man now clad in a demonic armour and was taller than Gryph. It also looked as if his skin had been replaced by that of his beast, as it continued to ripple over every inch of him consuming the dark grey cloak he wore. Even the bare hint of what I knew was his family's tartan and one he wore around his waist beneath the belt of his sword, transformed into a blood red sash.

"Gods," I whispered in shock and awe as suddenly his own wings from the combined beast burst from his back. They were a dark, navy blue that looked as if he had just brought with him a veil of night to this bright day. However, like this they looked far bigger and their reach forced the soldiers back, as each of them gasped in shock. They were sleek, as if built for speed, with each feather looking as if it were coated in something wet that had me questioning what.

But at the same time, a long scaled, dark and deadly tail started to appear from behind him. It rose up over his head like that of a scorpion, before creating the helmet part to his demonic armour. This was when it attached itself to his head, with the forked points running down his cheeks and curling back on themselves. This joined with the scales that were forging themselves into the right shape to fit its master's head with one goal of protecting it. However, there was one last element of his change that had me gasping in shock... his handsome face was now consumed by hatred. That once easy smile was long gone to sneering lips that curled as the beast in him snarled. Fangs emerged down that full bottom lip of his and his skin darkened at his cheekbones and around his eyes. Eyes that were now lost to an abyss of swirling darkness. Even his dark auburn hair looked as if it now floated under water, rising from his shoulders as if the power was rising from him in waves. But it was his scar that had my attention as it was glowing, as if there was a crack made in the Earth's crust and burning hot magma could be seen beneath.

Simply put... *he was utterly terrifying!*

"It can't be possible!" I heard the King at my back mutter, making me want to ask what it all meant, because it seemed to me that the Land of Dragons wasn't the only myth discovered today. I knew this when the King sucked in a deep breath when Trice's face darkened further before the shadow of a crown of ice hovered over his head.

This was before his demonic voice spoke and it was one that had not a single hint of an accent, but more like something that had been forged in the deepest levels of Hell.

"I CAN DO AS I WISH!" he roared in answer to the King's threat of not making demands of him.

"Calm yersel' doon, laddie, fur yer frightening th' lass," Gryph whispered, cautiously nodding in my direction where I knew even without a mirror that he was right... I was terrified. This was when he took a deep enough breath so that the next time he spoke his demon didn't roar his words, but instead drove home the threat with the depth of his voice.

"I can make you a promise, if you hurt her then my brothers and I will shift into something you have never seen before, something that will have your dragons cowering at the very sight of us and then we will slaughter every one of you and lay waste to your lands in a sea of flames and chaos!" I was left open mouthed and in total shock. Because if I hadn't believed before now that Trice had been destined to be a King of Hell, then now I was utterly convinced that this was his destiny!

It was of little wonder how he believed himself capable of fighting Lucius when it came to trying to win my hand. And it was only now that I was coming to understand one of Trice's greatest weapons. Because this was one of his secrets, the level of power he had at his fingertips. The one he held onto, that was captured deep within him as if too afraid to let it loose on the world. Gryph, seeing the situation as it was, could be seen speaking to him again, only this time it was in a language I couldn't understand. But whatever it was he said it invoked a deep and demonic growl from the powerful being now stood dominating the space.

I expected the King at my back to be more afraid of this side of Trice but other than being clearly shocked, he showed no fear. And the reason for this turned out to be because Trice wasn't the only one in the room with immense power. Meaning, that I soon realised there was a reason the man at my back ruled this Dragon Kingdom and it had little to do with being crowned but more to do with being...

Born in Dragon fire.

I knew this when the King's voice changed too as he became our next surprise. A darkness of his own spoke next and informed us all,

"Be careful, stranger of my lands, for you and your brothers… *you are not the only shifters in this room."* It was in this moment that I felt the hair on the back of my neck stand up and a crawling feeling creep along my skin. This was before I felt the hum of power coming from my back and rise up around me. This all happened before I felt the skin of his hand started to change at my neck, becoming hard as if it was now being covered in scales.

Dragon Scales.

"Oh shit," I whispered the second I felt it, something that ended in me sucking in air over my teeth. The same power Trice had was now at my back and changing the King right next to me! I knew this the moment he brought his other hand out in front of me, one that had been morphed into that of a beast!

A beast, just like the one he had been flying.

A hand that was now tipped with deadly talons that curled around as though they belonged on an eagle and would have rivalled even my father's demonic pet bird, Ava. White scales that were edged in black with the same reptilian skin underneath, just like the dragon we rode. Then he warned in that grated drag of his deeper voice,

"I don't need to crush her windpipe and mangle her delicate little neck to kill her, but with a mere thought I could flay her skin from her bones," the King said with deadly calm, making me say,

"Eww, graphic much." Something he ignored and instead proved when his hand ignited into the same blue, dragon's flame that surrounded the castle, telling me it wasn't from the power of the dragons, it was generated…

From their King.

"So you see, laying waste to my Kingdom won't be as easy as you thought, for I am no weak ruler!" It was at this point that I'd officially had enough! And I did this the only way I knew how to get the King's attention, just hoping it too hadn't changed. So I snaked a hand around my back and before he could do anything about it, I grabbed his man package! I also did this trying not to notice how considerably large it was and instead squeezed with all my might, making him now the one who sucked in air through his teeth.

"Right, now that I have your attention, I would like to point out that snapping my neck or setting me aflame won't get you what you want, and it most certainly won't get me what I want!" He growled making me squeeze harder causing him to stop and listen to me.

"In fact, all that would happen is you would find yourself at war as Lucius, who I might point out is the son of the Devil, a being that would bring a wrath upon on your head and your kingdom that even your impressive shifter ass won't be able to stop... as in... *at all.*" I hissed this last part before I continued,

"Because, trust me, when I say war, I mean with the entirety of Hell and that of my own father's kingdom included. So how about we cut the 'whose dick is bigger' shit and just agree that mine's bigger." For emphasis I squeezed his balls again and he instantly let my neck go.

"Good choice, Dragon King," I said with a smirk in victory. Then I added for good measure,

"Now, let's talk about this deal we are going to make, should we, and no offence, lover boy, but there is only one man's lap I sit on and it isn't yours!" Then, after I said this, I tapped on his arm so that he got the hint and let me go. I jumped down and walked towards Trice, telling him,

"As impressive as that look is on you, sweetheart, do you mind as I am trying to negotiate here, and the Hellish Ice Man look isn't helping." At this I heard both Gryph and Vern snigger, making me point a finger at them and warn,

"And as for you two, you can behave as well!"

"But of course, My lady."

"Aye whitevur ye say, lass."

"Right well, as nice and intimidating as this room is, which is what I guess you were going with here, I am tired, I am hungry and I need to sit down before I fall down... and no, not on your lap, *Your Majesty,*" I said when I saw the King about to point to where I was just sitting but I finished it off with a bow in his direction.

"Then let me suggest before that happens and I lose my leverage to starvation, we seek a more comfortable space," the King said, obviously now more amused by my antics than angry that I had well and truly manhandled his man meat package... thanks for that one, Aunty Pip, I thought with a grin.

"This way if you please," he said holding out his arm for me to place my own in the bend of his and be led from the room. Trice, now being back to himself, shook off the remains of his power and opened his mouth about to argue, when I held up a finger and snapped,

"No, now it's my turn and puffing out cock feathers isn't the way!" Then I walked over to the King ignoring Gryph's laugh, when he said,

"By Gods, ah lik' this lass."

"I must say, she is an utter delight, is she not, brother?" Vern added making Trice growl back at him before saying between clenched teeth,

"Aye, a fucking delightful pain in mah ass!"

"I heard that!" I told him over my shoulder after I let the King lead me away, making Trice just wink at me in a sarcastic way.

"Don't think I don't know what you did back there," the King whispered down at me as we travelled down an open corridor that was arched and offered access to another private garden. But this time, it was one that had a lush fountain at its

centre that looked like water running down the branches of a carved stone weeping willow. Wow, sculptors must have had a field day with this place.

"What do you mean?" I asked when we had passed the sight, wondering what the King had meant by that comment.

"You created a big enough distraction so that we would focus on you and not fighting each other… *I believe you humans call it, defusing a bomb."*

"I don't want them getting hurt, I don't want anyone getting hurt, especially not those I care about," I told him whilst sneaking a peek at the brothers over my shoulder, who were thankfully following without any severed guard's heads in their hands.

The captain was also in front of them, with his guards at the rear.

"It is a noble sacrifice and not one that will be forgotten by either party, I can assure you."

"Despite what happened in there, I really did believe you when you said that you didn't want to hurt me," I said, now doing so as a way to judge his response and hopefully have it confirmed if this was still true or not.

"But of course, for what a waste that would be indeed," he said running his hand down the top of my hand that was still rested in the crook of his arm. This was before he used that same hand to reach out and push open a door at the end of the corridor that led into a gallery of some kind. Beautifully detailed paintings of landscape after landscape adorned the pale but smooth walls of the castle and one that was the perfect setting for displaying these masterpieces. Especially where such vivid colour seemed to explode off the canvas' at you. It made me want to stop and admire them and the King noticed.

"My sister is the artist and spends most of her days with

paint in her hair, much to the dismay of our mother." I smiled at this as it was clear that despite his teasing, he was extremely proud of his sister's talent. You could see the warmth in his eyes when he looked at them. Eyes that reminded me of the same blue flames he could obviously command.

"My mother is the artist in my family," I told him as if wanting to share this part of my life with him.

"You do not share in this gift?" he asked, and I laughed.

"Who, me? Are you kidding, even my stickmen have problems."

"Stickmen?" he enquired making me elaborate,

"Think rudimentary cave drawings and you will get the idea."

"Ah, I see," he said with a smirk.

"No, my talents lie mainly with dead people." At this his eyes widened making me laugh again.

"As in digging them up, not being the one to put them there… I'm an archaeologist, and my talent comes in the form of reading and researching… or at least that was my job until all this happened," I said with clear melancholy that hadn't been needed but just slipped out.

"But you are still a Princess?" he asked, obviously wondering what a royal was doing by having a job.

"Kind of, I mean yes, my father is King of all Supernatural life on Earth, but I didn't exactly want to follow down the family footsteps, if you know what I mean, not with me being completely human and all," I said as we approached a door at the end that looked more like one that would lead into a room or private space. But this was when the King laughed and said,

"Oh, but that is where you are wrong, Princess, for there are only four humans that will ever be granted access to our realm." I sucked in a breath, wondering what in all the Gods names combined could that mean.

This before whispering,

"And they are?" This was when he paused before pushing open the last door and telling me the shocking truth…

"Our fated humans… Our Queens."

CHAPTER ELEVEN

BROTHERS OF WOE

The door opened onto what was obviously a private library or office of some kind. Of course, the dead giveaway to this was that two of its walls were covered in ornate shelves lined with thick leather-bound books. At a quick glance, it also looked as if some books in particular had been well read as the spines were cracked and in less than perfect condition. I knew why when he leant into me and said,

"You're not the only one who's well read." After this he let my hand slip from the crook of his arm as we walked into his space, before motioning to a seating area saying,

"We will not be disturbed in here… *if you please."* He then took his tall, muscular self over to the comfortable looking living space that had an arch shape of carved armchairs. These nine, high backed chairs were all positioned around a beautifully ornate stone fireplace. One that reminded me of the Tree of Life that was situated in my father's temple back in the underground belly of Afterlife.

In fact, it also reminded me of the tree in the centre of

Lucius' winter garden on the top of his castle, because it was shaped the same. The roots appeared as if rising from the ground and created an open space in the middle. Well, this was carved the same way, only instead of a place you could sit inside, like Pip often did, in this one a fire was lit, crackling away and creating a warm glow off all the pale furniture.

The pale omber trees had been used to carve the ornate seats, that were curved waves like the wind had blown the wood making it grow that way. A large desk was situated on a higher platform, with a solid polished top and a network of carved roots covering every inch of the bottom. But then another quick scan of the room awarded me the little details, like artwork on the walls or the large ceramic pots that rose up like giant painted lilies or crimped tulips. It was what gave it its art nouveau style, with nature's beauty playing the biggest part.

A large steepled chair stood tall and proud behind the desk, as though it belonged in some English castle as it was worthy of any King to sit upon it. A tapestry style rug which looked like the whole kingdom was depicted on it, sat in front of the fireplace and was big enough to fill the living space. The only other form of decoration in the room was the now distinct style of paintings that his sister had obviously gifted him, and this time it was an incredible lifelike portrait of his Dragon, situated proudly behind his desk.

The other one was positioned in front of where he would sit, so he could look at it whilst working. And I knew why when I recognised it as being one of his Kingdom. It was a sight that no doubt reminded him of why he made the decisions he did...

For the good of his people.

I didn't know where these thoughts had come from, as I didn't know this man. I didn't know this Fae King that obviously had the power to shift where the rest of his kingdom did not. Just like I didn't know how I knew that he was born from Dragon fire. All I knew was that it was almost as if being close to him was projecting his life on to me and his rule encompassed. It was as if I knew that every decision he made was for the good of his people, and that included this one.

The one he felt guilt over making.

I frowned at this, narrowing my gaze when asking myself if his actions were ones he would feel guilt over, then why make them… had he been forced? I quickly realised that unless I gave him the time to explain then I wasn't ever going to find out.

So, I followed the King towards the seating area and watched as he flicked out his robe before taking his seat. His captain also did the same and I raised a brow in question at Balin, knowing now that he had lied. But then he too had obviously been following his King's orders to find us, which was why I wasn't surprised when he shrugged his shoulders at me and winked. This told me that he knew exactly where my thoughts had been in that moment.

In fact, I was just about to follow suit, minus the cool looking robe flicking, which I had to say on him looked kick ass. But before I could lower my ass to the seat, this was when Trice stood at the edge of the seating area and purposely folded his arms, declaring like some spoiled child,

"I wull remain standing, thanks." I rolled my eyes at him and said,

"Well, suit yourself, but my legs are killing me." Then I sat down and watched as both his brothers squeezed past Trice and did the same as I did, taking a seat opposite the Fae. Trice shot them a look that said it all, making Gryph be the first to respond,

"What? A'm wi' th' lass oan that one," he said rubbing at his thick, trunk like thighs, before swinging his weapon from his back and dropped it down with a clunk as the heavy weight of his war hammer hit the floor. It made a vase wobble nearby and we all watched it, me with a wince as I was expecting it to topple over and smash. Thankfully, we all let out a sigh of relief when it didn't, making Gryph whistle before adding,

"Och, sorry bout that, bit ye ken whit thay say, luck o' th' Scottish."

'Luck of the Scottish?' I mouthed at Vern, as I was pretty sure the saying referred to the Irish. Vern smirked back at me before he shook his head a little, telling me his brother had got it wrong. I tried not to laugh, hiding my own smile behind my hand before coughing in it and making Vern do the same. Gods, but we were like naughty children in a schoolroom trying to hide our giggles from our teacher.

Thankfully, instead of getting insulted the King just held up a hand and shrugged it off, telling Gryph with that gesture not to worry about the vase. And, well, I had to say that so far it looked to be going pretty good. Well, that was if Trice would give up the I want to rip your throat out stance and join us by sitting down. Something that after a couple of nods of my head when gaining his attention, he thankfully got the hint, but not before he rolled his eyes and huffed like a sulky teenager. Then he finally took a seat to my left. This meant that I was sat in the centre chair facing the fireplace directly, with the brothers on one side of me and the King and his captain on the other.

"Right, well, let's start with the obvious should we, your err… Majesty?" I said in an uncertain way making him grant me a soft look of amusement.

"My name is King Auberon, and you know my second in command, Balin, my Captain of the Guards."

"Oh right, yes introductions are probably a good place to start, I am Amelia as you know but these are…"

"Getting pissed aff wi' all this shit, that's whit we are!" Trice snapped, making me shout his name,

"Trice!" This was when he turned in his seat to face me and pointed out,

"May I remind ye, Princess, that we are oan a mission 'ere, one tae save a life, or did ye forget that 'n' wish tae continue wi' th' pleasantries after he had his hand aroond yer throat only a moment ago!" He said this last part directing his furious eyes towards the King, and my response to this was to release a sigh before I too turned my attention to King, now telling him,

"What he says is true, we are under a time constraint here... even if he was a little bit blunt at reminding me!" I snapped this last part at Trice, giving him my best pissed off look, one he just sneered at in response.

"Then let's proceed shall we and I will begin by telling you exactly what I want and how we may help each other in this negotiation," the King advised after first giving his own pissed off look towards Trice, and I got the impression it was because of how he had spoken to me.

"Oh, so tis a negotiation noo, fur a moment ago it looked lik' a kidnapping 'n' ransom, as ye threatened a Princess by ripping her throat out... or am ah mistaken, *yer Majesty?*" Trice said mocking his royal title.

"Trice! Gods, just stop, okay! Because you making digs at the guy who can help us is not going to get us any closer to getting back to Hell and getting out of here!" Thankfully, he didn't respond to this, so I took it upon myself to turn to the King and ask,

"What is it you want?"

"Simply put, I want to bargain you in exchange for my brother's return," he replied honestly and in a tone that didn't exactly say he felt any guilt about this. This made me wonder then what did he feel guilty for, as I had definitely picked up on it when first walking in the room.

"Your brother?" I asked in surprise.

"Your vampire King has him, or so I am told," Auberon replied making me close my eyes and want to groan as I rubbed my forehead as if a headache was coming on. Because this was obviously where things were about to get way more complicated. This is when I told him the truth,

"So, about this bargain you made with the witch, I hate to be the one to tell you this, but you should know that she was trying to kidnap me herself, meaning you wouldn't have had…?" He stopped me by holding up a hand and said,

"The witch's deal I had was not for you, for I didn't even know you existed." At this my eyes grew wide in surprise and what it now meant. This was confirmed as the King looked towards the McBain brothers, making them laugh and Trice said,

"Yer deal wis fur us?!"

"Your deal was for them?!" I asked the same, only screeching a little in shock.

"I believe now that the witch's plan was to use me in aiding to rid you of your bodyguards so she could take you with ease. However, that was naturally not how the deal was sold to me," he admitted with a small gesture of his hand as if this was obviously an inconvenience for him.

"What do you mean, just what was this deal you made?" I asked.

"I was told that these three men were part of the King's council and that this King of the Dead would trade anything or more to the point, *anyone*, to get them back." At this all three brothers suddenly burst into laughter, with Gryph slapping a beefy hand on his leg. I shot them a look telling him without words that it wasn't a good idea to laugh at the King.

"Well, ye wur fucked over that one!"

"Aye, as let's just say th' King dinnae give two shits stains aboot us vagabonds, 'n' we are nothing mair than a useful tool fur him tae use!" Trice informed him making me frown because that sounded bad and I hated believing that this was true. However, Lucius hadn't exactly given them any other reason to believe otherwise and that thought pained me.

"I'm afraid what my brother is saying is correct, for we are the last three the King would be interested in saving, of that I can assure you," Vern said, being a little more eloquent at it too.

"Yes, I am seeing that now. Lucky for me then that something far more important to the King made it through that portal and into my Kingdom, for I suggest we focus on that element of current events and move on negotiation… wouldn't you agree, gentlemen?"

"Well, it's nice to be considered as a gentleman for once," Vern said making his brothers roll their eyes, but Vern just shrugged his shoulders and merely said in his defence,

"I fear it cannot be helped, chaps."

This was when the King, who was sat on my right, leant close to me and said,

"Are we sure that he is related to the other two." I smirked and said a whispered,

"Looks can be deceiving." He smiled at this before nodding his head slightly before continuing,

"In the end it matters little, for I see a way for us to all get what we desire."

Aye, an hoo is tha' then?" Trice snapped with a fold of his arms making the leather across his chest groan against the simple dark green tunic he wore underneath.

"Well, you wish to go home, back to this realm in Hell ruled by your King and I know how to get you there. What I am suggesting is a simple exchange," he offered with a flick of his hand.

"Exchange?" I said wanting things clarifying.

"It is simple, for I will have your bodyguards escorted to the

Dark Fae realm, and from there they can use the portal that can access that particular part of Hell's realm in which you speak."

"And you know this for sure, do you?" Trice bit out again, now leaning forward with his hands on his knees.

"I do, for it is the very same one that my brother used when he was banished from this place," King Auberon admitted.

"Wait a second, so your brother was banished to Lucius' Kingdom?" I asked, now thinking that this may not be as dire as I feared as it meant that his brother might not be one of Lucius' captives at all… big phew moment for me there.

"My brother is under the protection of your King, this much I know, and now the time has come that I want him back. Now, for this to happen I need leverage and you, unfortunately my dear, will do nicely."

"Figures," I muttered making Trice give me a look that said it all… *pain in his ass once again.*

"So, I propose that your protectors get escorted to this portal, so that they may announce to your King of my intentions and be told that if he wants you back, then he must send my brother in exchange, for this is the only way that you will return to him." I swallowed hard once he had finished, knowing that this was pretty much the bargain in a nutshell. However, unsurprisingly there was one member of our group that was not happy with this arrangement.

"The hell we wull, I am nay leaving th' lass 'ere alone!"

"Trice… please, we can't…" I started to say when the King conceded quickly,

"Very well, that seems reasonable enough to me, after all, there are three of you," the King announced making Trice visibly relax for a moment, that was before the King added,

"He will stay and no one else." This was directed at Vern, making his eyes widen in surprise.

"Why th' bugger wid ye pick him!" Trice argued.

"Now, I say, brother, that was rather uncalled for wouldn't you agree?" Vern said making me try and hold in a giggle at his posh outrage. The King's lips twitched as a grin also played there and in that moment it was a bit like watching a cat playing with a mouse. Especially when he said,

"Well, he is after all the polite one and will fit in nicely within my Kingdom… besides, he is trustworthy is he not, for he is your brother?" At this you could see Trice gritting his teeth before he ground out the word as if it had been chewed and spat on the floor,

"Fine!" At this the King clapped his hands together in his victory,

"Excellent." It was in this moment that I definitely refrained from comparing him to Mr Burns from The Simpsons, as not only was it quite insulting but he wouldn't understand the reference either, so what was the point.

Now after this little detail was out of the way, there was only one thing left to discover before the two McBain brothers were to leave the Kingdom and onward to a journey back to their own King. A King who I knew Trice loathed even more than this one.

"We wull be needing th' name o' this brother o' yours?" Trice asked in his usual brutish way. But this was when the surprises just kept on coming from King Auberon, as he told us…

"My brother is Carn'reau…"

"King of the Dark Fae Realm."

CHAPTER TWELVE

A DEVIL OF A REASON

S hortly after this, we found ourselves back in the throne room and near the doors at the end. It was time for our goodbyes. The terms had all been settled as Gryph and Trice were to travel to the Dark Fae Realm. A place I'd just discovered was to be ruled by none other than Carn'reau himself.

The plan was for the brothers to bring him back and in return they would get me… or at least, Lucius would. And in my heart, this plan meant not only my freedom from this place, but also achieving what was and had been my main concern all this time. The fact that the moment the McBain brothers reached Lucius' kingdom, they could finally have a chance at stopping the execution of his brother. This above all else was much higher on my list, even before being reunited with Lucius.

Which was why, when Trice was saying goodbye, I grabbed him to me and hugged him, whispering,

"Please get there in time and stay safe." I felt his hand go to the back of my head and cradle it as he held me to him. He did this before he whispered back down at me,

"Keep yersel' safe, Amelia, 'n' trust na one bit my brother." I looked up at him in that moment as he allowed the space for me to move, then he cupped my cheek in a tender hold and told me,

"That includes nae trusting th' King." I looked back over my shoulder as his hand dropped, and saw that the King he spoke of was standing there expectantly, obviously now waiting for me to join him. I looked back up at Trice and nodded, conveying my silent agreement. Trice, in the meantime, accepted this and because of it, now looked slightly less tense before turning his attentions to Vern.

"I know," Vern said as if replying to some silent demand, and Trice hooked a palm to the back of his neck and pulled him close, so his forehead was now touching that of his brother's. Then it was in this moment he said it anyway,

"Keep th' lass safe."

"With my life, brother," Vern vowed making me get teary at the sight… well, that was until Gryph walked past and said,

"Noo, if we done wi' this mushy shit, let's git going. Amelia, ye be in mind tae go fur th' ballocks noo lass 'n' keep yersel' safe, I hae a feeling Dragons aren't ney th' only one that bites round ere." I chuckled at this and hit him on the bicep before telling him,

"Well, Gryph, that was really soppy and heartfelt… now get your handsome ass going before Mr Broody here changes his mind." He let out a full belly laugh, especially when Trice rolled his eyes at my comment.

"Remember whit I said, lass… no one bit Vern." I nodded again, as Vern came to stand next to me and the both of us watched together as the two McBain brothers left the throne room. Left to take on their own quest, and one that I was praying would be successful.

After this, King Auberon stepped up behind me and offered me his arm once more,

"If it pleases your lady, I am having dinner served early so that we may solve that pesky hunger of yours," he teased with a glint in his eye. At that moment, Vern stepped up next to me and offered me his own arm and said,

"My lady, it would give me great pleasure to be your escort, *now and always."* Vern added this last part whilst looking up at the King and making his intentions known. I looked at the ground and smirked, trying not to laugh at the sound of Vern as he was obviously keeping his promise to his brother. I put my hand in the arm of my guardian, knowing I was making the right decision. Then I said,

"I thank you, kind Sir, for that would be most generous of you." This was in my poshest accent, trying to sound like an English aristocrat when the King raised a brow in question at my response. But then again, he was most definitely amused, and I was just glad that I was able to keep the King on the right side of a good mood by not insulting him with my decision.

"Very well, I see this time I am forced to concede… but make no mistake, for I will get your beauty to grace my arm once more before our time is up, Princess." This, he promised after he had lowered his lips to my ear, doing so on the other side from where Vern was stood.

Then, before Vern could tug me away like I knew he was a second from doing, the King spun on his heel and walked ahead of us.

"I think this is the part where we follow him," I commented, making Vern grin down at me and say,

"You know, by gosh, I think you're right." I giggled and he held up a finger in silent warning for me not to say a word. So I ran my own finger over my lips to tell him they were sealed, making him wink one of those beautiful hazel coloured eyes at me and flash a dimple that dipped deeper when he grinned.

Then we both followed to what I presumed was the King's dining room.

"Come on, handsome, let's go and eat them out of Kingdom and home." Vern's grin said it all.

A little time later and with a full belly, I was being escorted to my room, one that I was thankful to find was next to Vern's. This was after finding just the two of us sat at an elaborate table that looked as though it had been made from polished, petrified wood, cut from a large slice of a tree the size of a redwood. It was big enough that it could have sat at least forty people around it, and seemed a little overkill for just the two of us. However, it was most definitely fit for a king, one that chose that moment to be absent, leaving me and Vern to the feast in front of us.

I couldn't help but giggle when 'posh Vern' whipped out his napkin in a camp way before tucking it down the neck of his black chest plate. Then he ran a hand through his floppy strawberry blonde hair and reached for the silver-plated decanter. One that was far too flowery and feminine for such manly, rough hands that grabbed it now. He then poured me a drink first in the dainty handblown wineglass that was decorated by vines of silver curling up the green glass cup.

In fact, the whole room made him look out of place and I loved watching him as he embraced it! He was such a loveable rogue, that he just made you smile. And honestly, this was even more so when he was inflicted with Nero's 'posh gentleman' spell. It also had to be said that, well, it certainly made it easier to understand him. But speaking of

Nero, I couldn't help it whilst I had this opportunity to ask him,

"So, when are you and Nero going to get together?" On hearing this, he nearly choked on his drink before gently placing his glass down and clearing his throat, after dabbing his napkin to his kissable lips.

"Excuse me?" he said, turning fully to face me.

"Okay, let me put in a way that less posh Vern would understand, as I know he's still in there and all... here goes, so when are you and Nero going to stop pissing around and admit how you feel about each other?" I asked, making him drag a hand through his hair again and say,

"Ah, now I see where this point is headed." At this I actually rolled my eyes at him and said,

"Come on, Vern, I know you like her."

"Yes, well, that might be the case, but I assure you, my dear, it is not as simple as that." At this I called bullshit, and told him as much when reaching out to grab a piece of star shaped bread that looked glazed in something sweet. So, basically, it had my name written all over it.

"Sounds simple to me," I told him with a shrug of my shoulders.

"It would, you are human," he said, as bluntly as posh Vern would allow.

"Ouch, was that a burn, from posh Vern... see what I did there?" I joked making him be the one to roll his eyes this time.

"Not everything is as easy as it seems." Was his vague response.

"Seems easy to me... shifter likes witch, witch likes shifter..."

"Witch is now a vampire," he stated casually, making my mouth drop at the same time the dainty cutlery that I was about to use fell to my plate with a clatter.

"What?!" I screeched.

"Surely you cannot be that surprised, for how did you think he saved her life?"

"I don't know, first aid, some CPR, some burny eyes Superman style... what, it worked for Lois Lane?"

"I am afraid I am not following your brand of insanity in this moment."

"Oi! Okay, fine, no comic book stories or cinemas in Hell, I guess. But my point is, I wasn't there, remember? So, I don't know what happened to her. I just... *I just left her.*" I said this in a sad voice that made Vern grab my hand and give it a squeeze.

"Nero told me what happened, you didn't just leave her, Amelia." I thought back to that moment on the boat when I wished more than anything that I could have gone back for her. To force her to get on that boat with me and not sacrifice herself so that I could escape. Maybe we could have faced the Hellhounds together, we might have had a chance!

But then, the second I had been told that she was still alive, I couldn't have been happier, bursting into tears of relief. A relief that was soon short lived for I was robbed of the feeling when it was soon followed by what came next. Finding out that my own words spoken to Nero had potentially caused Lucius to kill his own brother. Well, naturally that would put a downer on any happy moment.

"She's my friend. When we were locked up together, Gods Vern, I don't think I could have done it without her, and then she started talking about you and telling me how you both met and..."

"Wait, she did?" At this I smirked and gave him a knowing look.

"Of course, she did, who do you think she was most worried about not ever seeing again?" At this Vern released a deep sigh.

"It matters not now, for it is too late I am afraid." I frowned when he said this and crossed my arms, clearly affronted by this.

"Why? Because she's a vampire? I know you don't like them but..." I had been about to say more when he interrupted me and when he did, let's just say I dropped my attitude pretty quickly.

"They slaughtered my family, my entire clan," he blurted out and I gasped in shock.

"Oh Gods, Vern, I didn't know... I am... I am so sorry." I reached out and was now the one to hold his hand, squeezing it in comfort. But then the question that I didn't ask, yet was dying to, was that if he hated all vampires then how did he and his brothers end up with their souls being owned by the king of them all?

"I know what you're thinking," he said as if reading my thoughts. That, or he had already figured out my curious nature.

"You do?"

"You're currently asking yourself how is it that my brothers and I could be blood bound to a vampire King, when it was his kind that wiped out our clan," he said hitting the fang shaped nail on the head.

"Yeah, something like that."

"I do not wish to get into our sordid tale of woe, for alas it is not my place to, but I can tell you that the vampires that killed my people were rogues."

"They were?" I asked thinking at least this made some sense, as who better to deal with rogues than the King.

"But in exchange for revenge against his kind and the enemies against our clan, a deal was made and forged in Hell with the Devil," he told me, making me ask,

"Your enemies? As in Human?"

"They had been the ones to enlist the help of Vampires to eradicate us."

"Wait a minute, but if you made a deal with Lucifer, then how is it that Lucius owns your souls?" I asked, only now picking up on that important piece of information.

"It is simple, the King is the son of the Devil, and it is in his power to do as he pleases with the souls he collects." I looked away, shocked at this.

"Besides, the Devil also has a sick and twisted humour, for this much is true," Vern added taking a sip of his wine.

"What do you mean?" I asked frowning.

"Lucifer wanted to see just how far his little creations could turn and although it is still unclear as to how he accomplished it, the fact remains that when we became too powerful to be contained, he needed a solution." I frowned, wondering just where I had heard a story similar to this, as it seemed to be a common theme with the Devil and his 'creations gone wrong', my Uncle Adam included in that list.

"But I always thought it was Lucius who…"

"It was indeed Lucius who was charged with dealing with the rogues, as, unbeknown to the simple human warriors we were at the time, it was his responsibility to do so regardless, but it was always the Devil who our souls were sold to."

"Oh Gods, Vern, I had no idea, I always thought…"

"Yes, I know, and no doubt that's what my brother had you believe for a reason," Vern said making me realise it was true, Trice wanted me to believe that Lucius was the bad guy in all this.

"The truth is that the Devil entrusted our souls to his son, giving us away like gifts. It was a sick twist of fate, to now find our souls in the hands of the same creature that lay waste to what was our entire world."

"But I still don't understand why?" I admitted knowing that with the Devil, there was always a hidden motive.

"Why not, it is after all named Hell for a reason and he is the Devil. A deal was made with him and we ended up there after our revenge was complete. The irony was always to be that our punishment for our sins of revenge were that the very creatures we'd loathed, the creatures we wanted revenge on, that the King of all of them would be the one to own our souls. He would be our eternal Warden for an eternity in the prison of Hell. That was what our revenge cost us, and that is what the King is still to give back to us."

"Oh Gods… okay, so yeah, I kind of see why you hate him now." At this he laughed before downing the rest of his wine and refilling his glass. So I told him, after reaching out and taking his hand again,

"I promise you, Vern, I promise you and your brothers that I will do everything in my power to try and get your souls back and hey, if he says no, then I just won't have sex with him until he does." At this, Vern burst out laughing before choking on his wine as I leaned over and whispered,

"And he really likes sex." Then I winked at him and drank my own wine. But there was one last question in my mind, for I knew that the Devil was in the details.

"So, all three of you sold your souls to the Devil and for that, he turned you into shifters… I wonder why shifters?" I said almost musing to myself before Vern dropped the biggest bombshell on me yet.

"Ah, but I am afraid that's where you're wrong, sweetheart."

"What do you mean?"

"It wasn't all three of us that sold our souls." I frowned at this and shook my head a little, before asking in an almost fearful tone,

"Then who was it?"

"It was just one of us that made the deal with the Devil…" He paused as if pained. As if he didn't want to say it but felt too compelled to. Like fate was forcing the next three words out of his mouth, and with them condemning his brother…

"…It was Trice."

CHAPTER THIRTEEN

LITTLE MISS PISS POTTING

After the meal, and the bombshell from Vern I now had my head spinning over, we found ourselves with full bellies and ready to sleep for a week. Or at least I was. A meal, which I had to say included a lot of salad and therefore I was not surprised that everyone I'd seen so far were tall and slim. This was because there had not been one single ounce of fat on the table and in all honesty, I was really starting to miss cheese.

Vern had laughed at me of course when I had said this, as he just admitted to being glad that there was meat on the table, as I think he'd had some misconception that all Fae were going to turn out to be vegans. Now, I didn't have a problem with vegans, or vegetarians for that matter, as most of the time I wish that I had the willpower to join them. But, unfortunately, I was a meat girl through and through, and as for cheese... well, everyone who knew me, knew what I felt about cheese. In fact, I think even Lucius had commented once about how there had been more cheese on my chilli than actual chilli. I had just given him a look and said, 'and?' to which he had burst out laughing.

But then this had me thinking back to that day and how perfect it had been. Well, that had been until I had ended up being chased by Hellhounds and tackled to the ground by the witch in the freezing snow. Then yeah, minus that part and it would have been the perfect date.

But speaking of dates, it had been at this point that this one with Vern was ending, as the King had come back to retrieve us, ready to escort us to our rooms.

"I will be right next door if you need me... *for anything?*" Vern said this as a question, and managed to shake me out of my melancholy thoughts and away from times that painfully seemed like an age ago. *Gods, but I missed him.*

Vern added to this by looking distinctly at the King, telling me exactly what it was meant as... A warning to leave me alone. After all, he had a promise to his brother to uphold.

However, I also knew that having the King escort me to my room wasn't what Vern was making out that it was. Because, despite the King clearly being the flirty type, I knew that was all it was. Because he himself had admitted that the only full humans allowed in their realm would be their fated Queens. This then meant that he wasn't so different from any of the other Kings in my world who had been fated to find their own Chosen Ones. Something my mother and father's union had kick started for everyone else. Because if the Fates were to be believed, then this was because they all had some sort of connection to my mother. Of course, for most, this had been proven to be true, my cousin Ella for one, despite how stubborn they both were on the matter.

But this meant that I understood the King a little better than most would. As the King's heart was only ever going to be meant for one soul in the entirety of all realms combined and he knew that as well as I did. Which was why his flirting didn't bother me as I would rather that than incur his wrath, one that I'd merely had a taste of when negotiations had first started.

However, I was of a curious nature and anyone who knew me might have classed this as a flaw, one that often got me into trouble. But it was who I was, and it was why I wanted to know the King's story. It was why I wanted to know why his brother had been banished and no longer ruled the Dark Fae Realm, but more than anything, I wanted to know why he wanted to bring his brother back now and if there was a possibility of that happening without Lucius being the one to drag him here himself?

Knowledge was after all, power, and seeing as I was lacking in that department in this realm, then it was all I had left... well, that and my clumsy charms, I thought wryly. But these were answers to questions I knew I couldn't ask in front of Vern. Because I knew they weren't questions that would have been answered in front of someone the King didn't trust. And for some reason I knew the King trusted me. I knew this the moment I had asked the very question once a plan had been formed back in his library. I had asked him why Carn'reau had been banished and after a moment of looking forlorn, he had said in a distant tone,

"That, I am afraid, is a story for another time." This answer at least gave me hope that he might be willing to tell me that very story once we were alone, so that I may better understand what had driven him to these extremes. Also, he didn't seem like the kidnapping and holding to ransom type.

But then the problem I had with all of this was Trice's voice entering my head and telling me not to trust the King. Something I was finding very difficult not to do, because I didn't know what it was about King Auberon, but I felt his loneliness. I felt his compassion for his people. I felt his love for his Dragons and his adoration for his sister, even though she too had been absent during the meal. In fact, it felt as if I actually knew him, as though he had unknowingly been projecting elements of his personality and I kept picking up on them. I wanted to understand what would push a King like him into making such a rash decision in putting trust in a witch. To make a deal that clearly would have been the wrong one, for the King had just ended up another one of the witch's pawns. A way to rid herself of the McBain brothers by casting them out to a different realm and being imprisoned by a King who only wanted to bargain their lives for that of his brother.

What drove him to make that decision?

Well, I felt compelled to find out, which was why I made my own rash decision. Meaning the moment that the King and I both watched as Vern disappeared into his own room, I stepped closer to him and said,

"Can I request to speak to you privately?" The King's eyes widened in surprise for just a flicker of a moment before that amused smirk started playing at the corner of his lips. It was as if he had known this was coming, and I just hoped it wasn't him getting the wrong impression or believing another reason for this was of a seductive nature. Because no way! I mean yes, the guy was undeniably hot, handsome, and powerful enough to shift into a freakin dragon for the Gods be damned sake! But he wasn't my Lucius, and he was the only man candy I was addicted to and always would be.

"I had a feeling you were going to ask me that," he admitted, making me blush, and again I was tempted to point out that talking was all I was interested in but then he spoke again before I got a chance to.

"I will tell you what, Princess, go into your room and lie on the bed." My blush quickly turned into a crimson flame and I opened my mouth, realising the blunder I had made and tried to stop it in a mumble of words,

"No, I... well, I didn't... that's the last thing, I just wanted... no, not the last thing, because well, not that there is anything wrong with your erm *thing*... oh Gods, please stop me now." He laughed heartedly at this, before stepping closer and said on a chuckle,

"Calm yourself, all I want from you right in this moment is for you to rest. For if we have this conversation any longer you will faint in my arms and I will have no other choice but to carry you to bed, something I fear your well-spoken friend may not feel so forgiving about... *for he's listening by the door and waiting for me to leave."* This last part he whispered down by my ear and I could hear the smile in his voice that made me shiver.

"Ah, I see," I replied lamely, making him smirk down at me.

"I will call on you when the time is right, and when I believe you are well rested... *good day, my lady."* At this, the King bowed his head slightly and turned to walk away without saying another word. This was when I said,

"It's alright, he's gone now, my virtue is safe," before listening for what I knew was coming. Meaning I grinned to myself when I heard the door close next to mine as Vern was now assured the King had left. I shook my head and chuckled before I did what I was ordered by the King to do.

I slept.

Like the dead

Waking up in a room that literally looked like you were now living in a fairytale, naturally made me believe I was still dreaming. That was until I felt the aches in my legs that had me questioning the pain, because I didn't need anyone to pinch me to see if I was awake, as all I needed to do was stretch out my muscles and that did it for me. I sat up on the incredible carved bed I had been sleeping in and one that I had literally fallen into, still fully clothed.

But it was always funny how that happened, how the adrenaline just kept you going over and over and over again until finally someone said stop. And when you did, it meant that it was like game over the second your body knew that it could relax. It became an impossibility to move again until it was rejuvenated and re energised, which thankfully, I now was.

However, it also made me look down at my dirty crumpled mediaeval style dress that I was now so desperate to get out of, it wasn't even funny! I needed a shower badly. In fact, I felt like I needed ten of them! Or just something a little more substantial than standing in a bucket and having Trice throw water over me before being able to sit in a tub.

"Gods in heaven, please let there be a bathroom... please let there be a bathroom," I said to myself as I took in the rest of the space around me, something that barely even registered before I'd fallen asleep. As for the room, it also had me questioning what time of day it was or if the sun went down far later here than in the human realm, because daylight was still streaming through the large arched windows, ones that were framed with an elaborately carved wooden arch, that had elvish symbols decorating it. This also meant that I was yet to see this place at night, if such a thing existed here.

There was everything in the room that one would expect to find, a bed, a dressing table, a few chairs, and a place to hang clothes, yet nothing was as I had ever seen before. It was as if nothing was made with only a single purpose, as if its use came secondary to its beauty. In fact, it reminded me of all those grand manor homes I had visited whilst living in England on the days off from work that I didn't fancy spending at home in my little flat building Lego and watching reruns of Star Trek in my pj's. When I could be bothered to catch the train, I would go as far as I was able in the short time I had off. Because that was the beauty about England, you were only ever a stone's throw away from some of the most beautiful architecture in the world.

A romanticised era gone by of the likes of Jane Austen and Charlotte Bronte. A time when men were true gentlemen, and it was a custom to take your hat off when entering a room or rise from your chair when a lady rose from her own. But it was also within these homes that the gentry used as a means to show off their wealth. And what better way than to fill your home with the all the world had to offer in the way of elite craftmanship. Down to the very teacup you drank from, to the plates you ate your cucumber sandwiches off. The grand pianos that adorned drawing rooms, and fancy furniture that had been brought from the places these great lords and ladies would visit.

Everything was a show of wealth and I had to question if that was the same here. Or was it just that everyone in this realm was born into great craftsmanship. Then again, I had to remember that I was currently sleeping in a castle, and I very much doubted that a King such as Auberon would have anything less than the beauty he seemed so fond of. I thought back to Afterlife and knew that it was certainly a common theme with Kings, my own father included.

Therefore, I ignored the sleek, curled lines of this world's beauty, and the carved fauna that they welcomed into their homes with each design. And instead went in search of that all-important bathroom that my bladder so desperately sought.

"Thank the heavens!" was my response to finding a bathroom, complete with plumbing at last! The bathroom was all carved from quartz of some kind, including a bathtub that would have been big enough for me and the cast of Grease! It took up practically the whole room, and my first thought was how I wished that I'd started running the water before I took a nap as it would probably take that long to fill it.

"You pull on that chain there, in case you were wondering." I gasped in shock at now finding that I was not alone and spun around to find myself facing a young woman. One who was, aside from Pip, most likely the cutest girl I had ever seen in my whole life!

She had a mass of wavy hair that was a dark and deep purple at the roots before it shaded into a stunning raspberry colour then ending at the tips in a light pastel pink. It was most definitely unusual, but I had a feeling that it was also natural as it didn't exactly strike me as the type of place that sold hair dye. But then, other than the slightly pointed ears I could see poking through, she didn't exactly strike me as being Fae either. Because she was nothing like them, as in, *at all.*

But this was also because of her facial features, or what could be seen of them, as one half of her face was hidden by a curtain of her thick, wavy hair. She also had large, doll like eyes that were similar to her hair colour, being the same dark raspberry colour that was ringed with a lighter pinkish tone. A slight pink freckling dusted the skin at her cheeks and bridge of her small button nose. Perfect heart shaped lips that looked naturally pink like a rose shifted to one side, as it was clear she felt uncertain of being there as I hadn't yet said anything, being far too transfixed in looking at her. Gods, but she was like a perfect china doll, dressed like some fair maiden. But the closer I looked, the more I could see the tell-tale signs of who she may be.

Little paint splats dotted her hair and I looked to her hands to see the paint around her fingernails that she had obviously tried to scrub out but failed. This is when I smiled at her and said,

"Let me guess, you're the King's sister and awesome artist of this place?" I thought it best to lead with a compliment, and was rewarded by her beaming smile that made me want to tip my head to one side and saw, aww. Yes, she was that ridiculously cute!

"I'm Alvena, and I take it you're Amelia? Which means we both have names beginning with A… isn't that funny?" she said in a nervous way as if she couldn't help rambling.

"Call me Fae, as in the name, not one of you… although I have been meaning to ask do you prefer Fae or Elves?" I said blurting it out and making her burst out laughing, instantly relaxing now she knew she was in good 'random stuff to blurt out' company.

"Fae is just fine. Our ancestry speak of the elvish language, which is what we are taught by our elders, but it has always been classed as the Fae Realms like the city we are in now… it's called Calidad, in case you were wondering. So, are you going to pull the chain, or should I help… oh, and that's a piss pot over there as well, you know, in case you need that… which I would, as most do I suppose when waking," she said, now making me laugh for I think I'd found somebody as scatty as me, which was kind of a relief when finding a kindred spirit.

"Thanks, yeah I think I will, pull the chain that is and definitely need the piss pot, which we call a toilet."

"Yes, we call it that too, but I always liked piss pot, most likely because I wasn't allowed to say piss pot when I was younger or even now really, but well we are alone and therefore now I can say piss pot as much as I like, piss pot!" I burst out laughing at this and she blushed.

"I'm sorry, there's a reason I don't usually meet other dignitaries and they tell me you're a Princess so, yeah, I can be a bit awkward sometimes, it's why I like to paint, no one really to insult there my mother says, and no awkward moments around painting. I like painting… so anyway, enjoy your piss potting!" she said, suddenly turning round and walking out the door to then groan in frustration as if she'd forgotten something, which I knew she had when she stormed back in and told me,

"I forgot the reason I came here. Well, I didn't forget the reason I came here, I just remembered the reason I came here but the part I forgot was to tell you the reason I came here… I left you a dress!" she blurted out again before shaking her hair and making her hair fly around, as if she was silently chastising herself.

"It's on your bed, for you, erm, from me. My brother told me that you weren't wearing a nice one, so I have lots of nice ones… not to say it's ugly or anything. Okay, well I should be going to let you…"

"Piss pot." At this she smiled as if she too had just met a kindred spirit and said,

"yes, to piss pot…" Then she paused on her way out and told me, "I think we're going to get along really well," and I quickly said,

"Thank you for the dress." Strangely she waved an arm up in the air as if it was no bother and mumbled something as she left making her one of the cutest, yet strangest beings I had met so far. And I just knew that if there was one person in the world that I would love for her to meet one day, it would have been Pip.

As they too would have been kindred spirits.

In fact, I was still grinning to myself as I turned to face the rest of the bathroom and with one place in mind, I couldn't help but say out loud,

"Well, here's to piss potting."

CHAPTER FOURTEEN

THE STORY OF FOUR KINGDOMS

"Wow, she wasn't kidding about the dress," I said, as I stood there now staring at myself wearing a beautiful satin style dress that literally made me look like a Princess from a fairytale. This was after I'd had the most amazing bath, one that didn't take forever to fill like I would have thought. This was down to pulling on the chain and then being left to watch as it strangely filled from the bottom. But then the water level just kept on rising and rising, only stopping just before it was full.

Of course, this didn't stop me from having quite a few moments of panic as I was convinced that it would overflow. Meaning that I spent quite a bit of time looking for a way to stop it before it flooded the entire bathroom and then I would have had to go and find the King to tell him what I had done. In fact, these embarrassing thoughts consumed me as I wasn't exactly in a rush to explain to him how I was a total liability and threat to his Kingdom by just being here. And well, after tugging on the chain for about five minutes, swearing at it and praying to any God that had the power to control water, it finally stopped.

No thanks to the tugging, obviously.

Seriously, I was thinking there should be a sign somewhere for guests, like 'Will stop on its own, no tugging needed', that type of thing. I found myself sinking under the water, wishing that instead of being told so thoroughly about the piss pot, I would have been told not to worry about the water overflowing. Yeah, 'cause that would have been handy! Either way, after my freak out, I finally got to enjoy the bath, and that all important trip to the piss pot, of course.

I had even found an ornate wooden box filled with glass jars that I used for cleaning myself, and congratulated myself that I had manage to use the right things on the right parts. Then I got myself covered in a robe, that was an absorbent velvety material of emerald green. I had also wrapped up my hair in the same material, that I swear must have acted like a sponge, as my hair was almost completely dry by the time I unwrapped it.

After this the next blissful moment came when I got to use a brush, I know, small pleasures and all. But it felt like heaven against my scalp, and then I got to top it all off by getting dressed in the most amazing outfit! One that, yes, I did hold out at the skirt and twirl in it like a five-year-old girl in her first party dress. And man, but what a dress it was!

It started off white at the top and came down into a plunging V neck with an inch of gold silk that framed the edges. The material was thick but felt like satin to touch and was decorated with soft velvet flowers and vines in the lightest peach colour that was only barely seen against the white.

As for the sleeves, they were only made out of the same material at the top of my arms, where it was ruched until it reached a band of gold silk above my elbow. From that point a sheer peach material floated down past my hands and dipped into a tear shape, that skimmed the floor along with the skirt. A belt of gold hung low on my hips that too came down into V shape to mirror the neckline. A long length of gold then fell down the centre to my knees. It matched the rest of the dress only it had been embroidered with words written in elvish.

As for the skirt, it flowed out around me and the further down towards my feet was when the leaves got darker, ending up in a deep burnt orange colour. I was glad that I wasn't expected to wear heels with this outfit as my feet were still sore from walking. No, instead I found some cute little flat boots that the King's sister had left, which meant all I was left to do was slip my feet inside and tie them at the front with the ribbon that crisscrossed up the front of my ankle, like a little corsets for my feet. They were adorable and these too matched, being made out of white leather and had the same leaf pattern along the edges.

"I am seriously going to try and steal this outfit," I said to myself on a laugh as I looked at myself in the mirror. As for my hair, I had gone with the motto 'when in Rome' and I had brushed it as straight as it would go before taking two sections at the sides and plaiting them before joining them at the back of my head.

"Definitely a 'when in Rome' moment, although not sure what I'm going to do about the ears part," I said to myself, giving my outfit one last look in the mirror.

"Well, I would suggest cutting them, but I'm not sure your King would approve, or mine for that matter," the King's sister said from the doorway and I jumped at the sound.

"Sorry, I do that a lot… startle people that is, I think it's because I'm always… what is it my mother says, ah yes, lurking and stuff. Anyway, you're probably wondering why I'm here again."

"To enquire about the piss potting?" I joked, making her

look at me as if trying to gauge whether I was serious or not before she relaxed enough to laugh when I gave her a wink.

"Well, we will always have piss potting together… well, not the actual act of it, just the conversation of it… oh, what a nice day again… this way!" She shouted this last part suddenly, as if blurting something else out was her way of dealing with moments she considered awkward. Like trying to dig herself out of a hole by unknowingly jumping into a new one. And it seemed as if she was constantly berating herself for saying the wrong thing.

But then when I burst out laughing, which obviously helped to ease her fears, she grinned at me. Which was why I walked up to her and said,

"I really like you and you are officially my favourite person I have met here so far!" At this, her eyes widened in surprise as if no one had ever said anything like this to her before. But come on, wasn't she a Princess, because I'm sure that came with having loads of friends… *didn't it?*

I mean, she didn't seem shy but then I suppose in some instances, she did, like when she thought she had said the wrong thing. But then I had to say that I found her awkward social nature to be endearing and I really didn't know what she had to worry about, as she was so very beautiful.

But then I knew she was different, as you would have had to be blind in a place like this not to notice. And that in itself was strange, especially for a Fae being to be so petite, as so far most of the women I had seen were tall like the men, along with being slender. Basically, like your supermodels of the human world, only a whole realm of them. However, the King's sister was only an inch taller than myself and she had plenty of curves, with rounded hips, a dainty waist and definitely more in the breast department than I had seen walking around so far. Gods alive, but back in my world she would have been considered a knockout and have guys practically drooling over her!

But then her attraction didn't only come down to the way she looked, but it was almost like her soul just welcomed you in and this in itself made you wonder what had happened to this girl to make her so unsure. Like the uncomfortable way she held herself, as if someone had spent years stepping all over this girl's confidence. She didn't stand tall and proud like she had any clue how sexy cute she was. But instead, looked far more comfortable hiding in the shadows and trying to be a part of them, instead of that of the world around her. As if all she needed was just a mere glimpse of it to be enough to make her content, when secretly her only wish was to be as a part of it, as her brother was.

"Wow," I uttered and when she enquired about what I had said, I shook my head and told her it was nothing when in actual fact ever since I had arrived here, all that seemed to be happening was an overload of information I was sucking in. It was as if the King and his sister were projecting their feelings and pieces of their personalities onto me. It made me wonder if every Fae being I came in to contact with would be the same. But then I thought back to the walk I'd had with the captain and realised that no, it wasn't the same as I hadn't got anything off him.

So the biggest question now was, what was it about the King and his sister that seemed connected to me somehow? In the end, I found myself more pleased about it than freaked, because the things I knew about the both of them, so far were only good, despite our rocky beginning. Which meant that I had to trust my gut and in turn, meant going against what Trice had made me promise not to do, *which was trust them.*

But then how could I not? Because the girl in front of me now was a truly kind-hearted person, who I knew cared dearly for her brother and most definitely had issues with her mother. If anything, I think that her mother was most likely the one who knowingly bullied her into being who she was. This shy, cute wallflower surrounded by such striking beauty it made her feel sadly less than she deserved.

It made me wonder if her brother noticed it too.

"So, you are probably wondering why I'm here, you look lovely by the way, I knew that dress would be pretty on you and we are nearly the same height and they make our clothes so long anyway, mine always trail on the floor, so a couple of inches wouldn't really matter, I'm going to stop talking now," she said, making me laugh as it was clear this was what she did when nervous and in front of new people or for all I knew, anyone really. A barrage of words that would fly from her mouth just like it did with me on more than one occasion.

"I do that too you know, just so you know, and now I keep saying the word know," I said and the grin I received from her was definitely worth the admission.

"How do you control it?" she asked, and I thought about it for a minute before grinning to myself. Then I told her honestly,

"I don't control it, because it's a part of who I am, and you should never try and change a part of who you are."

"But why not?" Her question made me want to hug her, but instead I grabbed her hand and told her,

"Because there is someone out there who will enjoy it for themselves and never want to change you." In that moment she looked forlorn and admitted,

"There's no one like that here, trust me, the perfect palace saga continues and every time one of my mother's suitors gets thrown in front of my face, they end up leaving, disappointed that they wasted their time by making the journey." I dropped her hand and gave her shoulder a squeeze to get her to look back up at me. This was when I told her,

"I'm no expert here, but *maybe that's because they were picked by your mother."* Then I winked at her and she burst out laughing before giving me a genuine,

"Thank you, so far, other than my brother, you seem to be the only person who gets me in this place."

"Then that is your mission?"

"What is?" she enquired.

"To find a man who gets you and deserves you as you are, after you find that, then you'll know."

"I'll know?"

"Yeah… *that he is the one."* I said this last part whispered in her ear and then I took her hand and gave it a squeeze again, making her beautiful eyes widen for a moment before we left the room, now giving her something to think about.

I glanced towards Vern's door, and for a moment thought about telling him that I was leaving with the King's sister. But then, considering I was pretty sure she was taking me to see her brother, I decided against it, as I knew I needed to speak with him alone.

So I let her lead me back the way we had come and then towards her brother's office, as it was clear that this was most likely where he did most of his work conducting royal business and the rest of whatever Kings did in this realm.

"Ah, Vena, my beautiful sister, I see you brought our guest," the King said the moment we stepped inside, and I couldn't help but smile, seeing now the way his sister beamed at him. I was just happy that she had at least one person in her life that made her feel good about herself, even though I could still feel a slight wave of doubt coming from her. It was as if she believed his compliment was only said because he loved her and wanted to make her feel good, not because it was actually true. It was in this moment that I couldn't help but grab her hand and hold it out to put her on display and say,

"I totally agree, in fact I don't think I've ever met a girl so beautiful in all my life!" After I declared this the King granted me a soft and grateful look, as if my words had touched him as deeply as they had touched his sister, someone who was now looking astonished by my admission. Then she quickly announced with that runaway mouth of hers,

"I wish you could marry her, brother, she's so lovely and other than you, the only other person that's kind to me here." At this my heart broke for her.

"I agree with you, she is most certainly lovely, but as you know it doesn't work like that, my dear sister. Besides, she has her own King." At this a whirl of raspberry hair blurred as she whipped her head around quickly to look at me, now astonished.

"You do? Well, you never said." I tried not to laugh.

"We have had more of a conversation about the piss pot, so I didn't really get chance," I replied winking at her.

"I'm starting to see now why you two get along so well," the King said clearly amused.

"Well, whoever this king is, I hope he's nice to you, oh is he the one that doesn't mind your…"

"Runaway mouth?" I finished for her.

"Yeah, that." She blushed, making the pink freckles on her face deepen in colour.

"He's the one." At this she gave me a dreamy look and then turned to her brother and said,

"Then we must help her get back to her one." I grinned and looked back at the King in a judging way, as it was clear he hadn't told his sister everything about the reasons we were here. He cleared his throat after a moment of having me making him feel uncomfortable, then he said,

"And that we will, sister. Now, I hate to dampen your happy mood, but mother is looking for you." At this she groaned, rolled her eyes and let her head fall back, before she turned to me and said,

"Do you have a horrible mother?" I laughed as her brother scolded,

"Alvena!"

"No, I don't, I'm sorry, my mother is… well, *she's wonderful,*" I told her feeling the pinch in my heart and tears pricked my eyes at the thought of how worried she must be. How worried they both must be! It made me think of how badly I'd treated my mother believing what her and Lucius had done. It was in that moment that I'd never wanted to hug my mother so much in all my life and how grateful I felt to her for giving me all of those wonderful memories of what a real mother should be like.

She never made me feel downtrodden or inferior and she always had my back whenever I argued with my father about being human and allowing me some freedom. She never once made me feel less of who I was just because I was different than everyone else around me. No, if anything she made me feel like the most special person in the world and I know that if I hadn't had my mother growing up, then I would have felt even more alone than I was. Because she had lived her life as a human, she knew what I was going through and how important certain things were to me. Simply put, she was the best mother I could have ever hoped for and now I missed her so badly my heart ached.

"Well, I guess this is my cue to leave, either that, or my brother has a crook in his neck… or he will if he keeps trying to motion for me to leave… which I get now that he didn't actually want me to actually say that out loud, instead just leaving quietly without bringing attention to it…okay, well I'm going to go now… erm, I hope I'll see you later, Fae… seems a bit weird calling somebody Fae but I guess it would be like you calling me human." I burst out laughing at this, especially when her brother groaned with exasperation.

"I agree, call me Emmie, it's another nickname of mine, as for some strange reason, I seem to have a lot of them."

"Great! Isn't that great, brother? I will be the only one in the realm to call her this, it means we are true friends," she declared grinning and then in some awkward way that I think she believed was my own custom, she pulled me in for hug that wasn't relaxed in any way. But I patted her on the back all the same, which meant she left after this with a big grin on her face. Not surprisingly, the moment the door was closed the King sighed and started to say,

"My sister, she is…"

"Perfect in every way," I finished off for him, looking to the door and grinning to myself, because she was just one of those people you wanted to be around, and she didn't even realise it.

There was nothing fake or superficial about her, she was just a person who couldn't help but be themselves and it was awful to realise that she was being persecuted for that by her own mother. I was just glad that she wasn't being persecuted for it by her brother as well, or she truly would have no one in this realm.

In fact, I had never wished for someone to meet their true love so much in all my life, for she deserved to have that person who spent his time building her up, not tearing her down. Someone who didn't try and mould her into some perfect royal wife, but instead allowed her to just slot in there as easily as stepping into a pair of shoes. I had only met her two times and had, I confess, a strange conversation with her about the toilet. But even that was enough to know that she was a good person, and good people deserved happiness.

"You know that's the happiest I've seen my sister for a long time, so whatever you said to her to achieve that, I thank you and am in your debt."

"Does this mean you're willing to let me go with a stick and a handkerchief full of food tied to the end." At this he laughed and said,

"Not quite yet, no… if you please," he said motioning to the chairs we had sat in before, only this time he wanted me to take the seat closer to him, which I did.

"I believe you wished to know the story of my realm and why my brother was banished," he said coming right out with the reason we were meeting like this. I had to say, it was refreshing.

"I do, if you would be willing to tell me." He bowed his head once to tell me that he was, so I remained quiet and let him begin.

"I am not sure you are aware, but the elemental realm is made up of four lands, the Dark Lands, my own you know being the Dragon Lands, then there is the Land of Souls, and what pieces all of these lands together is the Land of Gold."

"Gold?" I asked surprised.

"Naturally, it is the richest of all our lands, for it's very sands are speckled with gold dust, which is why it is classed as a heavenly place."

"Classed as… you mean, literally?!" I asked shocked.

"Essentially, yes, it is our form of Heaven, for when one of us dies and our soul is judged, if it is deemed to be one pure of heart, then this is where we will end up." I frowned in question before asking,

"So, I take it you have a Hell then?"

"Of sorts, for this is the Land of Souls, where those that have committed sin are doomed to spend the rest of their eternity under my brother's rule." I took this in and after a million questions all raced to the surface, I picked on one and stuck with it, asking now,

"So, I'm confused, does this mean you don't have any Gods?" At this he smiled and told me the biggest shock of all,

"My sweet girl, we four Kings that rule of these lands…"

"We are the Gods."

CHAPTER FIFTEEN

RIGHTING WRONGS

I sucked in a startled breath and he smirked before telling me,

"You are so shocked, I am surprised at this."

"Why?!" I shouted more surprised by his question.

"Because you are a scholar, are you not?" he questioned, and I couldn't help but feel another twinge in my heart for this had often been Lucius' nickname for me, calling me his little scholar. It didn't feel right coming from anyone else and my face must have said as much.

"Oh, I see I have offended you in some way." I felt bad when he said this so assured him,

"No, not at all and you're right, I'm a historian... scholar," I added softly.

"Then you will be aware of your own history, where many Kings were thought to be the descendant of the Gods they worshipped, were they not?" Okay, so yes, he had a point.

"This is true, especially for the Egyptians, for no one believed it more than they... but I should point out that just because it was believed it didn't make it true, and I have a feeling that you're not just saying you're a God because you're trying to impress me here." At this he laughed, and it was a handsome sound, a deep timbre that would make most girls swoon no doubt.

"No, I am not just trying to impress you, despite that you are most certainly worthy of achieving the task," he said giving me the compliment and making me blush.

"Your own people, at one time or another throughout your history, have themselves worshipped us as their Gods, my brother Carn'reau especially, for he was known as the God of War and was worshipped by many tribes. Some of which were led by Genghis Khan, who you must know yourself, given your chosen profession, nearly ruled your world and dominated the largest land mass of your world's history." I had to say, the King kept shocking me.

"I am surprised you know so much, considering I was always under the impression you didn't really like humans... what was it again, thought us as inferior beings?" I asked with a grin so as not to offend.

"Not inferior exactly, for that is not how I would ever put it," he said, obviously now being put in a difficult situation as he was, in fact, taking to a human now, despite what he thought.

"But?"

"But yes, it is known that not all my brothers feel this way, but then your kind's own history does not exactly lend you any favours in that regard." Ah, so this is when we were to get to the nitty gritty as my mum used to say.

"Care to elaborate on that?"

"Oh, come now, you know of your own history most likely better than I, just how many wars are fought over greed and power? Can you really say that your Kings have put their Kingdom's first, put the lives of their people first?"

"Alright, I will agree that not all wars over history have been fought with the people's best interest in mind. But actions of a few should not then taint the good actions of many. Not all humans are power hungry megalomaniacs." At this he laughed and said,

"No, and I have proof of that sat next to me right now, which makes me wonder how my brothers' views would change, should they have been the ones fortunate enough to sit with you now." I blushed again at his compliment and whispered a quiet,

"Thank you."

"So, I guess seeing as you're fated to a human, that's why your history is so good?" I asked thinking back to what he said, and wondering just how the other 'kings' felt about being fated to a human then, if this was what they thought of us? Because, wow, that was going to make for a good match… *not.*

"I make it my place to know your history along with that belonging to my own realm and those that surround my own, for power is knowledge, is it not?" He pointed out my favourite saying with a gesture of his hand, making me take notice again at how big it was.

"I agree, in fact if I hadn't been such a bookworm growing up then I would know nothing of my own culture," I admitted.

"Ah, you are a protected only child, I assume?"

"I was an only child for a while, yes, and being the only human born to supernatural parents, wasn't exactly easy for them or for me. But I am not an only child, as I have two brothers," I told him, wondering why I did. Especially considering we were getting somewhat off topic now.

"And these brothers of yours, are you as close to them as I am to my own sister?" he asked, and again I found myself answering him,

"Quite honestly, not as much as I'd like to be."

"And why is this not the case I wonder?"

"I thought it was me asking all the questions?" At this he shrugged his shoulders.

"I believe in the exchange of information and that it should be gifted in equal amounts," he told me, making a good point.

"Well said, I see you're a very diplomatic King." He laughed and gestured with his hand,

"I often try to be."

"To tell the truth, I found out about my brothers when I was sixteen."

"So late?" he questioned as most people would.

"It was kept from me and let's just say I wasn't too happy when I found out that it had been. My brothers were… *are,* beings of extreme power, and being the only human and feeling sort of persecuted for that with an over-protective father, admittedly I took out my bitterness on them. One, especially."

"And you regret this?" he said as it was easy to guess.

"I do. Theo, my brother, well he's a really great guy and he's funny and kind. I spent so long of my childhood wishing I wasn't alone and wishing that I had someone who I could be close to, like a brother or sister, that well… when it actually happened, I was too overcome by bitterness to see the positive side it brought me. To let myself see that I had been asking for this very thing all these years and when it finally happened, I wasn't in the right place to accept it. So, if I had the chance, would I go back and change things, yes, most definitely." After I had told him this he looked touched that I had confided in him, as he gave me a tender look before telling me,

"Time is all relative."

"Excuse me?" I asked as hearing him say this surprised me.

"I believe a very clever man once said this in your realm… yes?"

"That he did," I agreed.

"Then I think you will agree with me, that the time is what you make of it. For it is never too late to right a wrong, just as I myself have learned."

"Is that why you want your brother back, to right a wrong?"

This was when he told me,

"Not just to right a wrong, but to right the biggest wrong of all…" I held my breath before he continued with a look of shame…

"To right the reason why my brother was banished."

CHAPTER SIXTEEN

FAMILY OF GUILT

"What do you mean, why was he banished?" I asked making him close his eyes as the memory was a painful one.

"Time. It was all, I should have…" King Auberon said, and I knew it was only to himself, for I was not to understand any of it. So this was when I braved touching him, reaching out with my hand to offer comfort, resting it on his forearm. The material of his tunic felt more solid, more tense and I wondered if this was the difference between what they wore… did the men of this world wear a more stern, stiffer material whilst they wrapped the females up in the softest silks?

Or was it just the King who preferred the discomfort? I didn't know, but with the feel of his muscles tense beneath my palm, the next thing I wondered was if I had been wrong in touching him? However, he didn't pull away but instead covered my hand in his much larger one, looking down at it now as if just realising that he wasn't alone in his suffering.

I knew then that he was finding comfort in my presence and

STEPHANIE HUDSON

in that moment, I was happy to be the one to give it to him. But then I also felt the question behind the feeling. He wanted to know if this was what it would be like ruling with a queen by his side. Someone to grant him the strength when making difficult decisions, like the one he knew he was soon to face when his brother walked back through the doors of his throne room.

This was when I could stand it no longer. I had to offer him something. So, I spoke his name, as any girl would,

"Auberon." On hearing this, he finally raised his head to look at me and those eyes belonged to a man whose gaze you could have lost yourself in.

"Tell me," I whispered making him nod, for I could feel his need to get it off his chest.

"To tell you of this tale, this painful past of my family's mistakes, I must first go back to beginning." I nodded for him to continue, fully aware that he now kept my hand in his grasp as if needing it there.

"You see, the four lands that make up this realm were once ruled by one King."

"One?" I questioned.

"Yes, one. A great King who brought prosperity and peace to what once was battling territories. But it was prophesied that a darkness, an evil force, would sweep the land and destroy all that my father had built. He spent many years of his life trying to discover a way to prevent this from happening, when eventually, it was one of our own oracles, an Oracle of Light who gave him the answer."

"And that was?" I asked, soon to be once again surprised by his answer.

"For him to marry four wives." I scoffed back a laugh and said,

"Erm, not to be disrespectful here, but are we sure he

170

actually met this Oracle of Light and didn't in fact just want four wives?" At this he threw his head back and laughed heartily, releasing my hand as he placed his own to his chest as if he couldn't contain his amusement. This was before informing me on a chuckle,

"Trust me, I can believe having just one wife is quite enough, but four of them to make happy is not as easy as you would believe… my mother is proof enough of that." I thought on this a minute and even just thinking of the heartache and trouble that Lucius went through with me, well then if there were four of me, then I could very much imagine that would push him over the edge completely. He would no doubt have himself committed.

"Good point," I said, admitting to it after just a thought. He gave me one of his soft smiles in return as if he knew where his comment had led my thoughts to.

"Needless to say, my mother is quite a handful," he added no doubt trying to make me feel better.

"So, back to these four wives that your father had lots of trouble with… your mother included." At this he chuckled again.

"It was prophesied that he would need to split his power between four rightful rulers, and to accomplish such he went in search of a wife from each of the lands. Once these fated four were found, he bore four sons and four daughters, which is common in our people."

"You usually have a boy and a girl, like Twins?" I asked.

"The son's always born first, and it is custom with our people for mothers to become pregnant soon after, then after carrying the child to term, a daughter is born," he told me, and I was fascinated. Well, it would certainly make planning easier and picking out baby clothes, as I doubted they had the technology of an ultrasound around here.

"So, this means you have three brothers and four sisters?"

"Yes, but I know what you're thinking."

"That I don't I envy you at Christmas time?" I joked making him laugh.

"I am not close to my other sisters and there was only one brother we were all close to but unfortunately… well, this was also when all our troubles began." The sadness in his tone made me realise that we were obviously getting to the most difficult part of his story.

"What do you mean?"

"When our father had four sons, he granted each of us the land as our Kingdom to rule. Carn'reau, became the King of Dark Fae, a land which is known for breeding the best fighters, the strongest of our kind."

"Hence the whole God of War thing… Gotcha," I said nodding and he gave me a look as if he was endeared by my reactions.

"As you already know, I was granted the Land of Dragons, which only became this after I was born."

"Why did it change?" I asked interrupting his flow once again because, well, I was too curious not to ask.

"Because the first dragons were born with me, I am their heart and with my birth, also came their own." This naturally shocked me, especially given the relaxed way in which it was said. But then again, I suppose to his people it was a story that everyone would know, and common knowledge.

"Is that why you're part shifter?" At this he smirked and replied,

"It has something to do with it, yes."

"And what about the other lands, are they shifters too?"

"Upon my word, what a curious human you are." I laughed and said,

"That's a bit of an oxymoron, don't you think?"

"How so?" he inquired raising a perfectly shaped brow.

"Well, considering you're talking to a human and all... curiosity is kind of in our DNA and is in our nature."

"Ah, but of course, how could I forget all my history?" he said teasing me, making me smile.

"As for the other lands, my brother Regin, was granted the Land of Souls, hence why he is often referred to as the King of Sin."

"Catchy, well in the human realm that name's sure to get him a date."

"Yes, I am sure," he agreed wryly, before astounding me again when he added,

"Well, he is the equivalent to your Devil." My mouth dropped a little before I could speak again.

"Wow... so I take it that he's the bad boy of the family?" The King's face lost all humour as he said a single, stern sounding word,

"Indeed."

"And what about your other brother, I take it he is the King of the Land of Gold." It was in this moment that any other emotion fled him and sorrow inevitably took its place, and I soon knew why.

"My brother, Callon, he was the peacemaker of the family, the last of the sons to be born."

"So, the baby of the family... wait, what do you mean... he was...?" This was when it dawned on me.

The sorrow.

"Unfortunately, this is the part of the tale that certainly darkens our history."

"Go on," I urged softly.

"My father ruled all four kingdoms until the time came when he was to leave this world, as back then we were simply Princes born with a single purpose, to one day rule. It was all we knew, our whole focus was our kingdoms. Whether it was taught in battle and how to wield a sword, or learning the delights of politics," he said grinning when I made a face like I'd just smelled something bad.

"Our whole life was centred around the day we were each to become King, but it was one always to be soured by the loss of our father."

"You loved him?" He released a heavy sigh, admitting,

"Yes, very much so, he was a good man… but then, towards the end…" This was when his face darkened and I gave him the time he needed, not wanting to push too hard. A decision that paid off when he said,

"He changed. A madness gripped him and not long before his final resting days, awful news came to us here in the city that my brother Callon… he had been killed." I gasped and my hands flew to cover my mouth.

"Gods," I whispered, pained by his loss.

"The news came via our uncle, my father's only brother, Haleth. He told our father how it happened, despite his state of mind being in a fragile place."

"Oh no, I think I see where this is going," I whispered as gently as I could. Not only from fitting the pieces together but also from the waves of frustration, anger and pain I could feel coming from Auberon.

But there was one emotion that overruled them all…

His Guilt.

CHAPTER SEVENTEEN

FAMILY OF BETRAYAL

"Tell me, what happened?" I asked having a bad feeling about what he was about to tell me next.

"He told my father that Carn'reau had been responsible for his death." I sucked in air through my teeth and even started shaking my head, knowing for myself that I could never imagine it to be true. His uncle was a liar! I mean it wasn't to say that we were best buddies in Hell or anything, but even I could see how loyal he was to Lucius. And that in itself told me how loyal he would be to his own family. I just couldn't imagine it.

"And so I see on your face, that you to do not believe this," the King said as my own feelings were clear.

"No, I don't. I may not know your brother well, but I have witnessed his loyalty to Lucius, I know he wouldn't do this." At this I surprised him.

"You know of my brother?"

"A little, I mean he tried to kidnap me once, for Lucius that time, but I know what you're thinking, and trust me, kidnapping attempts happen a lot and kind of come with the job description when being a Chosen One… a little tip for you there and one to remember for the future, yeah?" I said, making him shake his head a little as if he was still trying to process all I had said.

"I will take your word for it and most definitely take it under advisement for when I am gifted with my own Chosen." I grinned at this and refrained from saying, 'poor girl', as I almost felt responsible for whatever may face her in the way of possessive paranoia. I just hoped he didn't take it to extremes like Lucius wanted to when threatening me with shackles and a ball gag.

"So I take it your father believed Carn'reau was guilty, due to his failing health?"

"I do not know everything that my uncle said to him that day or what evidence he provided, but whatever it was, it was enough to convince my father and get my brother banished. This meant that he was never to become King of the Dark Fae Lands as he had been born to do." I swallowed hard, unable to imagine the pain that Carn'reau must have gone through. To lose his brother, father and his intended Kingdom all in one foul swoop. No wonder he had ended up where he had, which is why I said this very thing,

"So that's why he ended up being in Hell then?"

"The King who you belong to, it is his realm that lies next to my brother's, and in order for my brother to survive being away from his own realm, he needed it to be close enough so that he could still draw from its energy, the power and essence he would need to survive," Auberon said, and it all started to make perfect sense.

"So he made a deal with Lucius." At this he nodded and agreed,

"This is what I believe, yes, for I do not know for sure as I have not seen my brother since the day he was banished." Wow, that was going to be one hell of a reunion… *literally*.

"And now you want him back… so why now, I don't mean to be disrespectful or anything, but hasn't your father been dead a while?" I asked.

"This is true, and I am ashamed to say this but up until recently I too also believed my brother to be responsible." I gasped in shock.

"You did, but why… how? 'Cause no offence, but even I can tell that it was the evil uncle!" On shouting this, then I could tell I had just astonished him.

"You think this?!"

"Erm… yeah, I mean, don't you?" I asked doing so a bit more tentatively this time.

"I do not wish to get into the sordid details of my family's past misdeeds but …"

"No offence, Auberon, but you kind of already are," I stated firmly, interrupting him and making him release a frustrated sigh.

"You are right, what is it you humans call it, opening a can of worms, I do believe?" As soon as he said this, I was suddenly slammed with an image of me and Lucius sat in his Lamborghini speeding down a German highway. We were on the way to his mountain fortress, *his home.*

It was when he was trying to convince me to move in and basically telling me that from that point on, my life had entirely changed. Every conversation he tried to have with me, I referred to as being a can of worms that I didn't want to open. It was laughable if I thought about it right now, as in that moment I would have given anything to go back to that time to open every single one of them. To talk about our future, one that I was admittedly terrified of. But I had been so blind back then as I wanted nothing more than the chance to prove to him how committed I was to him. There was no more running from it, no more running from him! I was in, three billion percent!

Gods, but all I needed now was the chance to tell him that!

I just wanted him back. I wanted to go back. Even when dealing with mercenaries and exploding helicopters and car chases, well it all seemed a lot simpler than what my life faced now. I couldn't believe all the things that had continued to happen to me since that point. In fact, the only break I'd had from any of it was when I had been on the run from Lucius for all those months.

It had been my small slice of normality, despite most of the time I had continuously had to look over my shoulder expecting to find him, for deep down I knew that I could have only got away with hiding from him so long. Now I just felt foolish and all of those months had been nothing but a waste of time! A time I missed out on and I hated myself for being so foolish, as I couldn't get back that time. The time that I could have had with the person I loved the most in the world!

"In truth, I feel immense guilt and shame when thinking of how I allowed myself to believe my brother to be the cause of Callon's death. But until the new evidence that recently came to light, then I am just as guilty as the other and I tell you now, Amelia, I am not proud of this fact," he said jarring me from my own feelings of guilt and focusing on his own.

"So you want him to come back and reclaim his throne, to make amends?" I asked.

"It is not just as simple as that," he said as if still feeling that shame for what he was yet to say.

"How so?"

"After our brother's banishment, our father still had a problem on his hands for after his death there would still be two kingdoms left without kings to rule them." Oh dear, I could sense again what was coming. Which was why I said,

"Oh no, I've got a bad feeling about this." His look said it all.

"Our father had no choice but to appoint his own brother as ruler of the Dark Fae Kingdom, something it turns out that he had been hoping for, so he could one day use this to his advantage."

"Of course he did," I commented dryly as it was obvious that this uncle of theirs was the bad guy in this picture.

"That he did, for he has spent this time amassing a great army, as his ambitions have now been proven to be greater and stretch much further than being content with his own lands." And yep, there it was.

"He's trying to overthrow you... that's it, isn't it? That's the proof that's come to light! Your uncle's ambition has proven to you that he was the one responsible for your brother's death, not Carn'reau." The second I said this, I saw his face and knew it to be true even without his words.

"Among other things, but yes, in this you are unfortunately correct, and as for my other brother, well..."

"Oh shit, don't tell me, the devil of a brother is..."

"Just as ambitious to take over all our lands, including that of our fallen brother's."

"Gods, no offence but I thought my life was complicated." At this he laughed once without humour.

"But wait, if your brother was killed, then who rules his Kingdom in his place?"

"That is my sister, Rina. She was born of those lands and just a year apart from Callon. She was the obvious choice for my father, but unfortunately my powers are limited in protecting her lands as well as my own, especially from my uncle's oncoming army."

"And what of your other brother, this Regin, won't he help you now that he knows the truth?" I questioned and this time, instead of looking amused or even upset, it was the first real time that I saw him grit his teeth and look angry. In fact, it was so scary that I was just thankful it wasn't directed at me as his eyes started to glow like blue fire. He actually had to close his eyes and shake his head a little as if to calm that beast inside him.

"It seems my brother is now in league with my uncle, as he too has a mighty force and an army of dead, ready to unleash on mine and my sister's kingdoms. I fear that without Carn'reau's return, then all will be lost in this realm and will soon fall to the darkness and hatred that lies within the hearts of my uncle and my brother."

"Just as was prophesied," I said looking down at my lap and speaking my thoughts aloud.

"Yes, this wasn't lost on me also."

"But I thought you said you all loved your brother, Callon. I take it that you meant Regin too?"

"Ah, but that is where it gets more complicated still, for you see the King of sinful souls, always had somewhat of a dark heart yet what light it did hold was held solely for our brother, which meant that when he died, what light that had been inside him was quickly consumed by bitterness and hatred." I shook my head a little as I tried to follow all this, which is why I said,

"So, he doesn't know that it was his uncle who killed him!?"

"No, for if he did, then he would surely direct his armies towards another enemy, for he would kill our Uncle without hesitation." I let out a heavy breath before saying,

"I know this may sound like a really blindingly obvious question here, but why haven't you told him?"

"As endearing as that question is, you do not know about our family enough to comprehend the complication surrounding our relationships. Not between our kingdoms or each other for we were never close as brother's, and Callon was the only glue we had to hold an already fragile pane of glass together."

"But you were all to be Kings, surely you had that in common?" I questioned.

"Despite our lands once being united under my father's rule, that union has long since been fractured to the point where we might as well be islands drifting off into a traitorous sea apart from each other. For my brother's blind hatred and cold heart sees nothing but what happened that day as being the fault of Carn'reau, and our uncle has manipulated that fact from the very beginning with his eyes set firmly on the throne to rule them all. My brother is but a pawn in his game of power," he told me, making me officially hate this uncle of his… oh, and want to slap some sense into this brother of sin!

"So that's it, your uncle was jealous of his own brother's rule and wanted what he had?"

"It is indeed, for the same Oracle that told my father of his future to marry his four wives and bear four sons to rule separate kingdoms, was one who did not live long after that, for a mysterious death befell her, which is one that is no longer so mysterious at all."

"Gods, but your uncle has been planning this all this time," I surmised.

"He believed that my father would appoint him as the next ruler, but I think now that he knew something about his brother, for his heart was too full of dark desire. Haleth was never about the people but only about greed and his own selfish desire to gain more power. It was a sickness, a hunger that has grown to the point that he cares little for who or what he destroys in his ambition for power. He must be stopped at all costs, for this is my last chance to save the people of my world." As soon as the King had finished, I couldn't help but place a hand over his own just like I had done not long ago. Just like I had done with his naive sister, who no doubt had no idea that any of this was going on. Because he no doubt wanted to protect her from the dire future of his people should he not succeed in defeating his uncle.

The King looked down at my hand before looking down at me, as even sat down, the height difference between us was almost comical. But still I felt compelled to say what I did next, just like I had done to Vern.

So, I made him this vow,

"I promise you, Auberon, I promise you that I will do everything in my power to help you, and I am sure... no, I'm certain that your brother will return. Trust me, Lucius will stop at nothing to get me back and from what I have seen of your brother's loyalty, then he will do this for him, he will return for his King."

"I hope you are right, little Princess, and all I can hope for is that when my brother returns, he does not hold that same dark twisted bitter hatred for a world he once loved... for a world that banished him... *I hope he can forgive me.*"

The moment he said this, I couldn't help but think of Lucius and his own brother and in that moment I started to pray like never before! I prayed to every God that would listen, to the very Fates themselves that the McBain brothers get there in time. Because I knew that Lucius would never forgive himself if he executed his brother. He would never forgive himself if by his hand he gave him an unjust death for something he never did.

Oh, I had no doubt that he would forgive me, and he wouldn't have blamed me, for I didn't know that was his brother. But I had been the one to say the words to Nero.

I had been the one to tell her of the traitor and told her who he was, meaning whether it was known or unknown, it was still my fault as much as it was his. A guilt I would forever hold as no doubt Lucius would also.

The only thing I had left now was to hope and pray it didn't come to that, and that Lucius discovered the truth. Discovered the truth about what he believed was his own…

Brother's betrayal

CHAPTER EIGHTEEN

LUCIUS

LIVING NIGHTMARES

"Where the fuck is she!" I roared in anger which had long ago consumed my mortal body, for my demon permanently perambulated the floors of my castle like some caged beast clawing at the confines of my own prison made. For that was exactly what this place felt like, knowing that she was out there and,

Not. Fucking. Here!

"There has been no word, my Lord," Carn'reau said, making me want to snap something in half and feel bones crushing beneath my palm. I felt like a wild eagle with wings that were fucking useless for they had nowhere to fly to that I knew would help. Knowing that I had to remain here in case my brother managed to escape his bounds was a Hell within this Hell. Just another thing for me to be furious with him for, as if betrayal wasn't enough, I thought bitterly.

Something, that pacing my brother's office, wasn't helping, for being surrounded by the things he held dear was fucking with my head! Because all it did was remind me of better times together. Persia… what had it been about that fucking place that had drawn us in like moths to the fucking flame! I hated the idea that it had been her fucking father, but all evidence suggested just that. And now I knew why…

My fated Chosen One.

Speaking of which,

"I do not understand how it is taking so long!" I snapped, hammering a fist down on yet another desk, Dariush's carved one of a Persian army fighting the Romans was long ago in pieces and beyond repair. But this had not been the first time this question had been grated through teeth and come out sounding raw, for I was fully aware of the time ticking down. Because I knew what was coming. I knew what I had to do, and I didn't relish one fucking second of it!

My brother's execution.

I wanted Amelia back and if I was honest, it wasn't solely just so I knew she was safe. It was more for selfish reasons, for I needed her comfort right in this moment like never before. I couldn't remember the last time I had done something that was as difficult as this without Amelia being the cause or reason. Like the night that I intended to break her heart and make her run from me without ever looking back. Of course, this had backfired, giving my first experience of raw fucking panic not long after she had run from my nightclub believing I was an utter bastard.

But, despite the bloody outcome of that night, even then everything I had done had been done with purpose. Had been done for the greater good, if you will. I had been convinced that what would keep the girl safe was severing any ties before they could be made with me. I thought back on what seemed an easier decision to make back then. Of course, at the time, seeing her that way, all dressed up to impress me, looking like the innocent little virgin she had been... well, fuck me, but I had needed a fucking sainthood just for having the strength at turning down such temptation!

Fucking perfection, even then.

But now I had tasted her, claimed her little moans of pleasure and screams of desperation and rapture, then no fucking way I could be that strong again! She was mine, in every way possible and fuck me, but I wanted my girl back!

Yet, despite this, a niggling feeling at the pit of my stomach told me something was coming. Another fucking impossible decision I would have to make, just like the one I was being forced to make in regard to my brother's death.

Gods be damned, but it had been one thing after another that had faced us since I first got to claim her. Since she first stepped back into my world and unknowingly sealed her fate the moment she smiled at me. The moment I saw her in that dress and heard her laugh. The moment I saw the weird toy shit in her apartment.

Everything she did made her mine, and little did I know that with every minute spent with her, she was entwining a web around us both. One that grew tighter and tighter until I took control. And all because I told Dom, my once King, that I would stand in his place and go to see his daughter. The plan had been simple, indulge in the sight of her for an evening, tease her cruelly, all before getting what I wanted and walking away. Walking away and taking the memory of her with me to last the next ten fucking years!

But then could I really be surprised, as often all it took was one taste for an addiction to start. And one taste was all it took for this king to fall under her spell, one she had no fucking clue she had been weaving.

Her web of love and addiction.

And all from a single night when stepping up to her back and announcing to her my presence. Back in that museum where everyone else around us could have been slaughtered and in pieces on the floor for all I cared, for I would not have noticed... *not when she was in the room.*

These thoughts were a fucking eye opener for me, considering where we were now, in the very last place I ever expected to be waiting for my Chosen One! Waiting for my fated Electus to be brought to me, brought to my very own Kingdom of Death of all places! It was a nightmare, nothing short of a Gods be damned nightmare! And one I was being forced to fucking live through just as she was. I vaguely remember an easier time where most of my worries centred around her future and how I could entwine it so tightly with my own, doing so that she would never have chance to escape it. How I did everything in my power to ensure Amelia's happiness when living in my mountain castle, without her precious job or little fucking apartment in Twickenham.

As for now, then all my fucking worries just included trying to keep the girl alive, and doing so long enough so I could get her back to some shred of normality! And well, not being down in Hell would certainly help with that... *fuck!* But I was still so angry at her for what she did. For this all began when she didn't listen to me and stepped through the Tree of Souls!

Anger was most definitely a fire that burned brighter the longer I was here and in my demon form. But without my Amelia to help calm me, to keep me grounded and not lose the last shreds of my humanity all together, it was getting harder by the second. Because this was what it was like to be a ruler in Hell and exactly why I had no fucking desire for any of it!

In fact, I didn't know how Dariush had done it for so long without losing himself completely. It had been one of the reasons he had been so good at it and if it had been possible, then I would have abdicated long ago and thrown the fucking title at him whilst running out the door! But fucking Lucifer, old daddy dearest, wouldn't have allowed that, no, not for his favourite son or greatest accomplishment to slip completely through his fingers.

Asshole.

But only what must have been an hour later and Carn'reau, just like the last time, was walking in my office. And just like last time the same fucking words snapped out of my mouth like a live wire lashing out electricity.

"I don't know what is taking them so long!" I ground out through my teeth as my second in command could see how close to the edge I was. A laughable statement considering my demon had fully taken over both my appearance and very near the last of my senses. But even in this demonic body, one that hummed with unleashed power, I was still aware enough to think of the guilt I would feel when bringing down that fucking blade on my brother's head. Even despite knowing of his guilt. knowing of his betrayal.

This was Hell alright.

My personal one!

"What is it ?!" I pratically barked at him the moment I realised his response to this hadn't been his usual, 'there has been no word, my Lord' but instead silence… until then finally,

"I have received word from my men." I sucked in a breath and closed my eyes, waiting for whatever news was to befall on me now.

"And did they find them? Did they reach the portal?" I asked knowing that there was only one portal that would have been safe to use to get back to my realm. It was also the reason why I had my men stationed there at the ready for them. However, in that time one of Carn'reau's men must have reached back to him with word.

"Speak!" I ordered through clenched teeth with my fangs pressing painfully into my lip.

"I am sorry, my Lord, but there is no sign of them and nor has there been any evidence of them ever making it through the portal," he said giving me the reason behind his reluctance.

"Then something must have gone wrong," I said after growling and snarling the word,

"FUCK!" This was before swiping everything that was on the desk to the floor, hating that this was being done in what was or had essentially been, my brother's office, a place where he had stationed himself to rule in my stead. It only ended up being a sickening reminder as to what he had done, for I still couldn't understand it! I couldn't understand why, what more fucking power did he need! What more could he possibly want! I was never fucking here!

And speaking of who else wasn't here,

"What is being done?!" I asked gritting out the words as I leant over the desk with my taloned hands curling long gouged slices out of the stone desk. Because I felt as if I was falling. As if I was spiralling out of control and falling into a deep pit of despair. That I was drowning in it trying to drag my way out. Yet, in reality, all I was doing was looking down at the top of the desk, trying to find my Chosen One in Hell.

Yeah, that was all, I thought bitterly.

"Avarolo made the decision to keep half of our men at the portal in case they make it through."

"And what of the other half?" I asked knowing I would go bat shit crazy if he told me they were on their way back here. Thankfully, this wasn't the case, for I shouldn't have underestimated the commander of my armies. I knew this when he informed me,

"They're on their way to the town after first acquiring a portal master to make it through. I'm yet to hear back from them but feel as if we will have a better picture of what happened once the town has been interrogated."

"Make sure it is it is thorough," I added like the cold hearted bastard I was.

"I instructed as much," Carn'reau said only now seemingly disappointed that he couldn't give me more. But I cared little for that in that moment or his sentiments. No, all I could focus on was questioning what the next fucked up shit was that had happened to her this time? All I could hope for was that whatever had befallen upon them she, at the very least, had three of the strongest shifters in Hell protecting her. This was my only consolation, for I owned their souls and right now I was willing to do anything to get my Chosen One back. Meaning that one thing the McBain brothers better hope for was that when they did finally get back here, they had my Queen with them, for if not, I didn't know how long those souls would last against my fury.

"I hate to ask, my Lord, but…"

"Don't!" I warned, knowing of which he spoke, which was why I rose to my full height and started walking from the room.

"My Lord?" He questioned where I was going and I looked behind my shoulder and told him,

"I am going to speak with my brother… and this time, I will tear a confession out of him!"

Even if it meant…

Cursing my Soul.

CHAPTER NINETEEN

BROTHER'S BETRAYAL

"You look like shit, brother." This was the first thing Dariush said to me when I walked into his cell after he had lifted his weary head. I released a deep breath, one that was both in relief at seeing that he was still where I had left him and one that felt like I was breathing in razor blades at seeing him that way. He was still chained by eight different points that connected his body to the walls. This was of course so he was unable to create a portal and escape, although admittedly, I almost wish that he would, just to save me the pain of what I knew was coming.

This was when I raked a frustrated hand through my hair and admitted,

"I feel like shit." This of course made him laugh before commenting,

"Well, I would offer you a drink but as you can see, my hands are tied."

"And you are out of whisky," I replied, making him laugh before looking around the room and saying,

"Yes, well, I suppose we are the only ones to blame for the shit amenities this place has to offer… I am dying for a piss!" I laughed at that and shook my head as if trying to rid myself the guilt I had no reason yet to feel but fucking did… because well, this was Hell, and I wasn't ruling in it at the moment, I was just fucking living it!

Of course, it did ease my suffering somewhat when seeing that despite all the torture he had received by my hand, he still looked as if there was not a single wound on him. Lucky bastard, as only the evidence of a single hit was of the blood that I had spilled in dishing them out.

"I take it no word of your Electus returning?" he asked me then with all seriousness and I frowned before enquiring with suspicion,

"You sound as though you are waiting for it so she may save the fucking day." At this he tried to shrug his shoulders but forgot that he was tethered to the walls and had very little in the way of movement.

"Just a feeling that she will be the key to ending this madness of yours, that's all," he said, making me force down my anger and try to keep my cool. Something that seemed fucking laughable these days, for my soul couldn't have gotten any darker.

"I spent the night looking for any shred of evidence that suggests you're innocent," I told him, for I had, which meant I only had one thing left to go on, hence why I was there now.

"Oh, and how nice for you to come all this way down here yourself to tell me that you found some and how now you have come to your fucking senses and are going to let me go!" my brother quipped angrily.

"Not exactly," I replied keeping my calm… *for now.*

"No, I didn't think so," he agreed as if he had been expecting this and I didn't know what made me more frustrated, that he had given up all the possibility of his innocence being discovered or that he knew there was no evidence to be found at all. That I had been on a fool's errand all this time.

"So, you are down here to tell me that my time is up, is that it?" he asked, for he had little in the way of gauging time down here.

"I want to know why?" I asked, feeling the increasing weight against my chest like a fucking blacksmith's anvil had been placed there.

"This again," he muttered.

"I want to know why you betrayed me!" I snapped, being driven by his blasé response.

"That's hard to say considering I didn't," he stated, lifting his head up now to scowl at me, with those olive-green eyes of his glowing a deeper shade of amber as if the fire in his heart was burning brighter. He was also minus clothing on his torso, long ago been torn off to inflict more pain on his vessel's skin. Not that it had made much difference, as he was one hard bastard to crack!

No, in fact, most of the time I just believed he had enjoyed the pain for he would often laugh and ask me if that was all I had. Infuriating fucker! He had me even questioning at times if I had in fact lost my edge, becoming soft thanks to time spent with my Chosen One, where the only pain I sought to inflict was the kind married with pleasure.

I snarled at the memory and roared at him,

"You had everything! You ran my entire Kingdom for fuck sake! What more could you want, Dariush, was it power? Was it to make sure that I didn't decide to suddenly come down here and pick up where I left off? Or was it to make Daddy proud?" I sneered making him growl back,

"Fuck that and fuck you! I wasn't lying when I told you where my loyalties lay, brother!" He yanked hard on his chains making them rattle enough that some of the stone cracked. This forced me to heal the stone so he wouldn't break free, for in that moment he looked more like a wild beast than a man of Persian decent, with his black hair loose and wild around his snarling features because the same demonic ink of power stained our veins, something that now showed under the skin around his eyes.

Oh, yes, he was killing mad… *and he wasn't the only one.*

"Ah, yes, that loyalty to the blood you share, not the blood that created you," I said remembering these words being spoken not long ago and not only believing them, but at the time finding comfort in them too.

"You hiss out that vow like my loyalty is an insult to you, yet it is me you insult! As if you have found proof of it never existing." I laughed at that and held out my hand in a gesture to point out the obvious as to where he was now.

"You are going to regret this," he snarled back at me through gritted teeth.

"I already do," I threw back at him, making him visibly jerk.

"So that is it then, you're truly in the depths of your dark soul believing the I was the one betraying you all this time?" At this I couldn't stand it and looked away, tearing my eyes from my guilt and pain.

"I see even now the doubt you have, brother, for if that is the case then why be so rash into making the decision…"

"You think this decision is being made lightly, as if it is something that I am rushing into at just a mere whim!" I shouted back in disbelief!

"So, you do this to prove strength to our people, is that it?"

"You know the longer I keep you here without action is every minute our fucking kingdom will consider it as weakness! I do not need another fucking war to battle, not when I will soon need them to fight by my side, not adding to those against me!"

"So quickly it has turned from us into you," he said as if this saddened him to think that I was actually facing this alone. I took a deep breath, hating how my love for him was manipulating me into taking action. No, I needed to focus on what reasons brought him here in the first place, which was why I reminded him of his own actions and my last chance at a potential proof we all needed.

"I saw you there, I looked into her memories and I saw a portal being created at the mouth of Tartarus, to where the harpies lair was found. The eye was there and so were you!"

"That's impossible!" he shouted back at me as if he truly believed it.

"I thought so too until I saw it for myself!."

"Then what you saw was false, because I was never there!" I growled low and pushed,

"You're calling me a liar!?" He took a deep breath as if he needed the calm before first applying logic.

"So, you saw my face, that is what you're telling me, you actually saw my face there!?" I thought on this a moment looking back through Nero's memories, and that was the one part that had me doubting this whole thing.

I had never seen his face.

"My Chosen One spoke of you, she told the witch, Nero, that my brother was the traitor!"

"Then we both have another brother we did not know about, for I can assure you it wasn't me!"

"Now, that would be convenient," I commented sarcastically, which is when he made a viable point of his own,

"Yes, it would, for ask yourself, brother, how would she have known that I was your brother, for correct me if I am wrong, but I think I would have remembered you introducing me as such!" This question was thrown back at me and I had to say, it was one that had plagued me all night.

Because I too had wondered how my Chosen One had found out that Dariush was my brother. But then without all of the gaps to fill in during her time spent at the harpies' lair, then I honestly didn't know what happened. I didn't know enough, for he could have declared himself as my brother to her during this time for this very reason. To create doubt should he ever be caught.

I was at a crossroads and on one side it was trusting the word of my Chosen One, the person that I would have trusted with my very life and much more. But then there was the other side. The side where my brother stood. A brother who, up until that moment, I had trusted with my very life many times over.

It was a cruel twist of fate, for which road I must travel down now, I knew would shape the foundations of my future for the rest of my lives. However many they may be left to live, given my current situation.

"But the timing, brother, do you honestly not see it for yourself, do you refuse to see how it looks! For the moment the Eye showed me what my Chosen One was seeing, was the very moment that the man responsible was creating a portal. The very same portal you made when arriving back. Explain to me how that is possible! How is that fucking possible, Dariush, if it was not you that was there creating it!? The only one powerful enough to do so!" At this my brother hung his head and started shaking it, as if he too couldn't give me an answer.

As if… *as if he just didn't know.*

"The very Eye, that I will remind you, held an interest to you beyond that it should have, and well before these events occurred," I reminded him.

"I merely wanted to know…" he started to say.

"What, exactly?! Where it would be and where my Chosen

One could potentially find it? I remember finding it odd when you asked me the question if my Chosen One knew where the Eye was, or if she would know how to find it. Fuck, but I should have known then!" I said in frustration with a shake of my head, getting angry at myself for being so foolish.

"I did not ask for that reason," he admitted in a deflated tone.

"No? Because I know the hex cast by the witch was not one used for her to be summoned to the witch, but for it to actually hold the reverse effect. I'm very intrigued to know how anyone would have known that Amelia would have been drawn to the Eye enough to find it," I told him, reminding him of this very conversation.

"But I …"

"Exactly, *you brother*… you were the only one that knew I had used the Eye for myself. I had also questioned that at the time if you remember and foolishly believed you when you said it was through the power of deduction that you knew." I'd known in that moment there was something he wasn't telling me.

"So that's it, guilty by association of knowledge!" he snapped.

"Again, I fear I have to remind you once more but was it not on your advice that I didn't have the Eye moved…? Think back, brother, trust in my words, for I have spent this night doing this same thing!" I informed him and again he hung his head as if defeated.

"I have questioned myself over and over why these events occurred, when there is only one answer to be found. You planned this. You planned this from the very beginning, and you used my Chosen One to get to the Eye!"

"NO!" he denied it on a roar, one I ignored and continued,

"I don't know how you knew but somehow, you knew that

she would be drawn to it. You knew that she would find it and when she did, that harpy bitch, along with the witch you have been working with, used the hex to get to her. It was the only way to ever get inside my domain and you knew it!" At this he didn't even bother denying it anymore.

"What's the matter, brother, have all your excuses run out?" I asked in that taunting way to try and drag it from him. I just wanted the truth. I wanted him to grant me this one thing, this last shred of proof that he actually gave a shit about the blood we shared. A lasting gift so it may finally alleviate some of my guilt when I had no choice but to take his life.

Something he was yet to give me.

But first I would need that last damning piece of evidence against him. The last and final answer to the most important question of all. The last chance at his innocence.

"Now, answer me this, when you arrived back at the castle, doing so at the very moment the one responsible disappeared, the very sight the Eye had chosen to show me... tell me, brother, if you weren't the one responsible, then where were you returning from?"

"What?" He seemed shocked by the question.

"Where, if not returning from the harpies' lair, did you return from?" I asked again, holding my body tense as if fucking praying for some proof left.

"I...I..." he stuttered out, frowning as if searching himself for it.

"Where were you, brother... for surely if there was anything left of your innocence, then that is your chance to provide me with your alibi... now tell me, *where were you?!*

"I...I can't answer that," he said in a pained voice.

"Why not!?" I roared in fury, which was when he raised his head and shouted back at me,

"Because I don't know!" I took a step back as if trying to

question where this response had come from. What did he mean he didn't know?

"Don't know or you just don't want to answer?!" I snapped.

"I don't know where I went, Lucius," he said again, and I felt my anger burning at my lungs in order to keep me breathing.

"That's a little convenient, Dariush, considering our current dilemma!" I bit back.

"Well, it's all I have to tell you, and believe me or not, it is the truth, for I will not stand here and lie to you! I will not make my death easier on you when killing me will only prove that I am innocent." I narrowed my eyes at him.

"And how exactly is your death supposed to prove your innocence?!"

"Because if there is a threat out there, and I am dead, and that threat continues, then you will know you took the life of the wrong man." He grinned this at me, emphasising each word like it was venom being lashed against my soul. I tore my face away, unable to continue looking at him. But then the next thing he asked,

"Now tell me, the girl, your Chosen One, she is not back yet, is she?"

"Excuse me?" I asked now feeling sickened by the tone he used when he asked me this.

"Funny, how the threat of my betrayal should be locked in here and yet she's still being kept from you… I do wonder, brother, who you will have to kill next, for perhaps then you will have finally taken the life of the real person behind all of this." At this I growled,

"If you think by throwing in my face and reminding me of the danger that my Chosen One is in right now will alleviate my anger towards you and direct it elsewhere, then you are sorely mistaken, for your death is surely coming. For a new day approaches by the minute and pretty soon, Dariush... *you will have run out of time."* I grinned at him before turning away and marching from the cell before I did something in that moment that I actually may regret.

Which was to give my brother a death he did not deserve, for having him tied up and in a cell to die by my hand was not our way in dealing with traitors.

No traitors...

...were made an example of.

CHAPTER TWENTY

EXECUTION

'My loyalty has and always will be first to the blood I share, not the blood that made me.'

Gods, but how these very words had plagued me! Over and over and over again I heard them being said in my mind like a sickness. As though I was lost in a world of madness and one that in this moment in time, I had never wanted to believe something to be true so much in all my years of taking an immortal breath!

I had been near desperate for him to give me the one thing that could have saved him from execution. If only he had been able to tell me where he had come from when creating that portal, then I might have been able to discover an alibi for him.

But he gave me nothing.

Fuck, but I was so enraged! I was so angry that he had nothing to give me but lies. Yet what was troubling me more was that he said he couldn't remember. Had this been just another excuse, for surely if my brother was so willing to lie to me then wouldn't this have been a better opportunity to lie further? To once again send me further down a rabbit hole of foolish hope to get lost in. Another fool's errand to grant him more time? Or was this my brother's version of just giving up? Did he foresee the inevitable death coming closer and decide there was no point prolonging the wait?

In truth I had no idea what was going through my brother's mind, for it was one I could not access... not unless he deemed it so, and there had been little point for he could have easily manipulated what I saw. But this endeavour had not been through lack of trying, for I had been trying to attempt it since the very first time I stepped into his cell after he had been forced into his chains. Before I have given in to the impulse of beating him to a bloody pulp. One he merely healed from over and over again.

"Any news of them yet?!" I asked with a growl of words as my commander Carn'reau walked into what was now unfortunately my office.

"I am sorry to inform you of this, my L..." I sliced an impatient hand down and snapped,

"Cut the 'lord' shit and get to it!"

"The remains of the portal master were found." At this I closed my eyes and let my head drop, asking in a dangerous tone,

"Any sign of them?"

"No, there is no signs of them, but a struggle definitely occurred. And there is something else."

"But of course there fucking is!" I said cracking my knuckles with a squeeze of my thumb in my fist.

"The portal master, he too had a hex cast upon him."

"Fuck!" I snarled slamming a hand down on the desk and feeling it crack.

"What is being done?!" I demanded.

"Witnesses remember seeing your Chosen One." At this my attention was fully on my commander as my head snapped up.

"Explain it all to me and leave nothing out." After this Carn'reau explained that my girl had been seen in some shithole tavern the night before. This was confirmed by everyone that was interrogated, as her movements were easily tracked from the very first instance she got off the boat. But of course, they were, as my troublesome little human was bound to get the attention of every fucking demon with the ability to see!

But these accounts were anything from her knocking on doors that surrounded the dock, asking for aid to much worse. Naturally, in the height of my anger, I wanted to go and kill every single one of them that refused her. But pretty soon, my anger was directed at yet another, this was the moment I heard the account of her trying to get into the town itself and being chased by a gatekeeper who tried to kill her.

She managed to get herself into a tavern, where it was clear she got into even more trouble. Thankfully, this was when one of the McBain brothers had intervened and I was frustrated to find that it was Trice. I was caught between a dagger's edge and a sword's blade for as much as I wanted her to be safe, the idea that she was being so in the arms of that Scottish bastard had my body close to becoming inflamed with fury! Especially seeing as I knew how much the fucker wanted her for himself!

However, the only good point to this account was the fact that Trice had saved her from her current troubles, and from the sounds of the screams that were heard, I can only deduce that the hex was thankfully removed. This, for obviously reasons, was the hardest part, as to know of her agony and being forced to listen to accounts of the sound of my Chosen One being in excruciating pain was never going to be easy to listen to.

It was at this point that I hissed,

"I should have fucking been there!" Wisely, my commander did not comment for in that moment it was clear I was killing mad and ready to rip anyone's jugular out. Doing so with little encouragement needed for if they had merely said something I didn't like the sound of, it would have happened. But then I knew that my guilt was also fuelling the rage that drove my actions to want to kill. Because just the thought of my girl lying in agony and being forced through the physical and mental torture of having a hex removed was like having my heart carved from my chest with a rusty blade!

For I wasn't fucking there.

I wasn't there for her.

I was not the one to be able to hold her through the pain and suffering she was forced to endure. And even without that guilty weight laying heavily against my shoulders, I had already been getting to the point that I was near desperate to have her in my arms, just so I knew that she was safe. *Safe with me and only me.*

I vowed, in that moment, that if I heard a single thing that Trice had done by taking advantage of her in any way, then there would be nothing in this world or the next, that would have the power to stop me from killing him! Not even the pleading sounds of my girl begging for his life to be spared would that stop me.

Someone was going to die today and if I knew that one finger had been laid on my girl, then it would be one more to add to the fucking list! For it was starting to look like today would be a day dedicated to death by hands.

And when in this Hellish realm, I was after all, the…

King of Death.

Speaking of which, Carn'reau informed me,

"It is time, my Lord."

At this I cracked my neck, which was so tense I was

surprised that when I stood, I didn't shatter my own bones. for the time had come that I had been dreading. That the hand of death was to be delivered and what was worse, it was a hand that belonged to me. For my brother's time had run out and what was worse, I was forced to do this with the extra worry lying on my shoulders as to where my Chosen One could be. The last she had been seen was leaving the tavern with the portal master and all three of the McBain brothers. At the very least I knew all three of them were with her now, and knowing my Amelia, my beautiful girl, I knew that she would stop at nothing until she got back to me. I knew this deep down in my core.

I had just wished for it to have been now, for I needed her counsel more than ever. But wishes were rarely granted in Hell, just as my brother was about to find out for his time in this world was now at an end.

So, I walked out of the office with purpose and for once, it was a death I would not relish in granting, for there in front of me now was my brother. I'd had no choice but to have him brought to the throne room as he was now, for he was too much of a liability to have just simply walked him in here. Not when he may have been capable of trying anything, like creating a way to escape. Which was why I had him brought out here in what would have been a torturous device for anyone, even one as powerful as my brother.

It was a Hellish version of the Iron Maiden, only without the person sized box that a body would have been put inside. this was because most demons came in different sizes than a human host, so it would have been pointless creating one in that image. Instead, I had discovered an old favourite of my brother's, one he himself used to use on prisoners. It seemed almost fucking poetic that it was now being used on him.

The āšipūtu cloak was known as exorcistic lore and said to

be created by Enki-Ea himself, the God of wisdom and exorcism in Sumerian culture. Mesopotamian magic was subdivided into four types, liminal magic, aggressive magic, your basic witchcraft, and the type used when creating āšipūtu cloak, being defensive magic. This was categorised as being when an evil force needs repelling, and that most definitely was the case here.

The āšipūtu was a long cloak that looked like a chainmail of triangular scales. each connecting plate was carved with a different incantation to prevent a demon's powers from being used.

Then, once placed around the prisoner, it would mould itself to every inch of its victim and start to burn these incantations into the skin. As if a demon was being bathed in holy water blessed by the Gods in Heaven.

I would have winced at the smell of burning flesh as my brother was brought forward, needing to be carried by my guards. Because wrapped up this way it was impossible to walk or have any use of your limbs for that matter.

Then, once positioned in front of the stairs that lead up to my throne, I made my way over to my brother, who had been laid on the floor like some wrapped up piece of meat. It was a sight that pained me to see, as his eyes were closed as if awaiting a swift death or trying not to think about the pain the āšipūtu cloak inflicted.

But a swift death would be one he knew I would be granting him, for I did not have it in me to make him suffer as I would have done to anyone else.

It was the least I could give him.

I walked with purpose towards my throne with Carn'reau a little way behind me. I positioned myself in front of my throne doing so now, so I could address my Kingdom. Of course, it was of little wonder that the entirety of the throne room was now full to the brim of my people all desperate to see the fall of the being who had ruled in my place for centuries.

I found myself growling at the sight, furious that these people were here to see the show and spectacle to be made of the fall of a ruler. Of course, had it been any other traitor, then I would have relished the sight, but considering who I was about to kill, well, it fucking sickened me. Yet, I tried to remember that no one knew that I was about to kill my brother other than Carn'reau. Meaning no one knew of the pain this would cause me.

I, therefore, had a brief moment to wonder what our own father would think when he found out what I had been forced to do. I shook away the doubts this thought caused me and instead focused my anger on the room. I knew I should have been using this moment as an opportunity to prove just what happens when my people betrayed their King. I knew I should have been following with my past sentiments in making an example out of a traitor.

But looking at him now, feeling the bile that wanted to rise up my throat and burn me from the inside out, well then, I knew I just couldn't do it. I couldn't make a spectacle out of his death. Which was why I looked up and let my demon loose, by roaring at every single one of them,

"GET OUT!"

I let the power roll out of me in a wave that pushed everyone back and soon had them running to save them from their Master's wrath. Then the moment the room was emptied other than those of my guard, I released a deep and heavy sigh, breathing as though my chest would barely allow it. After this, I walked down the steps towards Carn'reau and once there, I ripped off the cloak that had the ability to steal power. Doing so now, knowing that I only had the time it took for him to heal to end his life. Because I couldn't allow him to regain enough strength to create a portal to leave this place.

For time was not on my side, meaning I had no choice but to make this swift. Therefore, I pulled him up to his knees, ignoring the burnt incantations I could now see that marred his flesh, like scorched brands from a hot iron. I could even see them already starting to heal themselves, knowing I had to be quick. So, I allowed my armour to slither down my arm focusing all its energy into creating a weapon of death.

"Do you have anything to say, brother?" I wanted to give him his last words and the moment he spoke them, I nearly crumbled to my knees, for he looked up at me in that moment and said,

"I forgive you for what you are about to do, my brother in blood." Then he lowered his head ready for his execution.

Ready for my hand of death.

"Very well, may your soul find peace, my brother in blood," I whispered down to him before taking my stance to the side ready to sever his head, then I raised up my arm and without another word,

I swallowed painfully and let a single tear fall, at the same time,

So did my blade.

CHAPTER TWENTY-ONE

TIMING IS ALL RELATIVE

I n a split second the sight of my blade falling seemed to slow down to the point that it was as if time was being controlled around only me and my brother. Yet the bellowing of a command was heard in real time and I felt my eyes close as if pained by the sadness that consumed me because I knew within that one word roared out at me in desperation,

That I had been too late.

"STOP!" This mighty roar happened at the same time as other events. Events that I would one day look back on and it would seem as if I had unknowingly made a prayer to the Gods…

And. It. Had. Been. Answered.

That was because the doors at the end of my throne room were flung open at the same time a pathway of ice had travelled across the floor like a jagged bolt of lightning. One that had erupted from a source of great power, for it shot out so far and fast that it reached me in the time it took for me to open my eyes. And as soon as it was within reach, it shot from the floor and made it to my blade, shattering it. An explosion of ice became a sight that happened faster than the time being manipulated around me. I opened my mouth, roaring in my anger that was only heard when time was restored and when I looked up, I saw the cause.

Nero was there, now stood in the scattered destruction of my doors, the cause of which was standing there as well, with a mighty war hammer at his side… Gryph. But my eyes focused not on these two but the one who now stood in between them…

"Trice," I growled when seeing him with his icy blade in his hand just after he had used it to save my brother. I then looked down at the remains of my weapon, one that I was astounded to see had been destroyed, before looking back up at the shifter with deadly intent.

"You will pay for that, shifter!" I told him in a demonic tone that promised pain, now ignoring my own pain from having him sever a piece of my demon essence. One that had already started to flow towards me in order to reconnect with its host after it had been scattered along the floor.

"Aye, I reckon I wull, bit nae by you, fur 'twas yer woman who asked it o' me, whin she begged me tae save his life!" On hearing this I lowered my arm, letting it drop to my side and with it, ceasing the process of another weapon from forming.

"What did you say?" I whispered back at him before looking down at my brother and seeing him release a deep and heavy sigh. *Had he seen this somehow?*

It did not matter, for the shifter at my door had just saved my brother's life and at the request of my Chosen One! I knew then that the moment had been foreseen when Dariush managed to lift his head that wasn't on the floor as was intended. He looked towards where the shifter was now storming across the threshold, and muttered,

"Thank the Gods, she was found in time." My brother said this as if he knew. He knew this was his fate and that it was one tied to my Electus. It was as if he knew all he needed was my Chosen One to be found to prove his innocence. This was when things started to slot into place. How my brother was connected to my own Chosen One. The reason behind all the questions. The reason he was so interested in the Eye and wanted to know if I had been shown anything else, or why he secretly wanted Amelia to find it. None of it was because of betrayal. It was because…

He was searching for his fated one.

Gods, but just like her mother, Amelia was connected to those fated to find each other. It all made sense now. Amelia was the key to unlocking so much more than the discovery on how to save my people. But then, if this had been the case, why had my brother kept it from me? A question for another time, for in that moment I had more important matters that all centred around my own Chosen One.

Because as Trice and his brother now travelled the length of the throne room with their witch in tow it quickly occurred to me that a certain, very important someone was not following them and that panic, that blind fear penetrated my chest and I found myself taking a step back because of it before asking him in a dangerous tone ,

"Where is she?!"

"That is whit a'm 'ere tae tell ye, yer brother is innocent!" I looked down at him just at the time that he was getting up to his feet and snapped,

"Of course I fucking am, now answer him, where is she!"

"She's wi' th' King o' th' Dragon Lands, a city they call…"

"Calidad? That's impossible… how the fuck is she there!" Carn'reau snapped and it was the first time I had heard him really lose his patience, as it was clear he knew of this place.

"You know of this city?" I asked my commander. He nodded and told me,

"My brother's land." At this I snarled before turning back to Trice and snapped,

"And would you like to explain to me, shifter, just how my Queen ended up in the realm of fucking Fae?!" This was half asked by my demon side and came out as a warped version of my voice, one that sounded as if it had first been put through a fucking cheese grater!

Trice took one look around and I knew without being told that he didn't trust anyone to overhear what he wanted to tell me next. So, I calmed my demon enough to make the right decision and ordered,

"Nero, go cast a barrier at my doors. As for all of you, in my office, *now!*" I then let them all proceed me before offering a hand to my brother, one he knocked away and said,

"You can cut that shit right now, we have more important things to focus on than what passed between us." I dipped my head to tell him that I understood and watched as I felt the pieces of my liquefied armour return back to me, making me shudder as it remoulded itself to my form. Then I felt my brother clasp a hand to my shoulder and tell me,

"Now, let's concentrate on getting back your girl before you fuck this up again!" Then he walked past me, and I couldn't help but grin at his sentiment.

"Oh, I will get her back alright, *even if I have to burn a realm to the ground,*" I said to myself before turning on a heel and marching to my office to find out exactly what fucked up shit my little Princess had got herself into this time.

Gods have mercy on my ragged soul.

"Fucking Fae fairy bastards!" I snarled before striding through the doors and because we needed the privacy, I

refrained from ripping them from their heavy hinges in my anger.

"Explain!" I ordered as Trice gritted his teeth and for once, I knew I wasn't the cause but instead, Amelia was.

"We git tae th' portal."

"Aye, bit we wur double crossed," Gryph added as he too now was next to his brother, and both of them were looking grim… not exactly a good sign.

"We found the portal master with a hex and believed it to be the work of…" Carn'reau said, informing of them of what we already knew.

"The witch, aye, 'twas. she tried tae snatch Amelia bit I saved her 'n' pulled her thro' th' portal, bit I hate tae tell ye this bit th' witch git th' Eye instead."

"I don't give a fuck about the Eye, all I care about is that Amelia is safe!" I snapped making everyone in the room look to me with their eyes widened by my admission. Because the witch now had one of the most powerful weapons in her grasp. But I was just thankful that what the Eye had shown me, I now knew that no one but myself and Amelia had the power to touch it and to use its power. This was no doubt the reason the witch wanted Amelia in the first place, for it was not just her blood that she needed to command the Tree of Souls… *I knew that now.*

"Then a'm happy tae report that whin we left she wis indeed safe," Gryph said making me snarl my anger his way.

"And would you now like to explain to me why you fucking left her there in the first place!?"

"Because we dinnae had a choice 'n' th' only one o' us that wis allowed tae be left wi' her wis Vern." This came from Trice this time.

"Aye, th' posh Eejit." I knew by that quip I could only

assume that it meant that something had happened to Vern where his gentleman like manner had once again resurfaced.

"What did my brother want?" Carn'reau snapped this time, obviously knowing this was the case.

"Aye, real charmer that one!" Trice commented and I didn't miss his brother's reaction when Gryph shook his head a little at him, telling him not to go there. But it was too fucking late for that, as I was missing nothing when it came to my girl! This was the reason I gritted out,

"And what the fuck does that mean?!" My knuckles cracked again from my fists, as now I was thinking all manner of things and each and every one of them including a fucking Fae King trying to bed my woman!

"We made it thro' th' portal, 'n' all three o' us shifted th' moment th' Raiders turned up." At this I closed my eyes and held the bridge of my nose with a taloned finger ready to rip the fucker off if only to alleviated the pressure in the panic I felt mounting. A panic from trying to picture my girl surrounded by fucking Raiders!

"I take it you dispatched these men," I said as calmly as I could manage in that moment, but at this Trice and Gryph exchanged a look before the biggest of the two said,

"We made it thro' th' portal, 'n' all three o' us shifted th' moment th' Raiders turned up."

"Just get to the fucking point!" my brother snapped beating me to it this time.

"Yer brother's army turned up 'n' killed th' Raiders, surroondit us 'n' told us that we hud a common enemy 'n' assured us that by going wi' them thay wid help us," Trice said nodding to the only Fae being in the room.

"Ah, my cunning little brother," Carn'reau commented with a curl of his lip,

"Explain!" I ordered this time directed at my commander.

"Let me speed this up for you, brother, this Fae king gained your trust and took the girl as leverage," Dariush said folding his arms, that were now completely healed and were back to being his usual dark golden skin tone.

"Aye, that be pretty much th' wey o' things," Gryph agreed, making me rake a hand through my hair before slashing that same hand down and gritting out through teeth that felt close to cracking,

"So, let me get this straight, you are telling me that the King of a Fae realm now has my Chosen One, kidnapped and held to FUCKING RANSOM?!" I bellowed this last part allowing my demon his say on the matter. I was also very much on the edge of destroying yet another room, one that had barely been fixed since the last it was left in near pieces.

"I will kill him!" I vowed, after a moment of silence had passed between the brothers, telling me exactly that this was the way of things. Then I turned to my commander and told him,

"I am going to kill your brother!" Carn'reau nodded and with a fold of his arms said,

"Well, if you don't then I will. Now what does my brother want other than an obvious death wish?" Carn'reau asked the shifters and I had to say, their response surprised us all, my commander most of all.

"He wants ye."

"Me?"

"Why, what does this Fae King hope to achieve with the return of his brother?" I asked in place of my commander, who was obviously still trying to process this information.

"That he wid nae say, only that ye wur a King 'n' rightful heir tae th' Dark Fae Lands, 'n' wi' him wanting ye back, well mah guess wid be tae rule once more," Trice said.

"Fine, then we will leave at once." And just like that my commander was willing to forfeit the life he had made here in order to get my Chosen One back. He was willing to go back and face whatever fate awaited him and considering I knew he had been banished, then I didn't expect that it was for a happy fucking reunion! But that was how deep his loyalty to me ran, for it didn't even take him a moment to think about it.

"If that be case, they said they'd be waiting at th' portal tae escort ye back tae th' Castle," Gryph informed us.

"And Amelia?" I asked and they knew what I was asking. I wanted to know how my girl was holding up.

"She wis as feisty as ever," Gryph told me and I finally let out a breath of relief, one that was added to when Trice also helped put me out of my misery when he said,

"She is well 'n' unharmed, althoo she wis complaining aboot bein' hungry 'n' tired." On hearing this and knowing that she was safe, I relaxed because at least I knew that the King wouldn't do anything to what was his only leverage in getting what he wanted. Of course, now all I had to hope for was that she didn't do something stupid and reckless like trying to escape. Because in truth there was only so many times Amelia could get lucky with the rash decisions she made. Some of which I had to concede had paid off in the past. However, she was in a world she had no clue about and from what I had heard of the Kings of Fae, then they were unfortunately far from being weak creatures... my hard ass commander was proof of that!

But then my brief moment of relief was cruelly stolen from me when Trice added to his previous statement,

"Althoo I confess, I dinnae care fur th' wey th' King looked at her."

"Nae why did ye hae tae go 'n' say that, ye just coudnae leave it well enough alone, cuid yer." I ignored his brother's frustrated response and instead focused my attention back on Trice.

"Come again?" I said with my dangerous tone firmly back in place and my demon on edge once more.

"And how wid ye view it brother, bein' forced tae ride on th' back o' a dragon, in th' arms o' a King, 'n' then tae be collared by th' hand o' a shifter dragon as we wur forced tae do nothing fur fear o' him snapping her neck!" Trice said and I… lost… my… shit!

"Oh laddie, dinnae see whit ye doing?"

In this moment I lost it to Hell's fury after hearing every Scottish coated word that had been being said. This ended with me roaring loud enough to crack the walls, making them shake at the same time I hammered my fists down in the centre of the desk. A solid stone slab that cracked and fell was one that had not long ago replaced the desk before it.

"HE DID WHAT!?" I bellowed in undiluted rage.

It was in this moment that Gryph decided to take over, pushing his brother aside as if knowing what he was doing was trying to get a demonic rise out of me, because as much as him being here had offered me news that Amelia was safe, he purposely did so in a way that he knew would infuriate me. This was his own little slice of revenge… fucker!

The largest of the McBain brothers stepped up to me and gained my attention,

"Sire, whit my brother fails tae tell ye, is that th' wee lass, dinnae lik' bein' put in this position at all 'n' soon had th' bastards ballocks in her hand afore squeezing thaim hard enough he may ne'er be able tae faither wee bairn."

"And the outcome of this?!" I bit out.

"Meaning he let her go fur fear she wid rip th' fuckers aff. After she slid aff his lap 'n' told him thare wis only one man's lap that she wid ever sit on 'n' that wis yers. Then she told us tae shut th' bugger up 'n' starting th' negotiations. Ye shuid nae be angry, ye shuid be fuckin' proud." After the shifter's account, there was a collective sigh of relief from everyone in the room but Trice. Who was now smirking, and I was itching to punch that grin right off his face. However, I had more important things to do in that moment and all of them included getting back my girl. And if what Gryph had said was true, then he was right, I was fucking proud!

"You two, I want you both to go ahead of us and get back to my girl. Carn'reau, ready a regiment of your army, something tells me we may need it, for I do not wish to go there unprepared. I will not have this exchange go fucking wrong… because once I have my girl safe, you are free to do as you please." My commander nodded and moved to walk out the room when I stopped him with another word of warning,

"And be prepared, Carn'reau, for if I find out your brother has touched what is mine or harmed her in anyway, you will be the one to lose a brother this day, not I." He looked down over his shoulder at the floor as he listened before replying,

"I understand, my Lord, and I promise you, that I will stand by you if my brother has been foolish enough to do as such… or…" he paused long enough to look back at me and tell me,

"I may be the one to kill him myself."

I nodded after this, believing his words, for he had severed ties with that family long ago and declared his loyalty to me. I had to trust that that loyalty was still as solid as the foundations from which they were first built. As if he could read my mind he said,

"For I am with you in this, my King." Then he walked through the door to carry out my orders. As the McBain brothers followed suit, I warned,

"Do not lose her again, for I do not need to remind you what price is at stake if you do… a price I am close to paying." Trice looked as though he wanted to say something but with one look from his brother, he thought the better of it. Gryph bowed his head and said,

"We wull nae let any harm come tae her, fur oor vow o' life tae keep her safe still stands true."

"Then let us hope it doesn't come to that, for your life is what it will cost you… now go!" I ordered making them leave the room and just as my brother was about to follow them, I put a hand to his chest to stop him.

"Where do you think you're going?"

"Where do you think? To get your girl back!" he snapped.

"No, brother, your place is here, to continue ruling in my absence," I told him, making him ask in utter disbelief,

"You're still trusting me to rule, yet not ten minutes ago I was kneeling at your feet about to lose my head?" I would have winced had this been said with a more pained and accusing tone in his voice.

"I want to know how you knew that she would be the one to save you?" I asked, seeing if he would now trust me enough with the truth and I was only happy that at least some of it he was. Because it was in this moment that my brother put a hand on my shoulder and said,

"Because your Chosen One may have been prophesied to be your Queen, but long ago it was prophesied that she would one day be…

"My saviour."

CHAPTER TWENTY-TWO

AMELIA

THE TOUCH THAT MEANS EVERYTHING

Okay, so I had to admit, finding out that time ran a little differently here than in Lucius's realm had me freaking the Hell out! Because it meant that I didn't have hours to wait like I had naively hoped but in fact days. Of course, the good news to this was that it gave me more hope that the McBain brothers got to Lucius in time to save Dariush.

To save his brother.

However, on the not so bonus side of this snag in time, meant that I had days to wait, or should I say days to aimlessly pace the floors trying to play the 'guess what time it is' game. Which, trust me, was not fun, as in, *at all.* Thankfully, I had one companion in this, and she was lovely. It was of course the King's sister who had spent most of her time hiding from her mother and I was the perfect excuse to do this. She was also a woman that I had not been sorry to say I hadn't yet seen, and from all accounts not one that I ever wanted to as she sounded like the biggest cow bag bitch in the realm!

This was because of how she made my new friend feel. She was one of those mothers that was all about her son. The King was who she really cared for and the sister seemed to be more of an afterthought, one that the Queen had had to go through because fate deemed it so. Which meant to say that feeling bad for her was an understatement. It seemed as though the poor girl couldn't ever do anything right and it was little wonder that she preferred to hide herself away in her room, painting the world as she wished to see it.

Freely.

This was more like her prison than her home and the only sanctuary in all this was what she found in her painting. But now, having me here, she confessed to no longer feeling so alone. I knew this because at the end of every time we spent together, she would tell me that she considered that time as a gift. She also confessed to wishing that it would never be over, despite me secretly wishing the opposite. Because I needed to get back to Lucius and with each passing hour, it was getting harder and harder to face the doubt. To face the worry of all those 'what ifs' as the not knowing was the worst part about it all. And even in my sleep there was no rest for my mind, as I would just dream of him, waking to the sounds of his promises from the past. A vow he had made me when I had first run from him,

'Now, you listen to me, my girl, and you listen well, you and I will never be done, we will never be over, which means I will NEVER stop looking for you. I will fucking hunt you down to the ends of the Earth and beyond... so unless you want a hard time running, then I suggest you keep your ass there and be ready for me because... I. Am. Coming. For. You!' he had snarled dangerously, and I'd had no other option but to digest

224

his words and close my eyes against the sound of his threatening promise. Because that was what it had been and right now, even in my dreams I allowed my mind to take me back there. Back to this promise so I could hold on to it like comfort blanket.

But at the time my reply to this was,

'Then to the ends of the Earth is where it will be…'

And the ends of the Earth was where we now found ourselves. Because we were realms apart, no longer just countries between us as it turned out to be for months. So yes, my mind clung to this vow for a reason and it was one that admittedly my heart would hold him to.

Hold him to it until the end of my time living it.

Which meant that despite putting on a brave face every time I woke, my mind had spent the minutes of the day hanging on to my dreams of him and his promise. Of course, it helped when I would then get to spend my time talking to Vena, who wanted to know everything about my world. And I mean everything, as one conversation had led into another and another and before long there was little left for me to actually speak of.

She had wanted to know all about my family and my upbringing which, admittedly, compared to hers, I now felt bad complaining about. Even as I told her of the constraints set against me due to being being human, because when hearing of her own troubles, compared to her I had absolutely nothing to complain about.

This was because it seemed like every fun thing that they actually did here she wasn't allowed to do or ever included in for fear of causing her mother embarrassment. I found this a heart breaking admission, as all she ever did in her eyes was let her mother down. In fact, it seemed as if the only person who gave her any love at all was her brother, someone it became very clear she loved very dearly. I was actually starting to think that he was the only person in her entire life to have ever given her a compliment and even she admitted that as nice as they were to hear she always knew they were coming from a biased person.

That she could never fully trust them to be true.

I had to say I was utterly astounded by this, because to me she was a true beauty, inside and out! But then she had never heard a compliment come from another man before and even admitted to me that she wouldn't have known what to do if it ever happened.

I had first blurted out,

"Gods, are all the men blind here!?" This had made her blush and play with her fingers in her lap nervously which seemed to be a habit of hers. Then I had told her, that when it happens, as I had no doubt that it would, the very first thing she should do is trust it, for it was true. Her beautiful and unusual big eyes had widened at this before those freckles of hers had deepened to a darker pink. Gods, but she looked even more cute when that happened.

But then she asked me how would she know when she'd met the one. How would she know when she was in love? I told her of my own experiences with Lucius and about the feeling of being around someone when you're in love and what it was like.

That when you were with them it was like feeling your soul was being lit up and they were the only one that held the flame. Every laugh you managed to incite from them felt like a gift because you got to be the one that made them happy enough to smile in that moment. Every touch they gave you, as fleeting as it may be, was like sending a bolt of lightning to your heart, making it beat and speed up in a way that no other had that ability to do. It was a touch of discovery, where you felt everything they did, no matter how fleeting a time. Every graze of their hand or contact of skin, was amplified by a thousand. It didn't matter how long you had been together or apart, that touch…

Well, it meant everything.

But it was also more. Like the way the person who loved you looked at you, as if you were their entire world and all of the imperfections you yourself saw, they only ever saw them as part of the whole package that made you perfect just for them. But that's what soul mates were. They loved you for you and didn't try and mould you into something you weren't. If anything, they simply got to marvel at the sight of watching you bloom into who being with them made you. A better version of your former self because they would make you feel as if you were capable of so much more.

They could make you feel as if you could do anything.

Vena actually placed her hand on her chest at this point and released a sigh as if unable to picture it for herself.

Which is when I told her, that when you were with them you didn't need to be doing anything exciting for you to be excited. As some of the best times I had ever had with Lucius had been the times it had just been the two of us. The times when there was nothing able to penetrate our little world of blissful happiness. Although, admittedly, we hadn't had as many of those moments or even a chance at them as I would have liked, for a thousand more wouldn't have been enough!

Because what little we had experienced together only left me wanting more… craving more time. Something that felt as if it would never be sated, that I would never get enough of.

It made you want to beg for time both lost and the time yet to gain.

"So that is was what love is like," Vena had said in a dreamy way, and by the time I had finished she had her legs folded underneath her, sat on the bed, looking so childlike she was verging on ridiculously Pip level cute. In fact, she reminded

me a lot like Pip in a way, only without the added slice of crazy that went with her personality. Vena was a dreamer, but then she had little else in her life but to be one, so this wasn't surprising. She admitted to me that her biggest dream of all was experiencing everything life had to offer. She also admitted she hadn't been much further than the castle walls, and if she ever did get the opportunity to experience life outside the city, then it was always with guards who would barely even look at her.

Vena was beautiful, but even I could see for myself the clear difference between her and the rest of the Fae around her. To begin with she was much smaller and to add to that, curvier, something she told me her mother constantly chastised her for. Yet no matter how much she tried she could never change her figure and we laughed when she admitted to hating having to eat leaves three times a day!

But this in turn made her self-conscious and that insecurity had trickled into her personality, making it hard for her to converse naturally with others. She sometimes stuttered and other times blurted out random things, meaning the lack of a filter between brain and mouth. She was often a nervous wreck, unable to speak properly, and other times far too lost in her excitement when listening to my stories to let her anxiety rule over her actions.

However, whatever her mood, she was a delight to be around and even after only a few days, I knew that I would miss her terribly. I even considered trying to think of a way that I could sneak her out and take her with me. But then looking around this palace and I knew that one day in Hell for this girl and I was not sure her anxiety would survive it.

Besides, it wasn't fair of me to put her life at risk like that because right now there was no getting away from the fact that I was a walking, talking, target that would only end up making her the same.

But that didn't mean to say that I didn't want better for her. She was a good person, with a kind heart and she deserved to find the same in return. And where she lived may have been one of most beautiful place's I had ever seen in all my life, but there was no mistaking it for what it was, as here she was nothing more than a beautiful bird in a gilded cage.

I once asked her what her mother thought about her marrying someone, which is when she told me of the despicable jokes her mother would make on the subject. Openly laughing if ever the conversation arose, making it clear that no one would ever want her, saying that she did not have the grace and beauty needed to be Fae. In fact, it ended up being a good job I never came across the mother, because I think the first thing I would have done was punch her in the face and say,

'Now, let's see if you think a broken nose is pretty!'

I got so angry, one time I actually told Vena this, and she laughed so hard that she started hiccupping. And in the end, I was most thankful for Vena as our time today had certainly made my time here easier to deal with. The nights, however, I was not so fortunate. This was because the King would take a late supper so he could dine with me and we ended up being alone during these times, although how he had managed to get Vern out of the way I didn't know.

But I didn't think it was for any nefarious reason on the King's part, as I think this was also a way to keep his mother from me as I got the impression he wasn't too fond of her either. Which was why there were many times during these few meals that I wanted to ask him why he condoned his mother's treatment towards Vena. But then I also knew that it wasn't my place to interfere into his personal family life, despite how much I wanted to intervene on Vena's behalf.

However, it was one particular morning when I had just finished getting ready, being thankful yet again to Vena for her never ending dresses... Despite being locked away in a room most of the time, her mother still managed to scold her if she was ever seen in the same dress twice in one moon's month, which I gathered was like a regular month, only with the moon involved and playing a big part... So, after smoothing out the lines of another white dress, one very similar to the other, only with blue leaves this time, Vena rushed into my room. Then she told me the news that I had been waiting for.

She told me that a handsome stranger had turned up and was asking for me.

My eyes widened before I quickly raced from the room thankful that my shoes were already on. Because I cried out only one name at long last...

"Lucius!"

CHAPTER TWENTY-THREE

BONNIE LASS

I gasped, after calling his name, now running down the corridor towards the throne room. Then I burst through the doors ready to throw myself into his arms, knowing that this fairytale land had definitely warped my version of what would probably happen. But I didn't care, I just wanted to see him. I wanted him to hold me, to shout at me, yell at me for being so reckless and then madly kiss me, even if it was the angry kind. I just needed his touch, his kiss, his arms around me as it felt as if it had been so long and each day was getting harder and harder.

I needed my soul mate back.

But then, as I burst through the doors and saw that it wasn't Lucius at all, I had to hold myself back from crying. Hold myself back from falling to the floor like a little girl and crying out her loss. But not all was lost as the sight of Trice and his brother quickly incited another emotion from me and I ran towards them. This after only taking a few seconds to hide my disappointment, and shouted,

"Oh Gods please, please oh please, tell me he's…"

"He's alive, lass, Lucius' brother's alive!" Trice said and at this confirmation I threw myself into his arms. Then I couldn't stop the floodgates from opening as tears of utter relief were rolling down my face.

"Thank the Gods, you got there in time. Gods, thank you, thank you both, you saved him!" I said over and over as Trice cradled the back of my head and held it to his chest after wrapping another arm around my back. Another few minutes and this moment passed, and I pulled back to look at them both noting that they both looked tired. Then I grabbed Gryph and yanked him to me, which would have been useless had he not wanted the hug, as it would have been like moving a redwood rooted to the ground.

"Och! Aye alright, lass!" Gryph said as he too hugged me back when I tried to wrap my arms around him and not making it all the way around. Not with all that mountain of tattooed muscle on show. And I didn't care that he was near naked and only wearing his tartan across his bare chest like a sash. But then he was wearing trousers and his usual heavy looking shoulder armour to keep him warm. Oh, and not forgetting a thick leather strap decorated with the fangs and horns of his kills across his chest for carrying his massive war hammer at his back.

But I could tell he was holding back in fear of crushing me no doubt, as his arms were insanely huge, with biceps far bigger than my head!

"How was he?" I had to ask when stepping back and looking at them both again. And yes, I asked this even though I felt guilty doing so considering I knew how Trice felt about me. But I couldn't help it, I needed to know how Lucius was doing and more importantly, if he was actually on his way here.

"Furious, killin' mad, lik' th' wrath o' th' Gods wis cast doon upon us all 'n' set a light up his ass," Trice said making my mouth drop and his brother groaned with a shake of his head, making the end of his wrapped, flaming red mohawk snake over his shoulder. This was when I decided to look at Gryph for my watered down version.

"He wis mad, lass, bit happy 'n' relieved that yer are safe 'n' unharmed." At this I released my own breath of relief before asking my next difficult question,

"And Carn'reau, is he on his way here… will the exchange go ahead?"

"I think tis safe tae say, lass, that even if Carn'reau hud doubts o' comin' 'ere, that man o' yers wid hae ended up dragging him 'ere by his lang black locks," Gryph said and I laughed at this, knowing that it was probably true, because I hadn't been lying when I told the King that Lucius would have done anything to get me back.

"Tell me the truth, just how angry was he that I lost the Eye?" Trice gave me a tender look, which I turned away from and looked down at my feet in shame. This was before I felt him hooking a crooked finger under my chin and using it to raise my face up, before holding it there with his forefinger and thumb gripping my chin. Then he told me softly,

"He does nae blame ye."

I absorbed those words and hoped for them to be true, because I couldn't help but feel as though I had let him down. But then the next question I naturally asked was about time. More specifically on how long it would take before Lucius arrived. Unfortunately for me, this answer came as a disappointing one, as they just didn't know. Because it was unclear how long it would be until Lucius got there as they had no idea how long it was until he left after them. Only that he was making plans to do so but wanted to send the brothers ahead to ensure my safety as soon as possible.

Moments after I found out all they knew, the King arrived upon hearing that the brothers were back. He was also pleased to discover that he would soon be seeing his brother again as the exchange was going ahead.

However, I couldn't help but notice they had purposely left out the part where their own King was also coming for the exchange and he was killing mad at that. Meaning that I had a feeling this would end in two armies and two Kings butting heads like a field full of rams and fighting over who was more powerful.

Because one thing was certain and that was Lucius was pissed, and not in a happy drunk way. But as in the murdering, I am going to rip you limb from limb kind. And knowing Lucius as I did, then I knew he wouldn't let this go easily or without blood being spilled. Because in his eyes, anyone who thought they had the right to take me and use me as any kind of leverage was going to pay for the crime. This all despite the fact that I hadn't been harmed and that I had been treated well. I had been given a comfortable room next to my bodyguard. I had been well fed the entire time I had been here and well, as for the company, thanks to Vena it had been second to none.

And speaking about Vena, I could see her hiding in the shadows, as she admitted doing quite often so she could get a glimpse of anything happening in the kingdom. And right in that moment I could also see that her eyes were rooted to just one figure in the room…

Trice.

Gods, but if only I had the time to play matchmaker, as he would have been amazing for her! Yeah, okay so I knew that it was most likely a ridiculous notion, because as nice as Trice was, he was also a big scary, rough, dangerous shifter bounty hunter and Gods but what a mouthful that was! But I also knew that despite all these things, he could also be soft and gentle when it was needed. However, was he the soft enough soul that Vena needed. Trice had a kind heart, and his bravery was on near insanity levels! But he could also be very blunt, pig headed, stubborn and was always straight to the point and direct. Which was something I'm not sure Vena's anxiety would have been able to cope with. She needed someone to build up her confidence, not have the ability to tear it down in a moment of tactless comment coming out of their mouth. No, in that case maybe Trice wasn't the man for her after all.

Besides, the biggest obstacle would always be that he lived in Hell collecting the meanest of the mean as a bounty hunter. So not exactly the life for a naive Princess who only knew of her own world and by her own admission, it was not very much at that. I think Hell was a little bit too much experience for her to go through, which was a shame, as the look she was giving him now was like she had just found her Prince in dirty Armour.

In fact, I didn't even see a point where these two would even get to meet, as Vena was too scared to come out of her hiding place and Trice seemed oblivious to anything else other than the current situation we faced. This was until I excused myself to go to the bathroom. Because that's when I realised I had been wrong, as it looked as though they had got their chance to meet after all.

I knew this the second I walked out of the bathroom, as what faced me as soon as I did was Vena, who now looked like she was close to hyperventilating. As soon as I stopped walking she said,

"What does Bonnie lass mean?" I took a moment and grinned, trying not to laugh at her putting on a Scottish accent when saying these two words. Then I asked her slowly and in a knowing way,

"Why?"

"What does it mean… it means stupid doesn't it, although maybe ugly… yes that's right, ugly is probably what it means? Stupid and ugly, probably like a double insult… although, I confess that when he said it, he was smiling and I don't think I did anything wrong… although he did catch me and stop me from falling, which was nice. He didn't seem as if it was a nuisance… gosh, he's very handsome." At this my eyes grew wide as there was just too much of all that to take in.

"Okay, first off, don't insult yourself like that as I doubt anyone other than your bitch of a mother would say those things." At this she giggled because I swore, which she never did as I think 'piss pot' was her limit on that one. Then I asked,

"Now back up a bit, are you talking about Trice?"

"Oh gosh, even his name is lovely," she said in a dreamy way that had me grinning.

"Okay, Vena, focus for just a second here, are you talking about the tall one, big guy, very red hair, cute face but also scary as Hell, also half naked…" At this she chuckled again and waved her hand telling me no, it wasn't Gryph. Then she said in that dreamy voice again,

"No, I speak of the most handsome man I have ever seen, the one that looks like he could tame a dragon with just the look…"

"Sheesh, you have no idea," I muttered under my breath before she continued with her musings,

"I also wonder where he got that scar from, most likely fighting in some honourable duel." At this I nearly burst out laughing, but thankfully cleared my throat to mask it, as knowing Trice and his brothers it could have been from some drunken bar fight. However, I didn't say this but instead asked her somewhat more clearly now,

"So you fell, and Trice caught you, and then he called you a Bonny Lass… is that what happened?"

"Well, his exact words were…" she paused for a moment as if straightening up and making sure that she got his exact words right before she said them. For this was obviously a very important part of the whole exchange.

"Och… actually I'm not sure I'm saying that particular word right as I've never heard it before." Again I had to stop myself from laughing as she tried to mimic his accent.

"Okay, just leave that word out, what came next?" I asked again trying not to openly smirk so she wouldn't take it the wrong way and be offended. Then she said, trying again to mimic his accent and doing so slowly,

"He said… 'you mist be careful nae tae fall 'n' hurt yersel' fur a bonnie lass lik' ye needs tae tak' care'. Yes, I think that was it, but some words were strange. However, I think I got the gist of it." After this she quickly went on to tell me,

"He said this with his arms around me… he was very strong… then he set me back on my feet and nodded his head a little before grinning down at me and giving me… you know, the look we spoke of," she said, winking as if 'the look' was some secret of ours, which was sweet.

"Wow, that was quite an exchange," I admitted seeing now why this would totally have an impact on her.

"Oh it was! And he had such a handsome grin and one at me no less! But then he left and now I need to know what Bonnie lass means because I didn't understand that bit and fear I might have gotten this whole exchange wrong and misinterpreted *the look,*" she said with a slant of her head when saying these last two words. This was when my grin got even bigger and I told her without being able to keep the excitement from my tone,

"Okay, so are you ready." At this she smiled, smoothed down her dress and said,

"Yes, I am ready, hit me." I smirked not wanting to spoil the moment and say, it was really 'hit me with it' and instead left it for the good bit,

"Bonnie lass means pretty girl." At this her eyes widened, and she deflated onto the bed and said with a sigh,

"Oh, gosh."

"Yep." Then her eyes found mine and she said louder this time,

"Oh, gosh!"

"Yep," I said again before all the trouble really began as she grabbed my hand and said in an endearing way,

"I think I now know what it feels like to be in love." At this I had no other reaction to give but to pull her to me and hug her for what she had just said was probably one of the sweetest things I'd ever heard another person say.

However, as happy as I was that she was experiencing this moment, there was that little guilty part of me that knew in all likelihood that very little would ever come of this. That it wasn't through moments like this that you instantly fell in love and that what she was feeling was probably more lust than anything else.

Although, then was this really true, as thinking back to the day Lucius first saved me and I had felt the same way, believing myself instantly in love? Despite that what came next didn't feel so great but more like just another rejection. However, despite all of these things, when it came to my new friend, then in truth I just didn't have the heart to take this moment away from her. Because dreaming was all she had, and if Trice was now to become the centre of those dreams then who was I to crush them.

So I said nothing and instead let her bask in her moment wishing more than anything that Trice could have been the one for her. That he could have been everything that she ever needed and that she too could be the love of his life because Trice too deserved to be happy, as happy as I was with Lucius, and on a purely selfish level, then having him fall madly in love with someone else would make my life a little bit easier.

But I didn't want that for Trice just to make life easier for me, I wanted it more for him. and looking at this girl now, in all of her sweetness and thoughtfulness and tenderness and so much love inside that she had to give… Gods, but if only I had a wishing well in that moment then I would have thrown every penny I owned into it and wished for them to be happy together. As no two others deserved it more!

Unfortunately for me, reality was often a bitch and dreams had a way of biting you in the ass.

I knew this a little time later when I was back in the throne room and stood next to the King. A person that, in that moment, I probably shouldn't have been stood so close to. Not when the walls began to shake, and the screams of terror could be heard from just beyond the doors.

I knew then that my own King had come for me… *and he was bringing with him…*

The wrath of the Devil's son!

CHAPTER
TWENTY-FOUR

WRATH IN WAITING

T he moment I felt it, it was like a wave of terror that washed over the land. A darkness that I had long ago become addicted to. As it meant only one thing…

My King had come for me.

That promise, that vow he had made that he would always find me. That he would never let me go. It had never been truer than in that moment, but the only difference now was that he did so by bringing with him Hell's fury!

Because if there was one thing I could say for certain, as the grand throne room began to shake, then I would say that Trice had been right.

The King of Death and Blood was feeling *murderous.*

But in truth, I didn't seem to care. I couldn't seem to focus on anything else other than the fact that he would soon be walking through those doors. That I would be soon be in his arms once more. It was like a sickness within me. Like an obsession that had grown beyond all reason other than its one purpose and that was to get back to my Chosen One's arms, not caring how demonic they were. How deadly they were or what monstrosities they were capable of inflicting! I just wanted them around me!

Now!

Although, I had to say that when I pictured the moment of us reuniting one more time, I didn't account for the sight that met me now. I never imagined the beast pounding at the door, like the arrival of everyone's greatest nightmare. Even the King, who had been sat next to me, stood quickly and positioned himself in front of me. Doing so now as if to protect me from the sheer terror that was quaking the doors, making them splinter, despite how big they were. The very presence of Hell just beyond them that was terrifying his people outside, for you could still hear their screams of terror.

This was when I sidestepped a little so that I could see what was happening, doing so just in time to see the two double doors at the end fly open. Cracking with the force, despite how colossal they may be, they were nothing in the way of the powerful force that now came barging through them.

"Lucius." I gasped his name at the first sight of him.

Gods, he was magnificent!

Lucius, in all his demonic glory, and fully clad in his demon form, had pushed both doors open, slamming them so hard that they threatened the very creation that had them hanging there. Then he walked purposely down the centre of the room and it took him no time at all before he found me. And what he saw, well, it was clear to see, he most definitely did not like.

This was because another King stood in his way.

Oh no, he didn't like this at all.

Not. One. Little. Bit.

His huge demonic wings rose out to the sides and as the first line of the King's guards ran at him, he let loose that Hellish rage on the poor souls that we're trying to prevent him from getting to their King. He sidestepped, bending his body slightly so that one wing could simply swipe them all back. This made all four of the guards go flying back in the air, landing hard against the line of pillars. Then, with a glance to the other line of guards, he let the demonic armour slither down his arm to create his weapon of choice. It was a deadly sword that looked like a single black shard that reached the floor. One that I knew was sharp enough to sever demon heads. Meaning these Fae wouldn't have had a chance, even as they were now pulling their own swords free.

This is when I knew I had to act before the King's people got hurt… *permanently.*

"Please, you have to let me go to him!" I urged, but the King just looked down at me, in astonishment.

"Tell me this cannot be him!?" he said before looking back and finding now that Lucius by himself was like a one man army. His black and red armour was almost glowing with the power I knew flowed freely beneath. His demon was humming for vengeance, like a giant beating heart that wouldn't stop. Wouldn't stop until it had found me. Which was why I needed to reach him, to try and calm the beast that could only see one thing… another man was between him and his woman. I knew this when he roared at the King,

"GIVE ME MY HUMAN!" The King looked on in utter disbelief at the sight of him and who he obviously was to me. But I ignored this and stated again,

"I promise you, if you don't let me go to him, he will kill everyone here and destroy this place, he will stop at nothing… please trust me!" I said this last part by tugging at the neck of his tunic so he would focus on what I was saying. Although, Lucius saw this and as a result threw his arms backwards, leant his body forward and roared loud enough to cause pieces of the arched ceiling to crumble and rain down around us.

"You actually want to go to this... this demon! Are you insane, for he will kill you?!" The King argued and I could understand where it was coming from, as anyone else would believe the same thing. But he didn't know what I knew. He didn't know of the heart I owned that lay at the core of this demon. *But I did.* For he was one I had tamed once before, that night in Lucius' winter garden when I had seen him for the first time in his demon form. Seen for the first time the deadly beauty in the darkness around his eyes. The two pools of crimson fire that consumed those that belonged to his human... I saw it all. Yet that night, no matter how frightening he had been, he had come for me. He had saved my life and then cared for me in the gentlest of ways. He attended to the wounds on my feet by feeding me his blood and then carried me all the way back to his cavern. Once there he had set me in the bath to warm my cold and weary body and cared for me even more. That had all been down to his demon, and despite how scary he was now I still knew with utter certainty that he wouldn't hurt me. So, I turned back to the King and said,

"Please let me go, for he will only get worse, can't you see that!" I said as he knocked even more of his men back, many of which now lay bleeding on the floor in need of help.

"He will rip you apart, just look at him! You really wish to go to this monster?!" he barked back at me and I narrowed my eyes up at him and said with absolute certainty in my voice,

"Yes, now let me go so that I may save your Fae ass!" At this he released a sigh as if he knew he had lost.

"Very well, let it be your fate, for I will not sacrifice my people for a foolish life," then he held out his arm so that I may pass, and finally I had my moment. The King ordered to his men to stand down, no doubt worried that I would be caught in the crossfire despite his words.

So I ran, rushing down the steps, and as I did, I turned and looked over my shoulder to tell the King,

"You may think he's a monster, *but he is my monster!*"

Then I ran to Lucius, without a shred of doubt to cloud my judgement, for nothing could keep us apart in this moment, least of all his demon. So I ran and I kept running until at the very last moment he saw me. He saw me coming at him and instantly I took it as a good sign when his weapon disappeared, joining back with the rest of his demonic armour.

Then when I was close enough, he knew what I was about to do, and he was ready for it, and he caught me just before the impact would have hurt when throwing myself into his arms. Instead, he gripped my waist and lifted me to the right height to his face, so we could have this perfect moment. Because despite the bloodshed, that was exactly what it was! It was the moment that I could finally place my hand on his cheek and tell him with tears running down my face,

"What took you so long?" Then without waiting for my answer I kissed him, anchoring his lips to mine, by grabbing a fist full of his hair and holding him to me. The shock of my actions took him a second of surprise before he too was kissing me back and, in that moment, the entire room vanished. Everything went silent, in fact, it was almost as if everything around us just disappeared completely. It was as if the whole world evaporated into dust because nothing else mattered but the fact that we were in each other's arms once more.

And that kiss was all there was for me.

The kiss from the man I loved.

"Amelia, my Khuba, my sun, my Chosen One… I have you, I have you once more," he told me and again the tears continued to fall, as I placed my forehead to his and closed my eyes, just breathing him in. It felt like a lifetime, far too many memories in between the last time I saw him. Too many moments where

245

I'd ask myself if I was ever going to see him again! Far too many threats I had faced without getting him at the end to hold me, and having him here now opened the floodgates of my own emotions, to the point where I could barely breathe. I felt as though I was going to burst, and everything would come pouring out!

"I... I love you... so much Lucius... so very much," I said through my tears and I felt him grip me tighter before he lowered me to the ground so he could cup my cheek. Something which ended up being the whole side of my head thanks to how big his hand seemed in his demonic gauntlet. But this way he could look down at me and wipe my tears away with the back of a taloned hand, one that just proved my point... my monster would never hurt me, *he would only ever kill for me.*

"Found at last, my little human," he said as if mimicking the last time he'd said this in his own throne room. It was as if it had all been a cruel twist of fate for this to be happening yet again. Which had me asking, in a blur of tears,

"Why does this keep happening to us?" At this I knew the sound of my pain was breaking his heart for he closed his eyes cutting off the crimson world he saw, then he told me,

"I don't know, my Khuba, my love, but I know one thing, I am going to make sure it never fucking happens again!" I didn't know how he ever expected to accomplish this, all I knew was that I would do whatever he asked of me to try and prevent it, because I too couldn't allow this to happen again.

"I can't do this without you again, I just can't... I just can't, Lucius," I told him on a whisper, and he got down lower towards me and whispered back,

"You won't have to, for I promise you, I am not letting you out of my sight again." This sounded like a promise and one I had no problem with, for I didn't ever want to be apart from

him again. Which was why I said in a small voice still raw from being emotional,

"Okay, shackles and all." This made him grin down at me before agreeing in his sexy demonic voice,

"Shackles and all."

After this was when he must have realised that we were not as alone as we would have liked. Which was when his head snapped up and he hooked me around the waist, tugging me to him. Doing so after first moving his dangerous armour at his side so it wouldn't hurt me and now leaving his bare skin on show. Oh and a delicious hint of those rock hard abs and gills of muscles at his sides. Gods, but how I wanted him!

"You are the one who dared take what is mine!" Lucius' demon bellowed when finding the one he classed as being responsible. But to give the King his due, he didn't even flinch at the sight of what he knew was a formidable opponent. One, given what he had seen already, he most likely would lose to, as Lucius' powers were beyond compare.

"I am King Auberon," the King stated with his back straight, proud and unmoving.

"Then you are the man I am here to kill!" Lucius said making a step towards the King and giving me no choice but to try and pull him back. Then I shouted,

"Don't, please don't kill him!"

Thankfully, Lucius did stop but he did so just before he snarled back at me, most definitely getting the wrong impression. But with the King now seeing that Lucius' anger was directed at me, he foolishly intervened, no doubt fearing for my life once more. And in that moment I was torn as on one hand the thought irked me, but seeing as I knew it was something that came from concern, then how angry could I be with him for now being the foolish one. Noble but foolish.

"I am the one who had her brought here and kept her from returning, if your anger is with anyone, it is with me not the girl!" I swallowed hard the second I saw Lucius' eyes flash with crimson jealously.

"Then you will die for that offence, for no one keeps what is MINE FROM ME!" This time his wings spread out making me jump but instead of letting go, I merely clung on harder, because I knew he wouldn't risk fighting if there was a chance of me getting hurt.

"Release me, my Khuba," he ordered and I grimaced at how hurtful it sounded. But I stood my ground and snapped back,

"No, not a chance!" He growled down at me and warned again,

"Let me go, Amelia!" At this I clung on even harder and shouted even louder this time,

"NO!"

"If you do not, then be warned little one, you will force my hand in this." I closed my eyes for a few seconds at the sound of his harsh words and forced them to the back of my mind. Then I swallowed hard and hit him with what I knew was the truth.

"What, and risk hurting me, would you really do that?!" I snapped.

"To get to my enemy, *yes.*" I sucked in a painful breath and shouted at him,

"You wouldn't!" I challenged and suddenly I felt a hand collar my throat and squeeze as if in warning to prove his point. But thankfully it wasn't hard enough to prevent me from speaking as I told him,

"He is not your enemy!" This turned out to be the wrong thing to say, I knew that when he roared down in my face,

"You defend him! Is there more to this that I don't yet

know… *did he touch you?"* he asked in a dangerous tone before looking down at my body as if he would find the evidence there for himself in way of bruised fingerprints on my skin.

And I had to say, the pain of hearing this was as though he had taken a whip to my skin, lashing it over and over with every accusation thrown at me. All this time I had spent pining over him, desperate to get back to him!

And for what, to get accused of cheating on him!

Fuck me, but I was furious!

But then I also knew that with looking at him and seeing how close to the edge he was, that now was not the time to lose my shit as I wanted to. No, that would come later! But for now, I had to calm the beast, not taunt it or feed into his delusions. So instead, I decided on a new tactic that I hadn't yet used before, guilt and truth. So, I reached up with my hand and palmed his cheek, as best I could with him still holding me by the neck. Then, when I gained his attention it took his deathly glare away from the King. But at the very least his hold on me eased, doing so even more when I said softly,

"Hey, now listen to me, demon, I would never let another man touch me, you know this, for there is no one… *fucking no one, Lucius, no one but you, honey… no one."* I whispered making him now start to fight with himself. I knew this when he closed his eyes again as if trying to absorb my words and keep them in a place that would stick. He needed to feed on them. He needed to hold on to them and get his demon to focus on them instead of the death of the King who's blood he wanted to coat his hands crimson. And well, he wasn't the only one who had a building need and desire that needed sating. Only mine was one of a very different kind.

Because, oh Gods, just the sight of that bit of skin and a need of the likes I had never known shot through me. As in it literally hit me like a bolt of power that had me…

Fucking desperate!

To the point that my fingers were trying to curl into the sections of his armour plating and because it was connected to him, he could feel it. I knew this as he looked down at where my hand was practically clawing at him to get to more skin.

"Khuba?" He suddenly let go of my neck and I would have laughed at the sound of his demon sounding so unsure, but I looked up at him and started crawling my fingers up his chest, careful of his chest plate. Then when I reached a part that I could grab I tugged him closer to me and said, with a naughty bite of my bottom lip,

"I need you, demon."

"Amelia?" He questioned this time on a growl. Which was when I told him more firmly,

"I need you to fuck me, Lucius… *Right. Fucking. Now!"* I warned on my own growl, and his eyes then focused on the way I looked down the length of him and licked my lips slowly before sucking in my bottom lip and letting it go again. And when he saw that… yep…

My demon was getting hard… or should I say,

Harder.

At this he growled low and this time there wasn't an ounce of anger, but instead it was all from an aroused beast. This was confirmed when he suddenly lifted me up by banding an arm around my waist, after shuddering through the movement of his demonic plating. Doing so once again so he was free to do this without hurting me. Then, with me plastered to his chest and with the whole room having witnessed us practically eye fucking each other, it didn't come as a shock as to what would happen next.

Meaning that it was quite a turnaround of events when he walked up to the raised platform and snarled at the King,

"I need privacy!"

"Seriously…?" I heard the King mutter under his breath in disbelief when Lucius looked down at me and confirmed in a demonic voice,

"Deadly, *now which room?!"* I bit my lip and giggled before the Fae King nodded to his left, telling Lucius,

"Your woman knows the way." Which meant that he was suggesting the room I had been sleeping in, which thankfully wasn't far from here. Lucius nodded, looking fucking bad ass when doing it, and started to walk in that direction, and I thought now was a good time to say,

"Auberon, I'm sorry…" At this Lucius paused a step and growled down at me, getting the wrong idea again, so I quickly finished by saying,

"…But we will probably break shit." At this the King groaned in exasperation before waving out an arm and telling us to just go, whilst I swear that Lucius' demon purred! A rumbling sound from his chest before he warned,

"Behave, my pet, before I fuck you here in front of everyone, fucking Fae be damned!" This was when I raised myself up closer to his ear and whispered my own warning,

"Then you better walk faster, handsome…"

"…before I fuck you back."

CHAPTER TWENTY-FIVE

BLOOD REUNITED

We made our way down the corridor from the throne room and the second people saw us, they wisely ran out of the way making fearful noises.

"Well, it has to be said, we sure know how to clear a crowd," I teased his demon, because I wanted to see how far I could push him. I wanted to see if it was possible to get more from him. Maybe entice a little laugh or a grin, something more than just a sinister smirk. I wanted to push for all of these little things that I was yet to see from him in this form. Because when I knew he was so close to the edge, it was exhilarating, and I found myself rubbing against him, making him warn again,

"Behave, woman." Naturally, I grinned at this.

"I would if you would get there quicker!" I told him back, making him growl and start walking even faster. I think the only reason he wasn't running at this precise moment was because he was scared of his armour catching on me in some way. Armour that I kept playing with, because being so close to his other form and finally having the freedom to explore, well I had become fascinated with every inch of him. And he knew it too as he could feel everything. I knew this because I kept extracting little sounds from him, like soft growls and a snarl. And well, there was also that strange rumbling purr of his.

"That isn't helping," he commented making me hold back a giggle by rolling my lips inwards.

"Neither is you walking... *so... slowly,*" I teased back before reaching up and peppering the side of his face with kisses, something that made him groan.

"Gods, woman!" It was at this point that he held me tighter and started to jog, being careful not to jar me against his armour. But then when he slowed again as we entered a new hallway, I reached up and started to feel my way along his horns and stroked my fingertips softly down his folded wings.

"I will fuck you against this wall, if you continue with this quest of discovery you seem to be on, little fuckable pet of mine," he warned, making me shrug my shoulders and say,

"I'm game if you are." At this he groaned as if my response had backfired on his threat.

After this he sped up again, after I first motioned which way for him to go with a nod of my head. In fact, the next amusing thing to happen was the moment we reached the door. Because it was at this point that Vern was exiting his own room and what he found made him stop dead and do a double take. Which wasn't surprising considering what he found was me clinging to Lucius in his demon form, with my hand sneaking down and trying to grab his hard cock. Something he was in that moment trying to prevent by shifting his hips away as if I was some sexual deviant taking advantage of a shy demon.

"Oh hey, Vern," I said casually whilst running my fingers through Lucius' hair and kissing the side of his mouth. Then Lucius had me howling with laughter when he snapped,

"You have been relieved of your duty... leave, *for it will be loud.*"

"Upon my word, I will take my leave of you this instant!" Vern said before running past us as if he couldn't get away quickly enough.

"Do I want to know?" Lucius said in reference to Vern's posh voice that was now back with a jolly English vengeance,

"Right now..." I paused to look down at his straining cock and finished,

"...definitely not." At this he smirked at me knowing exactly why not, after all he had much more important things to do... like fuck his horny woman! Which was why he kicked open the door with way too much force and it meant that it now hung on its hinges being barely more than useless.

"I will fix that," he stated, before doing so with his mind and I knew the only reason was that so we could continue with our goal in gaining privacy. But then, as soon as we made it into the room and the door was firmly closed behind us, he placed me on my feet. Then I pouted at him when I watched as his armour started to disappear, which was when I held up a hand to stop him.

"Please don't."

"Amelia?" he questioned looking shocked.

"I don't want him to go..." this was when I walked up to him with a swagger and said seductively,

"I want him to play with me." On hearing this his demon came back in full force, and doing so as if nothing had the power to stop him. Then he picked me back up and he said,

"Oh, I will play with you alright, my pet, for now it's finally time I let my demon have a turn at fucking this sinful little body of yours." He ended this with a growl before crushing his lips to mine in a bruising kiss. At the same time, he pushed me up against the wall and Gods alive, but I felt as if I could drown in this man! Drown in this beast and die in the arms of this demon!

He was my everything and it felt as though he was swallowing me whole and taking me under. I got totally lost in his kiss and in the feel of every inch of him, now feeling as if I was getting drunk from the waves of arousal that kept hitting me and crashing into me like the ocean hammering the shoreline in a storm. But it just kept building and building and he hadn't even touched me at my core yet.

"Lucius, I… I…" I warned him what was coming… that being me, and soon!

"You will take what I give you, woman!" his demon snarled at me and that too only managed to turn me on further. I felt my dress being torn up my waist, ripping due to his claws that I was just thankful weren't catching my skin. I was still amazed how careful such a brutal demonic warrior could be and adored the fact, because there was something about having sex fully clothed with such a dangerous being. One that still took care of what he owned, and still wanted to fuck me in a roared frenzy of need. One that didn't allow for the time to get naked.

But I had to have him. I had to have him inside me, or I felt as though I was going to explode! Which was why I allowed myself to hum in pleasure the second I watched as part of his armour shifted, now revealing himself and flowing towards the back of him like it was a second entity. But then some of this travelled up his back and down his arms. This was just before he grabbed my wrists and with my legs wrapped around his hips, he pinned me to the wall with my arms over my head. Because his demon side was adapting his armour so it could be used as a tool to keep me locked to the wall where he wanted me. My eyes widened in fascination as I watched it continue to ripple up his arms before moving over his demonic gauntlet hands.

Then my eyes widened further in shock this time as I saw them form crude shackles, now anchoring me to the wall creating a sexual thrill that I remembered having when being tied to his bed in Hell. It was when he was administering his punishment for having me leave him in the Temple. He had manipulated parts of his unusual bed creating restraints, so I was left spread wide open at his mercy.

Well, by doing so now it freed his hands so he could cup my ass from behind, now lifting me up and making me spread my legs even further. Then he stepped back into me a second after his armour disappeared from the rest of the front of his body, now leaving a naked strip of delicious skin. One that was all muscle and hard, hot male. One that I was proud to call my own, get the gift of seeing it, touching it, licking it and biting it whenever the fuck I wanted to!

He was mine.

It was a primal thought indeed, but it was one I just couldn't help. It was as if seeing his demon now had made me want to stake my claim, as if it had brought out my own possessive demon. One that wanted to own every inch of him, which was why, in an almost desperate plea, a whisper escaped my lips,

"I need you to fuck me, hurry Lucius, I need you." His crimson eyes burned brighter on hearing this, for I knew what begging did for Lucius… he loved it! In fact, I think he even craved it and I fucking loved that I could give it to him.

Lucius didn't say anything to this but instead he just waited until the rest of his armour had disappeared completely so the only thing left for him to do was with his hard long cock that was now free. One ready to impale me with like I was begging him to do. Meaning that the moment he positioned himself at my core, I started to try and push down on it, to get him inside me faster. This made him chuckle in a sinister way as if he found my impatience amusing. But still he held himself there without thrusting forward like I was waiting for and I would have asked why, but he beat me to it, telling me what he wanted… no, more like what he demanded.

"Tell me you are mine, tell me you are mine and no one else has fucked this sweet pussy I own, no one other than me, tell me it now!" he snapped now on edge from his own words spoken.

"No one but you," I whispered instantly.

"And it is my cock you want, isn't it… the only cock that has ever been inside you, it's that cock you want, *isn't it?"* He snarled this warning, telling me to accept his claim and quickly.

"Yes!"

"Then tell me, my fuckable pet I own, tell me…" He paused before whispering this last part against my cheek in a growl of words,

"…how hard do you want me to fuck you?" This was when I practically growled back at him,

"I don't just want it, Lucius, I fucking need it, I need your cock, so hurry up and give it to me as hard as… AHHHH!" This was all I needed to say before it ended on a cry of pleasure and pain that merged into one. Because he hadn't let me finish before he thrust into me, and the second I felt my body being invaded by that solid length now powering into me, I screamed with pleasure.

At the same time his wings erupted behind him as if aiding his movements in gaining momentum as he fucked me in earnest against the wall. My mind was only focused on him and what he was doing to me now, for it felt like no time at all before I was screaming his name and coming so hard, that I saw black spots behind my eyelids. I vaguely heard a smashing in the background, and the cracking sound of wood, along with the deep and grated growls of pleasure coming from Lucius. This was as I felt more of his armour sliding its way up my legs and towards my backside. Once there it formed a ridge on the wall big enough for me to sit on, so now Lucius was free to use his hands as he had obviously been desperate to do… *and boy did he use them.*

One he used to collar my throat, holding my head back in a controlling hold, the other was then used to grab my breast in a firm, bruising hold. This was before then lifting it up as high as it would go, so he could feast upon the nipple. I cried out in pain as he bit down hard enough to pull through blood, but it also had me come again as a sensation of pain and pleasure all merged into one long shuddering eruption. I was a quaking mess, vibrating against the fucking wall as I felt my channel quivering around his cock.

"Again, give it to me again, Amelia!" he demanded of me and suddenly I felt my body being moved and I opened my eyes, forcing myself to focus on what was happening next. Lucius had moved me to the dressing table so he could bend me over slightly, trying to make more of a connection and going deeper and deeper. My body bowed backwards with my breasts standing high and as if begging him for more attention. I could even feel the blood from around my nipple trickling down the side of my breast before he leisurely licked his way up to it, then swirled his tongue around the hardened abused nub.

It was one of the most erotic feelings and yet something so simple, as just the feel of my own blood being drawn from this wild beast of a man pounding into me. Then his hand circled my neck again as his thrusts got harder, as if needing to keep me in place or I would go flying off into the wall and hurt myself if he didn't. I could feel my breast jerking hard with the brutal thrusts and again I was crying out my release, quickly losing count of how many there had been.

Then, after my cries had been spent through this last orgasm, he squeezed my neck once more before releasing me and running his solid hand down my collar bone, and his other hand to my hip, holding me steady as he continued to pound into me, slower this time. Then that hand continued down from my neck and in between the valley of my breasts and all the way down to my belly. Doing so in a slow tantalising way that matched his now slower thrusts as he hammered into me hard but slow. It was torturous as much as it was pleasurable for the next time I came around his cock, it was almost as if he was dragging it out of me in slow motion.

"Lucius… I can't… I can't, not again," I told him a desperate tone, making him grin down at me and it was pure evil. Especially as he could feel for himself as fluttering wave after wave quivered along the length of him. One that ended up being the longest orgasm yet as he wouldn't stop, he wouldn't give me even a second of reprieve from this sexual onslaught! No, he just kept giving it to me, just like I had begged for him to do, as if each slow drag of his cock against the inside of my core was enticing more and more out of me and in turn, feeding his sadistic addiction.

Hell, but it soon felt as if I didn't even know my own name anymore, for there was only Lucius. For there was only one name that I would repeat over and over and over again, and that was his. This demon that clearly wanted to fuck me into oblivion!

But then finally, after I lay now limp and close to passing out on the table, Lucius must have known I was close to my limits, being human. Which was when he decided the last destination to fuck me would finally be the bed, as there was one last part still to come, literally. Because I knew there was still one thing missing other than that of our combined release…. he wanted to be reunited with the taste of my blood along with having me be reunited with the taste of his.

I knew this when he lay me down without his cock losing

even an inch of our connection. My eyes fluttered open to see him now leaning backwards above me, so he could take in the sight of me. The sight of his sated little pet now thoroughly fucked. But the sight he granted me in return was one that burned into my mind. Because it was raw, and it was beautiful. Because with his length still seated firmly inside me, he was still all demon and now with his wings stretched out, it became such a demonic presence, that I felt myself capable of coming again just from the sight alone. It was that powerful.

"Gods, but you are utter fucking perfection!" he stated with a hard demonic voice, that sounded more like he was making a vow not giving me a compliment. This was before he suddenly dropped down on his hands and started to take me faster and faster, now with his wings powering him forward creating the air to move around us. It felt almost like we were having sex in the air, rising from the bed which I knew we weren't, I was just that high on him, getting high off the feeling of Lucius fucking me into the mattress like a madman, for he was totally losing himself now, I could see it.

"Yes, yes, yes, give me more, give me all I want, give me everything!" I said over and over again, and it drove him forward until eventually he looked up at the ceiling and his fangs extended dangerously. Then, before my eyes could register anything else, in a blur of motion he was at me, latched at my neck and bit into me.

"AAAHHHH YESSS!" I screamed out as my last orgasm ripped through me within seconds. I was screaming so much that barely any sound was even coming out anymore, for it was rough and ragged being dragged out of me. I wrapped my legs around his ass, locking my feet there, as they needed to, just for something to hold on to. But then I also reached up and grabbed the sides of his shoulder plates, as I needed the top half of my body to be anchored to him also. Then he reached up and cut into his own neck before forcing my head there. He guided my lips to the point where he was gushing with blood before he ordered,

"Drink from me, take from me what is mine to take from you. Drink me down and swallow me whole, for my blood is your blood. Drink me down and take me inside you, just as you will take my seed inside your body," he said, still thrusting inside me with his declaration, as I continued to do as he asked and drink him down, now getting high on both his blood and his words of ownership.

"This body I own, for you are mine... for all eternity! Do you hear me, mine for an eternity! I get to fuck you whenever I choose! For this addiction will never end. This obsession I have of you, I will never stop adoring you, I will never stop worshipping you, this body gifted to me from the fucking Gods themselves, and this heart I own. I fucking love you, my Chosen One!" After this he threw his head back, tearing his blood soaked neck from my lips as he roared his release. I did the same, long ago losing count of how many times I had come for him as what I had thought would be my last, hadn't been. But I should have known, for the sight of his own release always sparked my own.

But then my body had finally given up and hit its limit, I knew this when my head fell back and the last I was able to give him, was my own whispered words...

"I love you, Lucius... always."

CHAPTER TWENTY-SIX

JEALOUS HEARTS

A little time later, I woke to the most incredible feeling of fingertips brushing through my hair. I loved having my hair played with and there was only one man who knew this. Because there was only one man who had ever done it and because I felt it now, I couldn't help but smile knowing what it meant, even in my dreams.

Lucius was with me.

"It's nice to see my girl smiling," a soft voice hummed down at me and again my smile got bigger.

"I don't want to wake up if I'm dreaming of you," I told him, and I felt a body shift over me as my body gained a little more weight on one side. Then I felt lips at my ear before the most beautiful line was whispered,

"Then open your eyes and see me, for if you are awake, then we can live this dream together." The moment he said this, my eyes snapped open and I realised what he was saying was true. This wasn't a dream, he was finally here and what had just happened between us, hadn't been some drug induced sexual

fantasy on overload. In fact, thinking about it now and I could feel the soreness between my legs and the aches of my muscles that had no doubt been peppered with bruises during the act. Something that, given another ten minutes, I would be completely healed no doubt, thanks to the copious amount of blood that he'd fed me.

But I knew why this was, as it was always the same after we'd been apart for any length of time. Lucius wanted to keep the connection strong between us and the exchange of blood was the way to do that. It was as if the beast inside him pushed at him to do it, that the demon craved it as much as he craved me, because it wasn't some animalistic need to drink blood in order to survive. The tales of vampires were far from the truth. No, the exchange of blood was more like a deep-rooted need and for Lucius, it was a deep-rooted need to keep that connection with me as strong as it could possibly be.

As when Lucius said that he owned me, that I was his, body, mind, soul, and heart, well, he was someone who took those things quite literally. But, opening my eyes now and seeing his handsome face looking down at me, with those usual stern features now soft and tender, I released a dreamy sigh. Because he was lowering those incredible eyes down my face as if scanning every inch of me and marvelling at what he saw. And for the sight of him, well, as beautiful as the realm of Fae was, there was honestly nothing to compare with the sight that met me now.

The man I loved.

"I would say good morning, handsome, but I have no idea what time it is." At this Lucius smirked before telling me,

"It is time I take you home, sweetheart, that is what time it is." I hummed at how nice that sounded before asking,

"How long was I asleep?" I questioned stretching out my arms on a yawn.

"Not long," was his soft answer, making me look at him as if there was something wrong, which was why I asked by saying his name.

"Lucius?"

"You were taken from me again, Amelia." His pained admission caused me pain and I didn't know what to do other than hug him back and hold him tight. He soon got the hint and wrapped his arms around me, holding me close. Thankfully, this was made easier considering he was now lying naked next to me with not a shred of his demonic armour in sight. But both sides of him were what I believed to be living perfection, demon or the human vessel that lay naked in my arms.

"I'm here now and I'm not going anywhere, not without you." I felt him take a deep breath and cradle my head to his chest, tucking the top of my head under his chin, with my cheek close to his heart, one that offered me the comforting sound of it beating.

That's when I whispered to him,

"I'm not letting you out of my sight." At least I felt him chuckle once, before pulling back on my hair a little so that I was looking up at him.

"That's usually my line," he teased.

"I mean it, Lucius, I am in, three billion percent," I told him making him frown slightly in question.

"What are you saying, Amelia?" he asked after my strange declaration.

"I'm talking about opening every can of worms there is. I'm talking about quitting my job and moving to Germany, living in your castle or Transfusion or wherever you want me, I'm in… I'm in, *three billion percent*." At this I was rewarded with the biggest grin yet before he bit his bottom lip as if trying to hold back his laughter. But then his face got low, closer to me so he could whisper over my cheek,

"As sweet as that is to hear, I am afraid I raise your three billion percent by my infinity, for I will never let you go. Wherever you are, I will come for you as you may have been born for me and fated to hold my heart… *but you were made to rule with me and that is exactly where I want you, always.*"

"Oh, Lucius!" I threw my arms around his neck and buried my face there, letting myself once again get teary.

"Ssshh, come now, I am here, let me care for you." This turned out to be him biting into his own fingers, doing so hard enough for them to pool with blood. Then he snaked his hand down in between us and I ended up crying out at the shock when suddenly I was penetrated by his two fingers. Fingers now coated in his blood.

"Ahhh," I moaned around the sweet and divine intrusion and found myself rocking against his hand. But Gods, it was so dirty and erotic that I couldn't help but roll onto my back. And of course, he followed me, knowing what I was doing, so my legs could spread wider and I could take him deeper.

"My girl likes that, tell me, sweetheart, how much do you like my touch?" he hummed in my ear now plastered to my side and with his large frame half over me. Asking me this as he continued to coat the insides of my sex with his blood soaked fingers, healing me as he did, and also bringing me to the brink of an orgasm. I don't know what it was about having his blood there, but it was tingling with the whole of my insides and dancing along my nerves. Doing so to the point where I knew I was seconds away from coming, from falling apart under him. My shuddering body told him as much for I felt him grin against my cheek.

"You didn't answer me, pet."

"Yes, I love your touch," I whispered, making him hum against my cheek as if pleased. But then he pulled his fingers out and I moaned at the loss, crying a little as I had been so

close. But something had switched inside of Lucius, where he was now cupping my sex possessively, which was when he said to me,

"And tell me again, Amelia, tell me that no one else has been here."

"Lucius?" I asked in confusion, dizzy from being so close and asking myself where this was coming from. But then it hit me the second he shattered my euphoria.

"No other King, answer me, for I need to know?!" It was at this point that all arousal fled me, and another emotion took complete control. I was furious and as a result,

I totally lost my shit!

"Are you fucking kidding me? That is what you think of me! That I would fuck another King!" I snapped angrily, now rolling away from him and grabbing what was left of my torn dress from the floor to hold in front of me as I didn't remember when he had taken it off me. Too lost in the act to remember exactly, but I think it was when he was tearing it from me when moving me from the wall to fuck me on the dressing table. One that now looked considerably less useful for its purpose.

"It is clear that you do not want this King dead, is there a reason for that?" he asked in a tone that was totally unapologetic, and I couldn't help but scream at him,

"Yes, because I'm not fucking psycho, that's why! Gods, but what type of question is that!"

"A reasonable one!" he snapped back, and my eyes bulged before I shook my head a little as if this would help me in making sense of his new brand of crazy!

"If you think that a reasonable question is why I don't wish someone dead, someone who is not on my enemy list… and trust me here, Lucius, I'm racking them up… then you have been in Hell for far too long!" I threw back at him after raking a hand through my hair in an angry motion with the other fisted

267

to my chest, so I wasn't having this argument with him completely naked.

"You're right, I have been in Hell too long and so have you!"

"Well, on that we agree!" I snapped.

"So, there is nothing you want to tell me about your time with the King?" At this I narrowed my eyes at him in question, wondering what it was exactly that Lucius had been told or for all I know, had seen by an 'all seeing' magical cow named Dixie that they had stashed in the basement somewhere!

"And what exactly do you mean by that question?" I asked with a hand on my hip, and it was at this point that Lucius stood up and came towards me, now clearly trying to intimidate me.

"You're deflecting, sweetheart."

"Oh no, don't you sweetheart me!" I said wagging my finger at him, and I wanted to wipe the smirk off his face when he was amused at seeing it.

"You don't get to sweetheart me when we're having a conversation about you believing that I would EVER FUCKING CHEAT ON YOU!" I roared at him before he got closer and told me,

"A question, I do believe, you haven't yet answered!" At this I walked away, lifted both my hands and shouted,

"AAAAHHH!" Then I realised I'd dropped my dress and did this naked. Then I held up a finger and warned when his lips twitched,

"Not. One. Fucking. Comment!"

"About the irresistible body that gets me hard in seconds, no not a word," he said, and my eyes shot straight to the evidence of that, now standing proud and to full attention.

"Like what you see, sweetheart?" At this I growled and said,

"Not right now I don't, no! So he can go back to being Mr

Floppy for all I care, as I think it's best you channel all that extra blood back to your brain, as that's clearly where it is needed if you think I bloody cheated on you!" I threw back at him, making him snap,

"Mr Floppy… really, Amelia?"

"Oh, but of course, that's the part he focuses on," I muttered to myself.

"If you would answer the question, then this argument would stop and I would then prove to you how fucking Mr Floppy doesn't exist with me, Pet!"

"NO!"

"Why not if you have nothing to hide?" he said, folding his arms over his impressive chest that right now I just wanted to scratch 'idiot' in with my nails!

"Because you're insane, that's why!" I shouted back at him, doing so again with both hands in the air and dropping my torn dress again.

"Oh, for fuck sake!" I snapped at myself as I bent to retrieve it for the second time.

"Yes, and who is it that drives me to such insanity, I fucking wonder!" he replied making me point out,

"Yes, well it isn't me making you believe these things so answer me something, Lucius… what did you expect was going to happen? Did you think I'd viewed this time here as a fucking holiday, a chance to have some girly romance with a pretty King who is holding me to ransom… because let me tell you something, that would never fucking happen and you know why…?" I snarled making him snarl right back,

"Why?!"

"Because I don't need another King in my life, Lucius, as I have far too much on my hands dealing with your jealous shit!" I said poking him in the chest before stomping away towards the door.

"And just where the fuck do you think you're going!?" he barked at me from behind and I spun on a heel and motioned down at myself, telling him,

"Where do you think? To get another dress because some big buffoon, who is my untrusting boyfriend, ruined this one!" Then this point was made by my dramatic exit, one that was definitely flawed considering I was in the room with a vampire. Make that a very angry vampire King, who didn't want me to leave. Oh yeah, and he had powers where I didn't... *joy for me.*

Naturally, this meant that the door was pulled out of my hand and slammed in front of me. So I turned around slowly and said,

"Well, unless you are going to sing like a Disney fucking Princess and bring a chorus of woodland animals in here to sew my dress back together, then what do you suggest I fucking wear!?" At this he looked as if he thought I had finally gone bat shit crazy, before storming his way over to me, pushing me against the door and gripping the bottom of my chin to force my head up. Then he snarled down at me,

"Naked and fucked, that is what I fucking suggest!" and then he ripped the torn material from my hands, throwing it to the side before my cry of outrage was swiftly swallowed up by his brutal kiss. A kiss I was ashamed to say, I couldn't fucking resist!

Because I kissed him back with just as much desire and anger as he was showing me. Then, just because I could, I bit his bottom lip and sucked on it, swallowing the small amounts of blood I gained in the process. His growl was not of warning but of pure desire for he lifted me up in his arms and impaled me on his cock once more, proving it most definitely wasn't named Mr Floppy.

Then he told me with a growl of words,

"Time for round two, Princess!" My reply was to get closer to his face in challenge and snap,

"Bring it on, Vampy!" He growled again but this time it was matched with a grin before he was once again kissing me and this time, he fucked me against the door.

"YES!" I cried as my first orgasm hit and hit me hard, making the back of my head fall against the door with a bang. But I did this too hard and the second I came down from my sexual high, I muttered a little,

"Oww." He grinned down at me before saying a condescending,

"Aww poor baby, let me make it better." And then he did…
over and over and…

over again.

CHAPTER
TWENTY-SEVEN

CREATED A MONSTER

A little time later, and too many orgasms to have kept count, I looked up from his bare chest, glancing around the room and said,

"I don't think the room would survive round three." At this he burst out laughing, put his head back to the torn pillow, and muttered,

"Not with the sex monster I've created, then no."

"Ha… well you… and stuff… Nope, I'm too chilled from all the orgasms, so that's all the comeback I've got in me at the minute." He chuckled at this as I snuggled closer down into him.

"So, same time next Tuesday?" I joked after a moment of silence and again making him laugh.

"No seriously, I mean I like you and all, but I've gotta good gig going here, the food is great, the dresses are well… great until you ripped one to shreds, the room was great… well, until you broke that… you know what, never mind, I am coming with you." I smirked when I continued to be able to make him laugh, before he commented in a husky whisper,

"I don't remember hearing you complain, sweetheart."

"No, that's because you were swallowing it when you crushed your lips to mine… nice trick by the way."

"Ah yes, I will have to remember that one in future for when I'm trying to shut you up again." This time I laughed and slapped his belly that was rock hard and had not an inch of wobble to it, not like mine. So I told him,

"You know, you're funny when you're not being all psychotic killer on me."

"And living with you, sweetheart, I think you will find that to be my new day job," he bantered back, making me roll my eyes which ended with my chin being in his grasp as my head was tilted back.

"Did you just roll your eyes at me?" This dangerous question I knew came with a glint of hope in what was now his gorgeous silver grey eyes that held flecks of blue glinting in their depths.

"That depends," I said making him enquire,

"On?"

"On whether or not your demon can create a butt plug with its armour, because if it can, then I'm not thinking good things are in my future." At this Lucius burst out laughing, to the point where it was so hard, I was practically bouncing on his chest. Then, when he had calmed, he started running his fingers up the crack of my backside, paying a certain amount of attention to one area in particular making me gasp in shock. As even though the feeling was foreign, I had to confess that it was not entirely unwelcome. However, what he said next really did shock me,

"Oh, sweetheart, but when I take this fuckable virgin ass of yours, it won't be with anything but my cock and my fingers, *of that I can promise you."*

After this he sealed his promise with a kiss, swallowing my gasp of shock and surprisingly this time, it was one slightly less forceful, proving to me that despite his words and what had just happened between us, he could still be tender and gentle and above all, my loving Lucius.

But a few minutes later I knew the time had come for us to have a conversation, in the hope that this time it wouldn't turn into a screaming match. Although, I had to confess, it certainly ended well.

"Erm, honey, not wanting to poke at the possessive beast you have up your butt…"

"Up my butt?" he said faking outrage that I ignored.

"Or provoke round three, because like I said, I really don't think the room would survive. But I have to know, what the Hell was all that?" At this he released a sigh and admitted,

"My demon has been in Hell too long."

"Erm yeah, I agree but what does that mean exactly?"

"That my human emotions are somewhat being tested, strained if you will, and therefore this invokes a side of me that is more suited to Hell… *you look confused,"* he commented because I was scrunching up my face, making him poke at my nose in a cute way.

"That's probably because I am," I admitted.

"I'm not really explaining this very well, am I?"

"Not really, no, but at least you're trying to explain it, so Gold Star for that one." At this he gave me a wry look before continuing,

"You remember what my demon was like when I first saw you in Hell, the way it reacted to you?"

"It's a little hard to overlook, seeing as you don't ever forget when your demonic boyfriend collars you for the first time and pulls you along by a leash," I said, making him give me a look of understanding before agreeing,

"Point made."

"I thought you said that that was more of an act."

"No, that is what you said it was, for me it was a natural response to being angry at my Chosen One, for stepping through a portal into Hell when I asked you not to," he replied, and surprisingly this didn't come with one 'fucking' or a roar of anger, so plus on that front. But I still couldn't help but tease,

"Wow you're really trying hard not to shout or swear at me, aren't you?"

"Is it that obvious?" I laughed,

"Kind of, especially when you grit your teeth in that way, it's a dead giveaway, fangy."

"Fangy, really?" I tried not to laugh at this so I could ask in a serious tone,

"What, you don't like Fangy?"

"At this point I am not sure whether it is a step up from Vampy or not… or if it just makes me sound like some pet dog of yours." I couldn't help but laugh at this, and pat him on his side as I said,

"We could get you a collar this time." Now at this he growled playfully and tickled up my hip, warning,

"Behave, pet." I giggled before getting back to our conversation.

"Look, I get what you're trying to say, you're in Hell so your demon's testy, me being kidnapped and finding myself in these situations is probably not helping Mr Testy at the moment and it's probably making you a little bit crazy… say, *crazy enough to accuse your girlfriend of cheating on you?"* At this he really did release a sigh and ran a hand through his hair in frustration before the bottom of his palm covered his face where he held it there.

Then amazingly he admitted on a groan,

"That was wrong of me." This was when I pulled myself up

so I could look down at him. Then I lifted his palm up a little and took a peek so I could say,

"Wow, Lucius, is that an apology… *no way?*" I whispered sarcastically making him give me a pointed look from under his hand. Then I pulled it all the way off him and said,

"Look, as far as I can tell, seeing as Trice is who he is and most definitely wants to make it his new job winding you up like a chime bashing mechanical monkey… stay with me on this one…" I said when he gave me a 'what the hell is my girlfriend talking about now' look.

"Am I right in saying that he was the one who told you about me flying on the back of the dragon with another King and oh my God, if he didn't and I'm the one telling you now, then before you freak out that is not a euphemism for sex!" At this he laughed once and admitted,

"He might have said something to that effect." I let out a sigh… *Gods, Trice.*

"And let me guess, you decided to storm a castle in your demonic glory, slam open the doors, see me stood next to the King with him trying to protect me from, by the way, what he assumed was some crazed Hellish monster…"

"Your monster, if I do recall you saying." I smirked at this liking that he'd heard that.

"That's right, my monster, but that is beside the point, as you went from entering his throne room, seeing me, destroying said throne room, to assuming the worst… *of me*… and reached 'I want to kill him' status in seconds."

"That might be the way of things," he admitted making me smirk.

"Okay, well let me set the record straight once and for all… he isn't the only King waiting to meet his Chosen One, his *human Chosen One…*" Lucius gave me a look that had me quickly adding…

"And no, before Mr Paranoid comes back out to play, he doesn't think it's me, in fact, he knows it's not me! And he is most likely very looking forward to the day that he finally meets said Chosen One and kind of needs to be alive to do that." At this Lucius released a sigh of relief and said,

"Then I fear I owe you a better apology." I grinned big at this and said,

"I think there's a piece of the room we haven't destroyed over there, wanna give it a go, see what else we can break?" At this he chuckled. And I couldn't help but tease again,

"But wow, I must say it's definitely my lucky day, after all, orgasms in the double digits and an apology from my boyfriend, what's next, Lucius, you going to tell me you bought me a Christmas present and have relented your Grinch-like ways?" At this he burst out laughing, hooking a hand behind my neck and pulled me to him, telling me the only words I needed to hear...

"Fuck, but I missed you." And as for me, I lowered to his lips and whispered over them...

"I missed you too, handsome."

CHAPTER TWENTY-EIGHT

MEETING OF KINGS

A short time later and I had a new dress on, this time one of forest green that made me feel as though I should be running along some field somewhere, singing some elvish song. Thankfully, I had found this in one of the only pieces of furniture we didn't manage to destroy. But then again, I can imagine it would be hard to have sex in a wardrobe, so not really surprising.

But as always Lucius was amused by this random thought of mine and chuckled because of it. Then, after it had been quiet from inside of our now broken room and after it was clear the sexcapades had finished, there had been a knock on the door to inform us a meeting was taking place.

As for the room, well, after round two we could now add a broken mirror to the floor, as well as pieces of plaster from the walls, a broken dressing table, a chair that was a little more than splinters and a bed that now had no feet, as they had not been able to withstand the power of Lucius' mighty thrusts. Again, this was another thing I had said to Lucius in a moment of weakness at which he had thrown his head back and laughed at... telling me he would have to remember that one, whatever that meant, as I had no clue as to what he could be reserving that moment for.

But this was before pulling me in for a hug and kissing the top of my head, telling me sweetly,

"I missed my funny girl." I then looked up at him and said,

"Then maybe you should consider, I don't know, getting daddy to send comedians to Hell, it might lighten the place up a bit, comedy club here and there, we could make it date night." At this his lips twitched as he tried not to laugh again, but instead growled down at me,

"Keep being cute and talking, sweetheart, and you will find out whether or not this room could survive round three... *and four.*" He whispered this last part making me giggle.

But after this, came yet another knock on the door, at which point we were ready to leave. I was therefore surprised to find my good friend Vena standing there, only now, I had to say, she looked considerably more fearful as her wide eyes took in Lucius' intimidating form, and what a form it was... *yum.*

As for Lucius, he had decided to go a little more casual this time, and was now wearing loose fitting black trousers made of some kind of animal hide from a beast I didn't recognise. As for his deliciously, muscular torso, this was covered in a black style jacket that wrapped around him and tied at the sides, leaving his large shoulders and impressive biceps bare. I had to confess, it also made not touching him difficult, for all I wanted to do was climb him like a stripper pole, hold onto his neck, and grind my lady parts into him as if I was riding a mechanical bull.

Gods Fae, few dozen orgasms and he was right, he had made me into a sex monster!

Lucius' hair had also been pushed back, mainly through me raking my fingers through it as we'd made out a lot, and I swear even his lips looked slightly swollen from all the kisses we'd shared. I also noticed that he purposely hadn't healed his bottom lip because he kept licking it, doing it as if to remind him of me biting him there. I would catch him doing this and smirking to himself as if the memory of what came after it assaulted him in a comforting way. Or maybe I was wrong, and it just turned him on. Who knows, but either way, he was clearly happy about it.

But now here stood Vena, who looked totally in awe of him and I think half of it was being terrified and the other half was, well, it was Lucius, and he was gorgeous so that definitely added to the intimidation level.

To break the ice, I put an arm around her shoulders, pulled her close and introduced her to Lucius.

"This here is Vena, the King's sister and my new best friend, she's also an amazing artist, and was kind enough to look after me and bring me nice clothes. She's also been wonderful company, listening during the endless hours I was pining over you, clearly." At this Lucius' lips tipped up on one side and again it was as if he was trying to fight the grin.

"Vena, this here is my soulmate, Chosen One, Vampy, sometimes Fangy, Honey Pot, Boyfriend, who sometimes likes to call me, his eternal life's partner… isn't that right, snookums?" I said making her choke on her shocked reaction, meanwhile Lucius was desperately trying not to give in to the urge of laughter and instead raised a brow at me, as if trying to be stern but failing miserably. This was because it was hard to look stern and be amused at the same time. Then he held out his bare hand, for his other was of course gloved, and said,

"I'm pleased to meet you, Vena, and thank you for taking care of my girl and keeping her company." At this point I thought Vena was going to swoon, but she grabbed his hand and shook his fingers before doing as she was taught to do around royalty, she grabbed the hem of her dress and curtseyed. Then she cocked her head to one side to tell me silently it was time to follow her. This was when I discovered the real problem with Vena… she couldn't talk to men! In fact, I wouldn't have been surprised if the only male she had ever spoken to was her own brother. I could tell this the moment she tried to say something but got tongue tied and gave up even trying.

It was only when we were following her that Lucius enquired,

"When you say she kept you company, you didn't just spend all that time talking *at her*, did you?" I groaned before smacking his arm and saying,

"No!" But this ended up with me feeling his large muscle, making him raise a brow and say in a cocky tone,

"Found something you like there, sweet cheeks?"

"Mmm, maybe… *depends what it's used for,*" I said waggling my eyebrows and making him grin, whilst shaking his head before muttering,

"I have created a monster."

Moments later we found ourselves being led into the King's office, only this time, it was clear Lucius had something to prove… a little something called *ownership.* I knew this when he draped his arm around my shoulders and tucked me as close to his side as he could get me. I think, had it not looked weird, he would have had me with my legs spread around his hips and clinging on to his neck as if I was some pet monkey of his.

I gave his sister a wink in a silent goodbye, making her give me a little wave of her fingers in return. As she was walking out of the door, I noticed that Trice and his brothers had arrived ready to stand guard.

Vena froze to the spot at the sight of him and when Trice saw her, he nodded his head as way of hello, but not knowing what else to do, she curtsied to him as well and then spun the other way and began walking. I grimaced the second she bumped into a vase on a table, and just before I could hear the smash, I could just see Trice coming to her aid as the door was closing, making me arch my neck to try and watch.

"Amelia." Lucius said my name to grab my attention, as if not liking the fact that I had been spying, no doubt because he thought that I had been looking at Trice, who admittedly, was still a sore subject for him. But he hadn't known the reason for me looking was so that I may plot a matchmaking job in the future.

"King Auberon, may I introduce my…"

"If you call me Snookums or eternal life partner, we're gonna have problems, sweetheart," he muttered stopping me before he took over the introductions,

"I am Lucius Septimus, King of the Kingdom of Death and blood ruler of this realm of Hell," he stated, his voice firm and unwavering.

"Wow, when you say it like that, it sounds almost impressive," I teased unable to help myself, and thankfully it helped ease the tension in the room as the Dragon King couldn't help but smirk. At this point Lucius covered my mouth with his gloved hand after wrapping his arm around me to do so.

"Of course you know of my troublesome little human here, who is of course, my Chosen One and you have probably gathered by now that there is no stopping her wit and humour, other than gagging… which if she carries on, will be next on my list of punishments," Lucius said and my mouth dropped, smushed up against his palm.

"Smuttin' ump mow," I mumbled behind his hand.

"That remains to be seen," Lucius commented without malice before removing his hand.

"I am King Auberon, and I welcome you to my lands."

"Seriously, just like that, just after he had… okay, okay, I'm going to stop talking now, because you're welcoming us and everything and there's little gained in pointing out how you should not be doing that... okay, we should totally move on now." I started out after Lucius gave me a look that told me this was precisely why I should not be speaking. The King grinned and motioned for us to take a seat, where we found that his brother Carn'reau had already taken his place. It was clear that they'd had much to discuss and at least they both seemed to be in one piece. No visible dagger wounds showed or anything, which I assumed meant it had all gone well... unless they healed as quick as Vampires did and only ten minutes before had kicked the royal shit out of each other?

Whole new meaning to kiss and make up, I guess.

"Carn'reau, lovely to see you as always," I said with a grin, making him bow his head and hide his own knowing smirk.

"My Kings, Queen," he said as way of greeting and I didn't think it was a good idea to point out that it kind of sounded as though he was playing chess. No, instead I moved to sit next to Lucius, but this was when he had another point to prove, as he tagged me around the waist and lifted me before seating me in his lap. This was when I turned my head inwards and whispered,

"Smooth, caveman." To which he replied,

"I'll remind you of that when I'm showing you my club later."

"It's a date, handsome," was my witty reply before turning back to the King and his brother, feeling Lucius' chuckle behind me. As for the King's office and the view that it offered of the private gardens beyond, thanks to the wall of arched windows either side of the fireplace, I suddenly blurted out,

"It's dark!" To which all three heads turned to the window as if I had just pointed out some medical marvel or someone waving at us with their pants on their head... *either one.*

"She's easily amused," Lucius said, and I rolled my eyes before saying,

"No, she has just been wondering where night-time had been for the last few days."

"Ah, I see, well our days work differently here to your human realm, I believe night only falls every three days to your one mortal day," King Auberon said.

"So, does that mean three days of night-time too?" I asked thinking this was inconvenient.

"Yes, for that is the way of our moon cycle," he replied.

"Cool," I said because I didn't know what else to say.

"Now we've got that piece of chit chat out of the way, let's move on to the more important things, like you holding my Queen to ransom in order to get your brother back," Lucius said with a bite to his words and I muttered,

"And there goes the niceties."

"Yes, and for that I must apologise to you both, but as I have expressed to my brother, unfortunately I had no other choice." At this I could feel Lucius about to snap something when I turned to my side, held a hand to his cheek and advised,

"Just hear him out, honey." Then he nodded and I was amazed that it had worked. It was at this point that Carn'reau took over.

"Our uncle framed me for my brother's murder, it was why I was banished. For he then took possession of the Crown to rule over the Dark Fae Lands, and has spent this time amassing a great army."

"Yeah, basically he's one bad dude and he wants to take over all of the realm, and the King needed his brother back so that he can help him prevent this from happening… sorry, I just thought I would say it in a nutshell kind of way, because no offence but you guys say it all in a really fancy way, and I thought we were under some time constraints here, so thought I would fast forward events." Lucius released a sigh and made the point,

"I thought I was supposed to be the one hearing him out." I turned my head and muttered,

"oops… My B…"

"Don't say it," Lucius warned making me chuckle, knowing this was a common Pip saying, one he had no doubt heard to death, seeing as she used to be on his council.

"Well, she certainly keeps things entertaining," King Auberon commented and at this Lucius laughed, before tipping my face up to look at him, then he stroked a fingertip down my cheek with his leather hand and said in an adoring tone,

"That she does and one of the many things I have missed." I gave him a soft tender look in return, one that didn't need any words… *he knew.*

"So, this uncle of yours, do you have any idea when he is planning this attack?" Lucius said getting back to business.

"No, but from the sounds of the intel that my spies have gathered I do not think it will be long in coming." Auberon told us.

"My Lord, if you please." Lucius made a motion for Carn'reau to speak freely.

"I believe we may be able to help each other in these two instances." At this I saw Lucius smile for he must have known where his commander's thoughts lay, because the next thing he said was him assuming as much,

"You wish to combine forces and create an alliance that will benefit you in protecting your realm and in return, should I be in need to add to my own army, you will stand by our side in battle."

"Yes, something my brother told me you believe may be coming," Auberon said.

"You do?" I asked, making Carn'reau wince as if he had

spoken out of turn and all the men in the room were now keeping something from me, or at least they were trying to.

"We will speak of this later, my love," Lucius said, and I knew not to push it in that moment. But then, this was when it hit me, reminding me that these Fae Kings weren't the only ones that had their problems.

Which is why I suddenly blurted out,

"Oh shit, but we haven't talked about your brother or the Eye or harpies or anything, we just… well you know." I blushed stopping myself in time.

"We've been a little busy, sweetheart," Lucius reminded me when I really didn't need reminding, the walls of my sex were already doing that for me with a flutter.

"Oh yes, we know, *in fact my entire Kingdom knows,*" the King said dryly, making Lucius grin because he was more than happy with the knowledge of us being heard having sex throughout the whole land and no doubt reaching every male ear possible!

"Ah yes, about that, you see we had a little mishap in the room," I said trying to be diplomatic, but this was when Auberon waved a hand at me and said,

"You did warn me, and not to worry, for I will just bill your King." I think this was said in jest but either way, I took the bait and said,

"Yes, do that, he's rich you know, like sultan rich, has his own castle and everything, although he doesn't have a moat of blue flames or a pet dragon. Why don't we have a pet dragon, honey… oh Gods, please stop me now!" This was when Lucius grinned, pulled me to him and whispered over my lips,

"Ssshh," and then he gave me a quick kiss, and we carried on with the meeting.

"It is true we have much to discuss but I am afraid that for now it will have to wait for another time," Lucius told me and, in that moment, he couldn't have been more right!

In fact, he didn't even realise how right he was, because this was when I was the first to notice something wasn't quite right. I began to notice just what dangers had been lurking in the shadows in wait. It made me wonder why no one else had noticed but then again, I was the only one that had been fascinated with the dark just beyond the windows.

A darkness I hadn't seen for days.

That same darkness that an enemy had been lying in wait for, waiting for darkness to fall.

Because this was when two things happened at once, and it started with me grabbing on to Lucius in a desperate way and telling him,

"You're right, now is not the time... now is the time to fight! Look out!" I screamed the moment glass exploded around us.

Just as...

Chaos erupted!

CHAPTER TWENTY-NINE

WRONG DAGGER

After I screamed this warning, everything else that followed happened so fast it was a blur of motion. The glass shattered and became lost to the sound of my own screaming, one that echoed in my ears and a sound that was swiftly followed by the demonic roar of Lucius. I was picked up suddenly in his arms as he turned me away from the danger. Then his demon side erupted, starting with his wings. They expanded to their full length and protected us both as he dropped to one knee. But by creating that barrier between us and whoever it was attacking, the evidence of his protection came in the form of the distinct sound of blades hitting the floor behind us.

"Get out of here, to the door, Amelia, and don't look back!" Lucius told me firmly and I nodded without hesitation, knowing that I was going to do whatever he asked me to do. He let me go, placing me on the floor and then he stood, I watched as the rest of his demon form rippled over him, consuming every inch of him back into his demonic armour. Then he turned that

Hellish wrath onto the oncoming assassins that started to flood the room.

As for Carn'reau and his brother, they had already pulled their own weapons from the sheaths that hung at their sides and had started fighting the new enemy. A new deadly foe to face, one that looked like some dark phantom that once held the soul of a fighter. Every single inch of them was draped in an ominous black cloth that seemed to float around them like some deathly essence was following their movements. Each was dressed like some ghost of a warrior assassin, with dark armour over layer upon layer of this floating material. But that wasn't what made them so frightening, for we were now facing an unknown enemy. Each of them wore long arcane hoods that covered nothing but darkness, for there was nothing there where faces should be.

I counted at least fifteen of them, surely an easy number to fight for the sheer combined power of the Kings in this room. But unfortunately, that age old saying that I had grown up hearing from my father came to haunt me now.

That assumption was the mother from where all mistakes were born, and I had assumed too quickly that this would be an easy enemy to defeat. I knew this the moment I saw Lucius lash out at one of these phantom-like creatures, and it passed straight through him as if there was nothing there but its dark soul. As for their own weapons, these, unfortunately, were more real than they were, as the threat of their blades continued to clash against the Kings' weapons.

It was as if they were fighting ghosts!

It took me a second to take all of this in, but it was long enough that Lucius could still feel my presence in the room. He looked over his shoulder at me and ordered,

"GO!" I didn't need to be told twice. I got to my feet and ran towards the door, just as it was bursting open and the three

McBain brothers were running inside to join in the fight. As soon as Lucius heard it too, he was shouting out a new order,

"TAKE HER!" But unfortunately, this was too late, as there was no one left to take me, because the reason the brothers had burst through the doors was because they themselves had been attacked from their end and were now fighting the same enemy from the other side.

This then meant one thing… *I was trapped in the middle.*

That made it even greater odds against us, as the Kings hadn't yet managed to slay a single one. As for the brothers, they were now facing off at least the same amount and without anyone's blade penetrating these phantoms, it seemed we were all hoping for an impossible outcome. As for Lucius, the only outcome he was concerned with was getting me to safety, but without first fighting them back, he just couldn't get to me.

I knew that I couldn't just sit and hide somewhere in this office, hoping that it would all be over soon and I would be saved by these men. I was after all,

A Draven.

This meant that I got my ass moving and ran over to Trice and without asking, I grabbed one of the blades strapped to his chest and used it to arm myself.

"Hide, lass!" he snapped at me, which is when I told him,

"I wasn't born to hide, *I was born to fight!"* Then I spun around with my long dagger in hand and faced the oncoming phantom assassin that had managed to slip through where the Kings were trying to keep them back.

"Gods," I muttered as it was unlike anything I'd ever seen before or faced in a fight. Its entire body was dressed for one thing, darkness and the kill. Because now from up this close, then the only thing you could see on it was the dead of its eyes, white and glowing from deep within an abyss of darkness. As if its face was so far away and what I was looking into when

trying to see its face, was a glimpse of horror from the past. As if it was inside there, screaming to get out, to be let free of its warrior chains!

It was as if it was caught between two worlds, half alive and half dead. Which was why, with each movement they made, it was as if there were three of them. Like a memory following in the first's footsteps, each making the same movements one after the other. The first was the fastest and the two behind moved slower, as if there was a lag behind the ghost of its image. It was like a dark shadowed train, for as it swung out its sword towards me, so then did two others. It meant I was not only defending myself against one but three blows, which meant I had to move three defence steps in quick succession.

Because of this time delay of theirs, they still had the power to inflict damage and I didn't have one weapon to face as it lashed out at me again and again, but I had three all in a quick blur of each other. Which meant only one thing,

I had to be faster!

So, I rolled out of the way of one and slashed through the legs of the other and up the back of the last, each time my blade sliding straight through as if they were made of smoke. I knew then something had to be driving these ghostly figures… these phantoms of the dead. Something or someone had to be controlling them?! Question was, what could it be?

I didn't even know what it was we faced, but it became clear very quickly, that all of the men fighting now knew there was only so long I could keep this up, because they had something that I didn't…

Immortality.

They could heal quicker, move faster, and see the enemy movements before damage could be inflicted. How long they could hold this up for, I didn't know but I did know it was certainly a hell of a lot longer than I could. But then the moment another one got through I held my blade above my head just before it could slice down at me. One hit, two hits and finally the third hammered my own blade closer and closer towards my face, taking me to my fucking knees!

This was when I purposely fell back, so I could kick up at the second phantom that I had originally been fighting, as I noticed now, they only ever fought singularly. I had only a split second to think this odd as surely with their numbers it would have been easier to combine forces. However, they seemed to work in tandem, as one was pushed back another quickly took its place so that way the threat never stopped coming.

I didn't have much more time to think about it as the next was coming down at me, that was until I kicked my body up, and ended up travelling straight through its body! I cried out in sheer horror at what I saw as for a moment I was in a large black void of someone's mind that was completely filled by cage after cage of chained dead decaying warriors!

It was one of the most frightening sights I had ever seen, as in that single moment in time as I travelled through all the decaying men, they looked towards me and all screamed at me at the same time, so that when I landed on the ground after making it through to the other side of the phantom, I had my ears covered to drown out the ear bleeding sound of thousands of souls imprisoned by one being.

"Amelia!" Lucius shouted obviously hearing my torment and thought that it came from me being hit. So, I forced the pain of what I had just seen through from my mind and made my body stand, gaining my feet once more.

But I didn't regret what I had seen, for now I knew. I knew in that moment that this small army indeed had a master. A master pulling at the strings of its puppets, commanding them to do its will. As now I had formed a connection and I saw him, as if he was moving in a different time. As if everything around him was being distorted. And as I had crossed over from his prison void, I now had a name to go with the enemy we fought. He was a Wraith Master.

So with the echoing of screams still ringing in my head, I swung my blade out again and again, trying to force back the phantom who I knew now had no choice but to fight. Its screams were getting louder in my mind as every time a blade travelled through one from the Kings' swords or the brother's arrow, hammer or deathly ice blade, every time it sliced into the creature it felt the pain of it despite no damage being done.

I also saw for myself just how long they could last for, as their souls belonged to this Wraith Master and his use of them was...

endless.

I knew we only had one chance at defeating them, as there was only one real enemy to find and to fight. One still hiding in the shadows.

"SAVE HER!" Lucius shouted trying to get someone free enough to be able to save me, in his noble attempt to get me out of danger. But then by doing this, he had opened himself up for an attack and just as one of the ghostlike creatures had raised up his blade and was about to hammer it down onto Lucius' face, I reacted. I just reacted without thinking and I threw my own blade before realising that it would have no chance to do anything in the way of hurting the phantom. What it did do was fly straight through his shoulder and out the window.

But this was when something curious happened, as every one of the ghosts screamed, and now I wasn't the only one to hear it. Then every single one all grabbed a hand to their shoulders as if all of them had taken the hit. That's when I knew that finally...

I had found the Wraith Master in the shadows.

This was enough to get Lucius to be able to block the

oncoming attack in time, for it stunned the ghostly figure he had been fighting long enough for Lucius to dodge the blow. Then when it was safe to do so, he looked at me over his shoulder and I winked at him.

Then I pointed with my hand out towards the window the moment I saw the glowing eyes of white in the distance. The Wraith Master was hiding just in the garden beyond. He was the one that they needed to kill, which is when I told Lucius,

"You need to cut the head off the snake and he's out there, not in here!" Lucius looked to where I was pointing to and didn't need any more directions than this before he was charging towards the window, ready to run straight through it. However, the thing that he never saw coming and neither did I, was the Wraith Master had plucked my own blade out of his shoulder and in a fit of rage threw it back towards me.

Unfortunately, I only realised this a little too late as I went back a step from the force of something hitting me. This was when I looked down to where I now felt something foreign, something that I knew shouldn't be there.

That was when I saw it. When I saw my own blade now sticking out of me in a way that I knew I wasn't going to come back from.

I knew this the moment my world started to turn upside down doing so now in slow motion before I landed.

Before I closed my eyes and…

Before I died.

CHAPTER THIRTY

HEART OF DARKNESS

T he moment Amelia had figured it out, I knew there was only one thing left for me to do and that was take out the threat as soon as possible! Because, despite trying to get her out of danger, the second I saw the McBain brothers being forced inside while fighting their own dark force, I knew that we needed to keep them away from Amelia for as long as possible. I was killing mad anyway, so at least I had something to direct all of my rage onto. However, this soon proved useless as it wasn't like any of the fuckers could die!

Because hit after hit and strike after strike and yet nothing, for the bastards kept coming! But it wasn't just fighting one, it was fighting a small fucking army of the dead, as one was like fighting three, we weren't just outnumbered we were royally fucked!

They were not like anything I had ever fought before, for it was like fighting a ghost and how the fuck do you kill something that's already dead!? How do you fight a soulless being who was nothing but an empty vessel to fight you? It was only when I heard the King shouting to his brother of what the creatures were, that I fully understood it for myself.

"Wraiths." The word had been hissed from my own demon's mouth, bearing my fangs at them, and wanting nothing more than to take chunks out of them. But trying to fight them and concentrate on what my girl was doing as well, was becoming problematic... oh, who was I fooling, it had become near fucking impossible!

But then I shouldn't have been surprised, not when I finally did get to check on her only to find that she had a blade in her hand and was fighting back. Fuck, that was my Amelia! Gods, but if her father wasn't proud once I told him all that she had done, then I would beat the shit out of him for the offence! Because I was so fucking proud, as proud as I was angry at the fact that here we were again, with me trying to protect her from yet another fucking enemy, and the biggest kicker this time was that this one wasn't even ours!

But then finally she had done what none of us had and that was discovering its weakness. Doing so after scaring the shit out of me and landing on the floor in a painful heap, covering her ears as if she was trying to drown out a sound of some kind.

But soon she was forcing herself to her feet and pointing the way to end it all. Pointing in the direction I had to go. I didn't even think before I was running through the wall of windows and smashing my force through them before racing towards the threat I could now see in the shadows.

He was there fighting nothing and manipulating the movements of his wraiths we had been battling. He was so busy concentrating on the movements of his army that he didn't even see me, so that all I had to do was grab him by the neck. Then I lifted him up, choking the life out of him, knowing now that all those we had fought in the King's office were most likely feeling the same pain. In fact, I was just about to snap his neck and end it all, when I noticed the blood seeping from his shoulder.

This was when events started to play back at me, events that began with my girl. Because I remembered Amelia wanting to save my life and thinking she was capable of it as instinct took over. She threw her blade, discarding her only weapon to save me. It was one that flew straight through the Wraith I had been fighting, and out the window. This had been only moments before she informed me of the Master I held in my grasp now. Moments before she discovered the head of the snake I needed to slay. That's when I realised that she knew he was out here hiding because she must have hit him.

But then the horror of this started to seep into my subconscious, nagging at me that something was wrong…

In. A. Big. Fucking. Way!

Because now I asked myself only one question…

Where was the blade?

Where was the blade she had thrown and why was it not still embedded in his flesh? I looked on the floor briefly, hoping to see it there glinting in the grass from where he had pulled it out and tossed it aside… *but there was nothing* .

It was in this moment that dread started to flood my system and the moment I heard my name being roared in panic from back in the office, was when I knew the worst had happened.

"Lucius no! Don't kill him! You can't kill him!" This was being bellowed at me from my commander, for now Carn'reau was running towards me and before I could move, he tore my arm from the Wraith Master's throat, making him drop to the floor. Then, before my demon could snarl down at him for tearing the kill from me, he pointed back to the office and said only one thing that filled my veins with ice!

Stone cold dread.

"If you kill him… *she will die.* " This was when I tore my

angry gaze from him and looked to where my girl was. That was when I saw her.

"NO!" I roared like a furious beast as I could now see my girl laying on the floor with the blade she had once thrown now stuck out of her flesh. I didn't even remember moving, it was all natural instinct from there, as I was outside one moment and in the next, I was by her side, kneeling next to her. I took her head and cradled it, then I snatched the blade from where it was embedded in her own shoulder, just glad it had missed her heart. That it hadn't killed her instantly.

Meaning I could save her!

I instantly bit into my wrist, tearing flesh off to ensure I would spill lots of blood. Then I held it to her lips urging her to drink.

"Drink, come on... come on, Amelia, I said drink!" I snapped giving her little shake, and the utter relief I felt when she moved her lips against my wrist, well it was like a fucking prayer had been answered.

But then that was the sickening thing about the Gods, something I knew all too well. For as quickly as they were to give life, they were just as quick to take it away.

That was the same with prayers answered.

I knew this when she started to cough up the blood that she had consumed and was supposed to be healing her. She kept on bringing it up, unable to keep it down.

"NO!" I shouted before raising it to my lips biting in even further before holding her mouth open and letting it pour down her throat.

"Come on, Amelia, come on, baby, just swallow it down," I urged, this time my voice more soothing than angry. But again, she just vomited it up and the sight had me in utter fucking panic! This was when I decided to go straight for the source, ripping open her dress wider where she had been stabbed ready to place my bleeding palm over the wound. But then I hissed when I finally saw for myself the problem.

The King sucked in a sharp breath next to me, for he knew what this was. He started speaking but I wasn't listening. No, I only listened to her heartbeat, one that was barely beating.

"Come on now, Amelia, wake up, wake up for me... come on, open those pretty eyes for me... Gods, please... PLEASE!" I kept speaking to her, but she would not respond. Which is when the King lowered to his knee, now looking at the wound that was turning black and spreading out much further than it should have been. As if an infection was growing and getting closer to her heart. I heard people speaking around me again, the brothers were talking, asking what was happening but I was blanking it all out, just talking to my girl. I heard a roar of anger, a muffled sound of pain, even a girl's scream.

But I dismissed it all.

For there was only her.

Only my Amelia.

"Amelia, come on, baby, come on now... don't you dare do this... don't you dare fucking leave me again... no, no... I do not allow this... I WILL NOT ALLOW IT!" I bellowed in pain wanting to bring her back to me, my hands curling into her dress, her body. I eased knowing that I could hurt her, bruise her. I needed to calm... for she would come back. Her smile, she would show it to me soon. Open those eyes for me and say some witty remark making me laugh... Fuck! But I would never laugh again!

"Come on! Wake up, damn you! *Wake up... wake up... please wake up!"* This desperate plea ended up as a whisper said against her skin, as I cradled her head to my lips, whispering now on her forehead, one that was feeling cold now.

Then I don't know when it happened, but one thing did finally penetrate my brain and it was the sound of Carn'reau as he stepped up closer to me and began to tell me the fucking awful truth,

"I'm so sorry, my Lord." But I lashed out, shouting how it wasn't true! It couldn't fucking be true!

"What the fuck do you mean, she will be fine... she just needs my blood, that's all... we just need to find a way for her to take my blood," I said ending this softly down at her, now pushing back her hair from her face. Gods, but she looked so pale, she just needed my blood.

"I'm afraid what my brother says is true," he tried again.

"What the fuck did he say!?" I snapped only hearing half of what was happening around me for I could concentrate on little else, still talking to her, trying to get her to come around.

"She just needs time, just a little time as she's tired... yes, that's it, she is just tired is all, she just needs my blood and rest, don't you, sweetheart?" I kept saying like some fucking fool, so deluded that not even my demon was listening. No, he was fucking roaring at me for letting this happen!

But I wasn't listening to him either, not until I finally looked up at the King, and his pained eyes looked back at me. That's when I realised that my face was wet, and I raised a hand to my own cheek wondering what it was before seeing for myself that it was my tears.

And they wouldn't stop falling.

Because I knew. The horrific part of me inside knew.

"I'm sorry, there is nothing we can do."

"I'm so sorry."

"Her heart, it has given way to the darkness. The darkness that poisoned her." These words they kept on being said over and over again but I was no longer listening.

No, I was back to listening to the sound of my girl's heart as it started to slow down even further, and then eventually that soft thud inside her chest started to mark the beginning of my own heart breaking.

It marked the beginning of my real Hell.

It marked the beginning of the end.

Of when…

My Chosen One died in my arms. And my…

My heart turned to darkness.

ABOUT THE AUTHOR

Stephanie Hudson has dreamed of being a writer ever since her obsession with reading books at an early age. What first became a quest to overcome the boundaries set against her in the form of dyslexia has turned into a life's dream. She first started writing in the form of poetry and soon found a taste for horror and romance. Afterlife is her first book in the series of twelve, with the story of Keira and Draven becoming ever more complicated in a world that sets them miles apart.

When not writing, Stephanie enjoys spending time with her loving family and friends, chatting for hours with her biggest fan, her sister Cathy who is utterly obsessed with one gorgeous Dominic Draven. And of course, spending as much time with her supportive partner and personal muse, Blake who is there for her no matter what.

Author's words.

My love and devotion is to all my wonderful fans that keep me going into the wee hours of the night but foremost to my wonderful daughter Ava...who yes, is named after a cool, kick-ass, Demonic bird and my sons, Jack, who is a little hero and Baby Halen, who yes, keeps me up at night but it's okay because he is named after a Guitar legend!

Keep updated with all new release news & more on my website
www.afterlifesaga.com
Never miss out, sign up to the
mailing list at the website.

Also, please feel free to join myself and other Dravenites on my Facebook group
Afterlife Saga Official Fan
Interact with me and other fans. Can't wait to see you there!

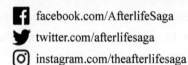

facebook.com/AfterlifeSaga
twitter.com/afterlifesaga
instagram.com/theafterlifesaga

ACKNOWLEDGEMENTS

Well first and foremost my love goes out to all the people who deserve the most thanks and are the wonderful people that keep me going day to day. But most importantly they are the ones that allow me to continue living out my dreams and keep writing my stories for the world to hopefully enjoy... These people are of course YOU! Words will never be able to express the full amount of love I have for you guys. Your support is never ending. Your trust in me and the story is never failing. But more than that, your love for me and all who you consider your 'Afterlife family' is to be commended, treasured and admired. Thank you just doesn't seem enough, so one day I hope to meet you all and buy you all a drink! ;)

   To my family... To my amazing mother, who has believed in me from the very beginning and doesn't believe that something great should be hidden from the world. I would like to thank you for all the hard work you put into my books and the endless hours spent caring about my words and making sure it is the best it can be for everyone to enjoy. You make Afterlife shine. To my wonderful crazy father who is and always has been my hero in life. Your strength astonishes me, even to this day and the love and care you hold for your family is a gift you give to the Hudson name. And last but not least, to the man that I consider my soul mate. The man who taught me about real love and makes me not only want to be a better person but makes me feel I am too. The amount of support you have given me since we met has been incredible and the greatest feeling was finding out you wanted to spend the rest of your life with me when you asked me to marry you.

All my love to my dear husband and my own personal Draven... Mr Blake Hudson.

Another personal thank you goes to my dear friend Caroline Fairbairn and her wonderful family that have embraced my brand of crazy into their lives and given it a hug when most needed.

For their friendship I will forever be eternally grateful.

I would also like to mention Claire Boyle my wonderful PA, who without a doubt, keeps me sane and constantly smiling through all the chaos which is my life ;) And a loving mention goes to Lisa Jane for always giving me a giggle and scaring me to death with all her count down pictures lol ;)

Thank you for all your hard work and devotion to the saga and myself. And always going that extra mile, pushing Afterlife into the spotlight you think it deserves. Basically helping me achieve my secret goal of world domination one day...evil laugh time... Mwahaha! Joking of course ;)

As before, a big shout has to go to all my wonderful fans who make it their mission to spread the Afterlife word and always go the extra mile. I love you all x

ALSO BY
STEPHANIE HUDSON

Afterlife Saga

A Brooding King, A Girl running from her past. What happens when the two collide?

Transfusion Saga

*What happens when an ordinary human girl comes face to face with
the cruel Vampire King who dismissed her seven years ago?*

Transfusion - Book 1

Venom of God - Book 2

Blood of Kings - Book 3

Rise of Ashes - Book 4

Map of Sorrows - Book 5

Tree of Souls - Book 6

Kingdoms of Hell – Book 7

Eyes of Crimson - Book 8

Roots of Rage - Book 9

Heart of Darkness - Book 10

Afterlife Chronicles: (Young Adult Series)

The Glass Dagger – Book 1

The Hells Ring – Book 2

Stephanie Hudson and Blake Hudson

The Devil in Me

OTHER WORKS BY
HUDSON INDIE INK

Paranormal Romance/Urban Fantasy

Sloane Murphy

Xen Randell

C. L. Monaghan

Sci-fi/Fantasy

Brandon Ellis

Devin Hanson

Crime/Action

Blake Hudson

Mike Gomes

Contemporary Romance

Gemma Weir

Elodie Colt

Ann B. Harrison

9 781913 904272